KNOWN SPACE

Larry Niven's *Known Space* series fuses the most exciting scientific concepts—including the first and most ingenious fictional treatments of the Black Hole phenomenon—with crisp storytelling and vivid characters. Readers of Niven's novels—such as *Ringworld* and *A Gift From Earth*—and the collected stories in *Neutron Star* will once again meet in this book such memorable characters as Lucas Garner, whose life spans the era between the First World War and the 22nd Century; the deep-space entrepreneur Beowulf Schaeffer; and the pivotal figure of Louis Wu. Now, for the first time in one volume, Niven has filled in the rich, complex background of this remarkable epic.

In an introduction to the book and notes to each story, Larry Niven discusses his writing and provides an invaluable guide to your own exploration of Known Space.

By Larry Niven
Published by Ballantine Books:

The Known Space Series:
A GIFT FROM EARTH
THE LONG *ARM* OF GIL HAMILTON
NEUTRON STAR
PROTECTOR
RINGWORLD
THE RINGWORLD ENGINEERS
TALES OF KNOWN SPACE:
  The Universe of Larry Niven
WORLD OF PTAVVS

Other Titles:
ALL THE MYRIAD WAYS
CONVERGENT SERIES
THE FLIGHT OF THE HORSE
A HOLE IN SPACE
THE INTEGRAL TREES
LIMITS
THE SMOKE RING
A WORLD OUT OF TIME

With David Gerrold:
THE FLYING SORCERERS

With Jerry Pournelle:
FOOTFALL
LUCIFER'S HAMMER

With Steven Barnes:
THE CALIFORNIA VOODOO GAME

Tales of
KNOWN
SPACE

The Universe of
LARRY NIVEN

A Del Rey Book

BALLANTINE BOOKS • NEW YORK

A Del Rey Book
Published by Ballantine Books

ISBN 0-345-33469-8

Printed in Canada

First Edition: August 1975
Fourteenth Printing: September 1992

Cover Art by Rick Sternbach

Acknowledgments

"The Coldest Place," copyright © 1964 by Galaxy Publishing Corporation for *Worlds of If*, December 1964.

"Becalmed in Hell," copyright © 1965 by Mercury Press, Inc., for *The Magazine of Fantasy and Science Fiction*, July 1965.

"Wait It Out," copyright © 1968 for *Futures Unbounded*.

"Eye of an Octopus," copyright © 1966 by Galaxy Publishing Corporation for *Galaxy Magazine*, February 1966.

"How the Heroes Die," copyright © 1966 by Galaxy Publishing Corporation for *Galaxy Magazine*, October 1966.

"The Jigsaw Man," copyright © 1967 by Harlan Ellison for *Dangerous Visions*.

"At the Bottom of a Hole," copyright © 1966 by the Galaxy Publishing Corporation for *Galaxy Magazine*, December 1966.

"Intent to Deceive," copyright © 1968 as "The Deceivers" by Galaxy Publishing Corporation for *Galaxy Magazine*, April 1968.

"Cloak of Anarchy," copyright © 1972 by The Condé Nast Publications, Inc., for *Analog*, March 1972.

"The Warriors," copyright © 1966 by Galaxy Publishing Corporation for *Worlds of If*, February 1966.

"The Borderland of Sol," copyright © 1975 by The Condé Nast Publications, Inc., for *Analog*, January 1975.

"There Is a Tide," copyright © 1968 by Galaxy Publishing Corporation for *Galaxy Magazine*, July 1968.

"Safe at *Any* Speed," copyright © 1967 by Mercury Press, Inc., for *The Magazine of Fantasy and Science Fiction*, May 1967.

Contents

Timeline for KNOWN SPACE by Larry Niven

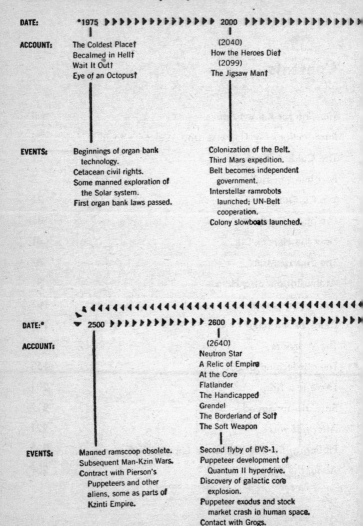

DATE: °1975 ▷▷▷▷▷▷▷▷▷▷▷▷▷▷▷ 2000 ▷▷▷▷▷▷▷▷▷▷▷▷▷▷▷▷

ACCOUNT:
The Coldest Place†
Becalmed in Hell†
Wait It Out†
Eye of an Octopus†

(2040)
How the Heroes Die†
(2099)
The Jigsaw Man†

EVENTS:
Beginnings of organ bank
technology.
Cetacean civil rights.
Some manned exploration of
the Solar system.
First organ bank laws passed.

Colonization of the Belt.
Third Mars expedition.
Belt becomes independent
government.
Interstellar ramrobots
launched; UN-Belt
cooperation.
Colony slowboats launched.

◁◁◁◁◁◁◁◁◁◁◁◁◁◁◁◁◁◁◁◁◁◁◁◁◁◁◁◁◁◁◁◁◁◁◁◁◁
◁

DATE:° ▼ 2500 ▷▷▷▷▷▷▷▷▷▷▷▷ 2600 ▷▷▷▷▷▷▷▷▷▷▷▷▷▷▷

ACCOUNT:
(2640)
Neutron Star
A Relic of Empire
At the Core
Flatlander
The Handicapped
Grendel
The Borderland of Sol†
The Soft Weapon

EVENTS:
Manned ramscoop obsolete.
Subsequent Man-Kzin Wars.
Contract with Pierson's
Puppeteers and other
aliens, some as parts of
Kzinti Empire.

Second flyby of BVS-1.
Puppeteer development of
Quantum II hyperdrive.
Discovery of galactic core
explosion.
Puppeteer exodus and stock
market crash in human space.
Contact with Grogs.
Louis Gridley Wu born.
Fertility Laws amended by
Birthright Lotteries.

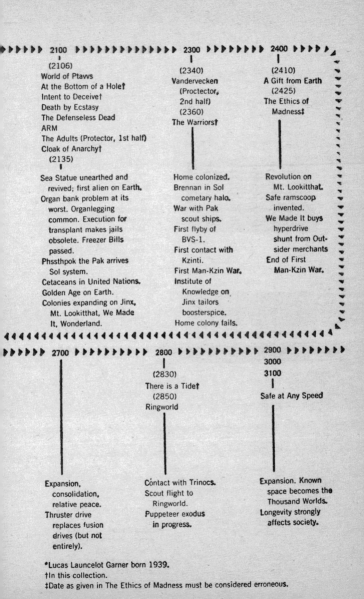

▶▶▶▶▶ 2100 ▶▶▶▶▶▶▶▶▶▶▶▶ 2300 ▶▶▶▶▶▶▶ 2400 ▶▶▶▶

(2106)
World of Ptavvs
At the Bottom of a Hole†
Intent to Deceive†
Death by Ecstasy
The Defenseless Dead
ARM
The Adults (Protector, 1st half)
Cloak of Anarchy†
(2135)

(2340)
Vandervecken
(Proctector,
2nd half)
(2360)
The Warriors†

(2410)
A Gift from Earth
(2425)
The Ethics of
Madness‡

Sea Statue unearthed and
revived; first alien on Earth.
Organ bank problem at its
worst. Organlegging
common. Execution for
transplant makes jails
obsolete. Freezer Bills
passed.
Phssthpok the Pak arrives
Sol system.
Cetaceans in United Nations.
Golden Age on Earth.
Colonies expanding on Jinx,
Mt. Lookitthat, We Made
It, Wonderland.

Home colonized.
Brennan in Sol
cometary halo.
War with Pak
scout ships.
First flyby of
BVS-1.
First contact with
Kzinti.
First Man-Kzin War.
Institute of
Knowledge on
Jinx tailors
boosterspice.
Home colony fails.

Revolution on
Mt. Lookitthat.
Safe ramscoop
invented.
We Made It buys
hyperdrive
shunt from Out-
sider merchants
End of First
Man-Kzin War.

◀◀◀

▶▶▶▶▶▶ 2700 ▶▶▶▶▶▶▶▶▶▶ 2800 ▶▶▶▶▶▶▶▶▶▶ 2900 ▶▶▶▶▶▶▶
3000
3100

(2830)
There is a Tide†
(2850)
Ringworld

Safe at Any Speed

Expansion,
consolidation,
relative peace.
Thruster drive
replaces fusion
drives (but not
entirely).

Contact with Trinocs.
Scout flight to
Ringworld.
Puppeteer exodus
in progress.

Expansion. Known
space becomes the
Thousand Worlds.
Longevity strongly
affects society.

*Lucas Launcelot Garner born 1939.
†In this collection.
‡Date as given in The Ethics of Madness must be considered erroneous.

Introduction:
My Universe and Welcome to It!

TWELVE YEARS AGO I started writing. Eleven years ago I
started selling what I wrote. And eleven years ago I
started a future history—the history of Known Space.

The Known Space Series now spans a thousand years
of future history, with data on conditions up to a billion
and a half years in the past. Most of the stories take
place either in Human Space (the human-colonized
worlds and the space between, a bubble sixty light-years
across by Louis Wu's time) or in Known Space (the
much larger bubble of space explored by Human-built
ships but controlled by other species); but arms of exploration reach 200 light-years up along galactic north,
and 33,000 light-years to the galactic core. The series
now includes four novels *(World of Ptavvs, Protector,
A Gift from Earth, Ringworld)* plus the stories in the
collection *Neutron Star,* plus the book now in your
hands, plus one other to be published in February of 1976
to be called *The Long ARM of Gil Hamilton.*

Future histories tend to be chaotic. They grow from a
common base, from individual stories with common assumptions; but each story must—to be fair to readers
—stand by itself. The future history chronicled in the
Known Space Series is as chaotic as real history. Even
the styles vary in these stories, because my writing skills
have evolved over eleven years of real time.

But this is the book with the crib sheets. The stories
published here are in chronological order. I've scattered

supplementary notes between them, to explain what is going on between and around the individual novels and stories, in a region small on the galactic scale but huge in human experience.

A few general notes are in order here:

1. The tales of Gil the ARM are missing. This book became so big that we had to cut these three science-fiction/detective stories—60,000 words' worth—to make room. Gil's career hits its high point around 2121 AD, between *World of Ptavvs* and *Protector*. We'll be publishing these stories in one volume sometime next year.

2. I dithered over including "The Coldest Place" and "Eye of an Octopus." They were my first and sixth story sales, respectively; and they aren't that good. Furthermore, "The Coldest Place" was obsolete before it ever reached print. But these two stories are part of the fabric of the series, so I've included them.

3. You may feel that Mars itself is changing as you read through the book. Right you are. "Eye of an Octopus" is set on pre-Mariner Mars. Mariner IV's photographs of the craters on Mars sparked "How the Heroes Die." Sometime later, an article in *Analog* shaped the new view of the planet in "At the Bottom of a Hole." If the space probes keep redesigning our planets, what can we do but write new stories?

4. I was sore tempted to rewrite some of the older, clumsier stories. But how would I have known where to stop? You would then have been reading updated stories with the facts changed around. I've assumed that that isn't what you're after. I hope I'm right.

5. The Tales of Known Space cluster around five eras. First there is the near future, the exploration of interplanetary space during the next quarter-century.

There is the era of Lucas Garner and Gil "the ARM" Hamilton: 2106–2125 AD. Interplanetary civilization has loosened its ties with Earth, has taken on a character of its own. Other stellar systems are being explored and settled. The organ bank problem is at its sociological worst on Earth. The existence of nonhuman intelligence has become obtrusively plain; humanity must adjust.

There is an intermediate era centering around 2340 AD. In Sol System it is a period of peace and prosperity. On colony worlds like Plateau times are turbulent. At the edge of Sol System, a creature that used to be Jack Brennan fights a lone war. The era of peace begins with the subtle interventions of the Brennan-monster (see *Protector*); it ends in contact with the Kzinti Empire.

The fourth period, following the Man–Kzin Wars, covers part of the twenty-sixth century AD. It is a time of easy tourism and interspecies trade, in which the human species neither rules nor is ruled. New planets have been settled, some of which were wrested from the Kzinti Empire during the wars.

The fifth period resembles the fourth. Little has changed in two hundred years, at least on the surface. The thruster drive has replaced the less efficient fusion drives; a new species has joined the community of worlds. But there is one fundamental change. The Teela Brown gene—the "ultimate psychic power"—is spreading through humanity. The teelas have been bred for luck.

A fundamental change in human nature—and the teelas are that—makes life difficult for a writer. The period following *Ringworld* might be pleasant to live in, but it is short of interesting disasters. Only one story survives from this period; "Safe at Any Speed:" a kind of advertisement. There will be no others.

There is something about future histories, and Known Space in particular, that *gets* to people. They start worrying about the facts, the mathematics, the chronology. They work out elaborate charts or they program their computers for close-approach orbits around point-masses. They send me maps of Human, Kzinti, and Kdatlyno space, dynamic analyses of the Ringworld, ten-thousand-word plot outlines for the novel that will wrap it all up into a bundle, and treatises on The Grog Problem. To all of you who have thus entertained me and stroked my ego, thanks.

Thanks are due to Tim Kyger for his aid in compiling

the Bibliography, and to Spike MacPhee and Jerry Boya-
jian for their assistance with the Timeline. They belong to
the above group and they saved me a lot of research.

—Larry Niven
Los Angeles, California
January, 1975

The Coldest Place

IN THE COLDEST place in the solar system, I hesitated outside the ship for a moment. It was too dark out there. I fought an urge to stay close by the ship, by the comfortable ungainly bulk of warm metal which held the warm bright Earth inside it.

"See anything?" asked Eric.

"No, of course not. It's too hot here anyway, what with heat radiation from the ship. You remember the way they scattered away from the probe."

"Yeah. Look, you want me to hold your hand or something? Go."

I sighed and started off, with the heavy collector bouncing gently on my shoulder. I bounced too. The spikes on my boots kept me from sliding.

I walked up the side of the wide, shallow crater the ship had created by vaporizing the layered air all the way down to the water ice level. Crags rose about me, masses of frozen gas with smooth, rounded edges. They gleamed soft white where the light from my headlamp touched them. Elsewhere all was as black as eternity. Brilliant stars shone above the soft crags; but the light made no impression on the black land. The ship got smaller and darker and disappeared.

There was supposed to be life here. Nobody had even tried to guess what it might be like. Two years ago the Messenger VI probe had moved into close orbit about the planet and then landed about here, partly to find out if the cap of frozen gasses might be inflammable. In the field of view of the camera during the landing, things like shadows had wriggled across the snow and out of

1

the light thrown by the probe. The films had shown it beautifully. Naturally some wise ones had suggested that they were only shadows.

I'd seen the films. I knew better. There was life.

Something alive, that hated light. Something out there in the dark. Something huge . . . "Eric, you there?"

"Where would I go?" he mocked me.

"Well," said I, "if I watched every word I spoke I'd never get anything said." All the same, I had been tactless. Eric had had a bad accident once, very bad. He wouldn't be going anywhere unless the ship went along.

"Touché," said Eric. "Are you getting much heat leakage from your suit?"

"Very little." In fact, the frozen air didn't even melt under the pressure of my boots.

"They might be avoiding even that little. Or they might be afraid of your light." He knew I hadn't seen anything; he was looking through a peeper in the top of my helmet.

"Okay, I'll climb that mountain and turn it off for awhile."

I swung my head so he could see the mound I meant, then started up it. It was good exercise, and no strain in the low gravity. I could jump almost as high as on the Moon, without fear of a rock's edge tearing my suit. It was all packed snow, with vacuum between the flakes.

My imagination started working again when I reached the top. There was black all around; the world was black with cold. I turned off the light and the world disappeared.

I pushed a trigger on the side of my helmet and my helmet put the stem of a pipe in my mouth. The air renewer sucked air and smoke down past my chin. They make wonderful suits nowadays. I sat and smoked, waiting, shivering with the knowledge of the cold. Finally I realized I was sweating. The suit was almost too well insulated.

Our ion-drive section came over the horizon, a brilliant star moving very fast, and disappeared as it hit the planet's shadow. Time was passing. The charge in my pipe burned out and I dumped it.

"Try the light," said Eric.

I got up and turned the headlamp on high. The light spread for a mile around; a white fairy landscape sprang to life, a winter wonderland doubled in spades. I did a slow pirouette, looking, looking . . . and saw it.

Even this close it looked like a shadow. It also looked like a very flat, monstrously large amoeba, or like a pool of oil running across the ice. Uphill it ran, flowing slowly and painfully up the side of a nitrogen mountain, trying desperately to escape the searing light of my lamp. "The collector!" Eric demanded. I lifted the collector above my head and aimed it like a telescope at the fleeing enigma, so that Eric could find it in the collector's peeper. The collector spat fire at both ends and jumped up and away. Eric was controlling it now.

After a moment I asked, "Should I come back?"

"Certainly not. Stay there. I can't bring the collector back to the ship! You'll have to wait and carry it back with you."

The pool-shadow slid over the edge of the hill. The flame of the collector's rocket went after it, flying high, growing smaller. It dipped below the ridge. A moment later I heard Eric mutter, "Got it." The bright flame reappeared, rising fast, then curved toward me.

When the thing was hovering near me on two lateral rockets I picked it up by the tail and carried it home.

"No, no trouble," said Eric. "I just used the scoop to nip a piece out of his flank, if so I may speak. I got about ten cubic centimeters of strange flesh."

"Good," said I. Carrying the collector carefully in one hand, I went up the landing leg to the airlock. Eric let me in.

I peeled off my frosting suit in the blessed artificial light of ship's day.

"Okay," said Eric. "Take it up to the lab. And don't touch it."

Eric can be a hell of an annoying character. "I've got a brain," I snarled, "even if you can't see it." So can I.

There was a ringing silence while we each tried to dream up an apology. Eric got there first. "Sorry," he said.

"Me too." I hauled the collector off to the lab on a cart.

He guided me when I got there. "Put the whole package in that opening. Jaws first. No, don't close it yet. Turn the thing until these lines match the lines on the collector. Okay. Push it in a little. Now close the door. Okay, Howie, I'll take it from there . . ." There were chugging sounds from behind the little door. "Have to wait till the lab's cool enough. Go get some coffee," said Eric.

"I'd better check your maintenance."

"Okay, good. Go oil my prosthetic aids."

"Prosthetic aids"—that was a hot one. I'd thought it up myself. I pushed the coffee button so it would be ready when I was through, then opened the big door in the forward wall of the cabin. Eric looked much like an electrical network, except for the gray mass at the top which was his brain. In all directions from his spinal cord and brain, connected at the walls of the intricately shaped glass-and-soft-plastic vessel which housed him, Eric's nerves reached out to master the ship. The instruments which mastered Eric—but he was sensitive about having it put that way—were banked along both sides of the closet. The blood pump pumped rhythmically, seventy beats a minute.

"How do I look?" Eric asked.

"Beautiful. Are you looking for flattery?"

"Jackass! Am I still alive?"

"The instruments think so. But I'd better lower your fluid temperature a fraction." I did. Ever since we'd landed I'd had a tendency to keep temperatures too high. "Everything else looks okay. Except your food tank is getting low."

"Well, it'll last the trip."

"Yeah. 'Scuse me. Eric, coffee's ready." I went and got it. The only thing I really worry about is his "liver." It's too complicated. It could break down too easily. If it stopped making blood sugar Eric would be dead.

If Eric dies I die, because Eric is the ship. If I die Eric dies, insane, because he can't sleep unless I set his prosthetic aids.

I was finishing my coffee when Eric yelled. "Hey!"

"What's wrong?" I was ready to run in any direction.

"It's only helium!"

He was astonished and indignant. I relaxed.

"I get it now, Howie. Helium II. That's all our monsters are. Nuts."

Helium II, the superfluid that flows uphill. "Nuts doubled. Hold everything, Eric. Don't throw away your samples. Check them for contaminants."

"For what?"

"Contaminants. My body is hydrogen oxide with contaminants. If the contaminants in the helium are complex enough it might be alive."

"There are plenty of other substances," said Eric, "but I can't analyze them well enough. We'll have to rush this stuff back to Earth while our freezers can keep it cool."

I got up. "Take off right now?"

"Yes, I guess so. We could use another sample, but we're just as likely to wait here while this one deteriorates."

"Okay, I'm strapping down now. Eric?"

"Yeah? Takeoff in fifteen minutes, we have to wait for the ion-drive section. You can get up."

"No, I'll wait. Eric, I hope it isn't alive. I'd rather it was just helium II acting like it's supposed to act."

"Why? Don't you want to be famous, like me?"

"Oh, sure, but I hate to think of life out there. It's just too alien. Too cold. Even on Pluto you could not make life out of helium II."

"It could be migrant, moving to stay on the night side of the pre-dawn crescent. Pluto's day is long enough for that. You're right, though; it doesn't get colder than this even between the stars. Luckily I don't have much imagination."

Twenty minutes later we took off. Beneath us all was darkness and only Eric, hooked into the radar, could see the ice dome contracting until all of it was visible: the vast layered ice cap that covers the coldest spot in the solar system, where midnight crosses the equator on the black back of Mercury.

This, my first story, became obsolete before it was printed. Mercury does have an atmosphere, and rotates once for every two of its years.

The sequel which follows fared somewhat better.

LN

Becalmed In Hell

I COULD FEEL the heat hovering outside. In the cabin it was bright and dry and cool, almost too cool, like a modern office building in the dead of summer. Beyond the two small windows it was as black as it ever gets in the solar system, and hot enough to melt lead, at a pressure equivalent to three hundred feet beneath the ocean.

"There goes a fish," I said, just to break the monotony.

"So how's it cooked?"

"Can't tell. It seems to be leaving a trail of breadcrumbs. Fried? Imagine that, Eric! A fried jellyfish."

Eric sighed noisily. "Do I have to?"

"You have to. Only way you'll see anything worthwhile in this—this—" Soup? Fog? Boiling maple syrup?

"Searing black calm."

"Right."

"Someone dreamed up that phrase when I was a kid, just after the news of the Mariner II probe. An eternal searing black calm, hot as a kiln, under an atmosphere thick enough to keep any light or any breath of wind from ever reaching the surface."

I shivered. "What's the outside temperature now?"

"You'd rather not know. You've always had too much imagination, Howie."

"I can take it, Doc."

"Six hundred and twelve degrees."

"I can't take it, Doc!"

This was Venus, planet of Love, favorite of the science-fiction writers of three decades ago. Our ship hung below the Earth-to-Venus hydrogen fuel tank, twenty miles up and all but motionless in the syrupy air. The tank, nearly empty now, made an excellent blimp. It would keep us aloft as long as the internal pressure matched the external. That was Eric's job, to regulate the tank's pressure by regulating the temperature of the hydrogen gas. We had collected air samples after each ten mile drop from three hundred miles on down, and temperature readings for shorter intervals, and we had dropped the small probe. The data we had gotten from the surface merely confirmed in detail our previous knowledge of the hottest world in the solar system.

"Temperature just went up to six-thirteen," said Eric. "Look, are you through bitching?"

"For the moment."

"Good. Strap down. We're taking off."

"Oh, frabjous day!" I started untangling the crash webbing over my couch.

"We've done everything we came to do. Haven't we?"

"Am I arguing? Look, I'm strapped down."

"Yeah."

I knew why he was reluctant to leave. I felt a touch of it myself. We'd spent four months getting to Venus in order to spend a week circling her and less than two days in her upper atmosphere, and it seemed a terrible waste of time.

But he was taking too long. "What's the trouble, Eric?"

"You'd rather not know."

He meant it. His voice was a mechanical, inhuman monotone; he wasn't making the extra effort to get human expression out of his "prosthetic" vocal apparatus. Only a severe shock would affect him that way.

"I can take it," I said.

"Okay. I can't feel anything in the ramjet controls. Feels like I've just had a spinal anesthetic."

The cold in the cabin drained into me, all of it. "See if you can send motor impulses the other way. You could run the rams by guess-and-hope even if you can't feel them."

"Okay." One split second later, "They don't. Nothing happens. Good thinking though."

I tried to think of something to say while I untied myself from the couch. What came out was, "It's been a pleasure knowing you, Eric. I've liked being half of this team, and I still do."

"Get maudlin later. Right now, start checking my attachments. Carefully."

I swallowed my comments and went to open the access door in the cabin's forward wall. The floor swayed ever so gently beneath my feet.

Beyond the four-foot-square access door was Eric. Eric's central nervous system, with the brain perched at the top and the spinal cord coiled in a loose spiral to fit more compactly into the transparent glass-and-sponge-plastic housing. Hundreds of wires from all over the ship led to the glass walls, where they were joined to selected nerves which spread like an electrical network from the central coil of nervous tissue and fatty protective membrane.

Space leaves no cripples; and don't call Eric a cripple, because he doesn't like it. In a way he's the ideal spaceman. His life support system weighs only half what mine does, and takes up a twelfth as much room. But his other prosthetic aids take up most of the ship. The ramjets were hooked into the last pair of nerve trunks, the nerves which once moved his legs, and dozens of finer nerves in those trunks sensed and regulated fuel feed, ram temperature, differential acceleration, intake aperture dilation, and spark pulse.

These connections were intact. I checked them four different ways without finding the slightest reason why they shouldn't be working.

"Test the others," said Eric.

It took a good two hours to check every trunk nerve connection. They were all solid. The blood pump was chugging along, and the fluid was rich enough, which killed the idea that the ram nerves might have "gone to sleep" from lack of nutrients or oxygen. Since the lab is one of his prosthetic aids, I let Eric analyze his own blood sugar, hoping that the "liver" had goofed and was producing some other sugar compound. The conclusions were appalling. There was nothing wrong with Eric—inside the cabin.

"Eric, you're healthier than I am."

"I could tell. You look worried, and I don't blame you. Now you'll have to go outside."

"I know. Let's dig out the suit."

It was in the emergency tools locker, the Venus suit that was never supposed to be used. NASA had designed it for use at Venusian ground level. Then they had refused to okay the ship below twenty miles until they knew more about the planet. The suit was a segmented armor job. I had watched it being tested in the heat-and-pressure box at Cal Tech, and I knew that the joints stopped moving after five hours, and wouldn't start again until they had been cooled. Now I opened the locker and pulled the suit out by the shoulders and held it in front of me. It seemed to be staring back.

"You still can't feel anything in the ramjets?"

"Not a twinge."

I started to put on the suit, piece by piece like medieval armor. Then I thought of something else. "We're twenty miles up. Are you going to ask me to do a balancing act on the hull?"

"No! Wouldn't think of it. We'll just have to go down."

The lift from the blimp tank was supposed to be constant until takeoff. When the time came Eric could get extra lift by heating the hydogen to higher pressure, then cracking a valve to let the excess out. Of course he'd have to be very careful that the pressure was higher in the tank, or we'd get Venusian air coming in, and the ship would fall instead of rising. Naturally that would be disastrous.

So Eric lowered the tank temperature and cracked the valve, and down we went.

"Of course there's a catch," said Eric.

"I know."

"The ship stood the pressure twenty miles up. At ground level it'll be six times that."

"I know."

We fell fast, with the cabin tilted forward by the drag on our tailfins. The temperature rose gradually. The pressure went up fast. I sat at the window and saw nothing, nothing but black, but I sat there anyway and wait-

ed for the window to crack. NASA had refused to okay
the ship below twenty miles . . .

Eric said, "The blimp tank's okay, and so's the ship, I
think. But will the cabin stand up to it?"

"I wouldn't know."

"Ten miles."

Five hundred miles above us, unreachable, was the
atomic ion engine that was to take us home. We couldn't
get to it on the chemical rocket alone. The rocket was
for use after the air become too thin for the ramjets.

"Four miles. Have to crack the valve again."

The ship dropped.

"I can see ground," said Eric.

I couldn't. Eric caught me straining my eyes and said,
"Forget it. I'm using deep infrared, and getting no detail."

"No vast, misty swamps with weird, terrifying monsters and man-eating plants?"

"All I see is hot, bare dirt."

But we were almost down, and there were no cracks
in the cabin wall. My neck and shoulder muscles loosened.
I turned away from the window. Hours had passed
while we dropped through the poisoned, thickening air.
I already had most of my suit on. Now I screwed on my
helmet and three-finger gauntlets.

"Strap down," said Eric. I did.

We bumped gently. The ship tilted a little, swayed
back, bumped again. And again, with my teeth rattling
and my armor-plated body rolling against the crash webbing. "Damn," Eric muttered. I heard the hiss from
above. Eric said, "I don't know how we'll get back up."

Neither did I. The ship bumped hard and stayed
down, and I got up and went to the airlock.

"Good luck," said Eric. "Don't stay out too long." I
waved at his cabin camera. The outside temperature was
seven hundred and thirty.

The outer door opened. My suit refrigerating unit set
up a complaining whine. With an empty bucket in each
hand, and with my headlamp blazing a way through the
black murk, I stepped out onto the right wing.

My suit creaked and settled under the pressure, and I

stood on the wing and waited for it to stop. It was almost like being under water. My headlamp beam went out thick enough to be solid, penetrating no more than a hundred feet. The air couldn't have been that opaque, no matter how dense. It must have been full of dust, or tiny droplets of some fluid.

The wing ran back like a knife-edged running board, widening toward the tail to where it spread into a tailfin. The two tailfins met back of the fuselage. At each tailfin tip was the ram, a big sculptured cylinder with an atomic engine inside. It wouldn't be hot because it hadn't been used yet, but I had my counter anyway.

I fastened a line to the wing and slid to the ground. As long as we were *here* . . . The ground turned out to be a dry, reddish dirt, crumbly, and so porous that it was almost spongy. Lava etched by chemicals? Almost anything would be corrosive at this pressure and temperature. I scooped one pailful from the surface and another from underneath the first, then climbed up the line and left the buckets on the wing.

The wing was terribly slippery. I had to wear magnetic sandals to stay on. I walked up and back along the two-hundred-foot length of the ship, making a casual inspection. Neither wing nor fuselage showed damage. Why not? If a meteor or something had cut Eric's contact with his sensors in the rams, there should have been evidence of a break in the surface.

Then, almost suddenly, I realized that there was an alternative.

It was too vague a suspicion to put into words yet, and I still had to finish the inspection. Telling Eric would be very difficult if I was right.

Four inspection panels were set into the wing, well protected from the reentry heat. One was halfway back on the fuselage, below the lower edge of the blimp tank, which was molded to the fuselage in such a way that from the front the ship looked like a dolphin. Two more were in the trailing edge of the tailfin and the fourth was in the ram itself. All opened, with powered screwdriver on recessed screws, on junctions of the ship's electrical system.

There was nothing out of place under any of the panels. By making and breaking contacts and getting Eric's reactions, I found that his sensation ended somewhere between the second and third inspection panels. It was the same story on the left wing. No external damage, nothing wrong at the junctions. I climbed back to ground and walked slowly beneath the length of each wing, my headlamp tilted up. No damage underneath.

I collected my buckets and went back inside.

"A bone to pick?" Eric was puzzled. "Isn't this a strange time to start an argument? Save it for space. We'll have four months with nothing else to do."

"This can't wait. First of all, did you notice anything I didn't?" He'd been watching everything I saw and did through the peeper in my helmet.

"No. I'd have yelled."

"Okay. Now get this.

"The break in your circuits isn't inside, because you get sensation up to the second wing inspection panels. It isn't outside because there's no evidence of damage, not even corrosion spots. That leaves only one place for the flaw."

"Go on."

"We also have the puzzle of why you're paralyzed in both rams. Why should they both go wrong at the same time? There's only one place in the ship where the circuits join."

"What? Oh, yes, I see. They joined through me."

"Now let's assume for the moment that you're the piece of equipment with the flaw in it. You're not a piece of machinery, Eric. If something's wrong with you it isn't medical. That was the first thing we covered. But it could be psychological."

"It's nice to know you think I'm human. So I've slipped a cam, have I?"

"Slightly. I think you've got a case of what used to be called trigger anesthesia. A soldier who kills too often sometimes finds that his right index finger or even his whole hand has gone numb, as if it were no longer a part of him. Your comment about not being a machine is important, Eric. I think that's the whole problem. You've never really believed that any part of the ship is a part of you. That's intelligent, because it's true. Every time the ship is redesigned you get a new set of parts, and it's right to avoid thinking of a change of model as a series of amputations." I'd been rehearsing this speech, trying to put it so that Eric would have no choice but to believe me. Now I know that it must have sounded phoney. "But now you've gone too far. Subconsciously you've stopped believing that the rams can *feel* like a part of you, which they were designed to do. So you've persuaded yourself that you don't feel anything."

With my prepared speech done, and nothing left to say, I stopped talking and waited for the explosion.

"You make good sense," said Eric.

I was staggered. "You agree?"

"I didn't say that. You spin an elegant theory, but I want time to think about it. What do we do if it's true?"

"Why . . . I don't know. You'll just have to cure yourself."

"Okay. Now here's *my* idea. I propose that you thought up this theory to relieve yourself of a responsibility for getting us home alive. It puts the whole problem in my lap, metaphorically speaking."

"Oh, for—"

"Shut up. I haven't said you're wrong. That would be an ad hominem argument. We need time to think about this."

It was lights-out, four hours later, before Eric would return to the subject.

"Howie, do me a favor. Assume for awhile that something mechanical is causing all our trouble. I'll assume it's psychosomatic."

"Seems reasonable."

"It is reasonable. What can you do if I've gone psychosomatic? What can I do if it's mechanical? I can't go around inspecting myself. We'd each better stick to what we know."

"It's a deal." I turned him off for the night and went to bed.

But not to sleep.

With the lights off it was just like outside. I turned them back on. It wouldn't wake Eric. Eric never sleeps normally, since his blood doesn't accumulate fatigue poisons, and he'd go mad from being awake all the time if he didn't have a Russian sleep inducer plate near his cortex. The ship could implode without waking Eric when his sleep inducer's on. But I felt foolish being afraid of the dark.

While the dark stayed outside it was all right.

But it wouldn't stay there. It had invaded my partner's mind. Because his chemical checks guard him against chemical insanities like schizophrenia, we'd assumed he was permanently sane. But how could any prosthetic device protect him from his own imagination, his own misplaced common sense?

I couldn't keep my bargain. I knew I was right. But what could I do about it?

Hindsight is wonderful. I could see exactly what our mistake had been, Eric's and mine and the hundreds of men who had built his life support after the crash. There was nothing left of Eric then except the intact central nervous system, and no glands except the pituitary. "We'll regulate his blood composition," they said, "and he'll always be cool, calm and collected. No panic reactions from Eric!"

I know a girl whose father had an accident when he was forty-five or so. He was out with his brother, the girl's uncle, on a fishing trip. They were blind drunk when they started home, and the guy was riding on the hood while the brother drove. Then the brother made a sudden stop. Our hero left two important glands on the hood ornament.

The only change in his sex life was that his wife stopped worrying about late pregnancy. His *habits* were developed.

Eric doesn't need adrenal glands to be afraid of death. His emotional patterns were fixed long before the day he tried to land a moonship without radar. He'd grab any excuse to believe that I'd fixed whatever was wrong with the ram connections.

But he was counting on me to do it.

The atmosphere leaned on the windows. Not wanting to, I reached out to touch the quartz with my fingertips. I couldn't feel the pressure. But it was there, inexorable as the tide smashing a rock into sand grains. How long would the cabin hold it back?

If some broken part were holding us here, how could I have missed finding it? Perhaps it had left no break in the surface of either wing. But how?

That was an angle.

Two cigarettes later I got up to get the sample buckets. They were empty, the alien dirt safely stored away. I filled them with water and put them in the cooler, set the cooler for 40° absolute, then turned off the lights and went to bed.

The morning was blacker than the inside of a smoker's lungs. What Venus really needs, I decided, philosophizing on my back, is to lose ninety-nine percent of her air. That would give her a bit more than half as much air as Earth, which would lower the greenhouse effect enough to make the temperature livable. Drop Venus' gravity to near zero for a few weeks and the work would do itself.

The whole damn universe is waiting for us to discover antigravity.

"Morning," said Eric. "Thought of anything?"

"Yes." I rolled out of bed. "Now don't bug me with questions. I'll explain everything as I go."

"No breakfast?"

"Not yet."

Piece by piece I put my suit on, just like one of King Arthur's gentlemen, and went for the buckets only after the gauntlets were on. The ice, in the cold section, was in the chilly neighborhood of absolute zero. "This is two buckets of ordinary ice," I said, holding them up. "Now let me out."

"I should keep you here till you talk," Eric groused. But the doors opened and I went out onto the wing. I started talking while I unscrewed the number two right panel.

"Eric, think a moment about the tests they run on a manned ship before they'll let a man walk into the life-system. They test every part separately and in conjunction with other parts. Yet if something isn't working, either it's damaged or it wasn't tested right. Right?"

"Reasonable." He wasn't giving away anything.

"Well, nothing caused any damage. Not only is there

no break in the ship's skin, but no coincidence could have made both rams go haywire at the same time. So something wasn't tested right."

I had the panel off. In the buckets the ice boiled gently where it touched the surfaces of the glass buckets. The blue ice cakes had cracked under their own internal pressure. I dumped one bucket into the maze of wiring and contacts and relays, and the ice shattered, giving me room to close the panel.

"So I thought of something last night, something that wasn't tested. Every part of the ship must have been in the heat-and-pressure box, exposed to artificial Venus conditions, but the ship as a whole, a unit, couldn't have been. It's too big." I'd circled around to the left wing and was opening the number three panel in the trailing edge. My remaining ice was half water and half small chips; I sloshed these in and fastened the panel. "What cut your circuits must have been the heat or the pressure or both. I can't help the pressure, but I'm cooling these relays with ice. Let me know which ram gets its sensation back first, and we'll know which inspection panel is the right one."

"Howie. Has it occurred to you what the cold water might do to those hot metals?"

"It could crack them. Then you'd lose all control over the ramjets, which is what's wrong right now."

"Uh. Your point, partner. But I still can't feel anything."

I went back to the airlock with my empty buckets swinging, wondering if they'd get hot enough to melt. They might have, but I wasn't out that long. I had my suit off and was refilling the buckets when Eric said, "I can feel the right ram."

"How extensive? Full control?"

"No, I can't feel the temperature. Oh, here it comes. We're all set, Howie."

My sigh of relief was sincere.

I put the buckets in the freezer again. We'd certainly want to take off with the relays cold. The water had been chilling for perhaps twenty minutes when Eric reported, "Sensation's going."

"What?"

"Sensation's going. No temperature, and I'm losing fuel feed control. It doesn't stay cold long enough."

"Ouch! Now what?"

"I hate to tell you. I'd almost rather let you figure it out for yourself."

I had. "We go as high as we can on the blimp tank, then I go out on the wing with a bucket of ice in each hand—"

We had to raise the blimp tank temperature to almost eight hundred degrees to get pressure, but from then on we went up in good shape. To sixteen miles. It took three hours.

"That's as high as we go," said Eric. "You ready?"

I went to get the ice. Eric could see me, he didn't need an answer. He opened the airlock for me.

Fear I might have felt, or panic, or determination or self-sacrifice—but there was nothing. I went out feeling like a used zombie.

My magnets were on full. It felt like I was walking through shallow tar. The air was thick, though not as heavy as it had been down there. I followed my headlamp to the number two panel, opened it, poured ice in and threw the bucket high and far. The ice was in one cake. I couldn't close the panel. I left it open and hurried around to the other wing. The second bucket was filled with exploded chips; I sloshed them in and locked the number two left panel and came back with both hands free. It still looked like limbo in all directions, except where the headlamp cut a tunnel through the darkness, and—my feet were getting hot. I closed the right panel on boiling water and sidled back along the hull into the airlock.

"Come in and strap down," said Eric. "Hurry!"

"Gotta get my suit off." My hands had started to shake from reaction. I couldn't work the clamps.

"No you don't. If you start right now we may get home. Leave the suit on and come in."

I did. As I pulled my webbing shut, the rams roared. The ship shuddered a little, then pushed forward as we dropped from under the blimp tank. Pressure mounted as the rams reached operating speed. Eric was giving it all he had. It would have been uncomfortable even without the metal suit arount me. With the suit on it was torture. My couch was afire from the suit, but I couldn't get breath to say so. We were going almost straight up.

We had gone twenty minutes when the ship jerked like a galvanized frog. "Ram's out," Eric said calmly. "I'll use the other." Another lurch as we dropped the dead one. The ship flew on like a wounded penguin, but still accelerating.

One minute . . . two . . .

The other ram quit. It was as if we'd run into molasses. Eric blew off the ram and the pressure eased. I could talk.

"Eric."

"What?"

"Got any marshmallows?"

"What? Oh, I see. Is your suit tight?"

"Sure."

"Live with it. We'll flush the smoke out later. I'm going to coast above some of this stuff, but when I use the rocket it'll be savage. No mercy."

"Will we make it?"

"I think so. It'll be close."

The relief came first, icy cold. Then the anger. "No more inexplicable numbnesses?" I asked.

"No. Why?"

"If any come up you'll be sure and tell me, won't you?"

"Are you getting at something?"

"Skip it." I wasn't angry any more.

"I'll be damned if I do. You know perfectly well it was mechanical trouble. You fixed it yourself!"

"No. I convinced you I must have fixed it. You needed to believe the rams *should* be working again. I gave you a miracle cure, Eric. I just hope I don't have to keep dreaming up new placebos for you all the way home."

"You thought that, but you went out on the wing sixteen miles up?" Eric's machinery snorted. "You've got guts where you need brains, Shorty."

I didn't answer.

"Five thousand says the trouble was mechanical. We let the mechanics decide after we land."

"You're on."

"Here comes the rocket. Two, one—"

It came, pushing me down into my metal suit. Sooty flames licked past my ears, writing black on the green metal ceiling, but the rosy mist before my eyes was not fire.

The man with the thick glasses spread a diagram of the Venus ship and jabbed a stubby finger at the trailing edge of the wing. "Right around here," he said. "The pressure from the outside compressed the wiring channel a little, just enough so there was no room for the wire to bend. It had to act as if it were rigid, see? Then when the heat expanded the metal these contacts pushed past each other."

"I suppose it's the same design on both wings?"

He gave me a queer look. "Well, naturally."

I left my check for $5000 in a pile of Eric's mail and hopped a plane for Brasilia. How he found me I'll never know, but the telegram arrived this morning.

> HOWIE COME HOME ALL IS FORGIVEN
> DONOVANS BRAIN

I guess I'll have to.

Wait It Out

NIGHT ON PLUTO. Sharp and distinct, the horizon line cuts across my field of vision. Below that broken line is the dim gray-white of snow seen by starlight. Above, space-blackness and space-bright stars. From behind a jagged row of frozen mountains the stars pour up in singletons and clusters and streamers of cold white dots. Slowly they move, but visibly, just fast enough for a steady eye to capture their motion.

Something wrong there. Pluto's rotation period is long: 6.39 days. Time must have slowed for me.

It should have stopped.

I wonder if I may have made a mistake.

The planet's small size brings the horizon close. It seems even closer without a haze of atmosphere to fog the distances. Two sharp peaks protrude into the star swarm like the filed front teeth of a cannibal warrior. In the cleft between those peaks shines a sudden bright point.

I recognize the Sun, though it shows no more disk than any other, dimmer star. The sun shines as a cold point between the frozen peaks; it pulls free of the rocks and shines in my eyes . . .

The Sun is gone, the starfield has shifted. I must have passed out.

It figures.

Have I made a mistake? It won't kill me if I have. It could drive me mad, though . . .

I don't feel mad. I don't feel anything, not pain, not loss, not regret, not fear. Not even pity. Just: *what a situation.*

21

Gray-white against gray-white: the landing craft, short and wide and conical, stands half-submerged in an icy plain below the level of my eyes. Here I stand, looking east, waiting.

Take a lesson: this is what comes of not wanting to die.

Pluto was not the most distant planet. It had stopped being that in 1979, ten years ago. Now Pluto was at perihelion, as close to the Sun—and to Earth—as it would ever get. To ignore such an opportunity would have been sheer waste.

And so we came, Jerome and Sammy and I, in an inflated plastic bubble poised on an ion jet. We'd spent a year and a half in that bubble. After so long together, with so little privacy, perhaps we should have hated each other. We didn't. The UN psycho team must have chosen well.

But—just to be out of sight of the others, even for a few minutes. Just to have something to *do*, something that was not predictable. A new world could hold infinite surprises. As a matter of fact, so could our laboratory-tested hardware. I don't think any of us really trusted the Nerva-K under our landing craft.

Think it through. For long trips in space, you use an ion jet giving low thrust over long periods of time. The ion motor on our own craft had been decades in use. Where gravity is materially lower than Earth's, you land on dependable chemical rockets. For landings on Earth and Venus, you use heat shields and the braking power of the atmosphere. For landing on the gas giants—but who would want to?

The Nerva-class fission rockets are used only for takeoff from Earth, where thrust and efficiency count. Responsiveness and maneuverability count for too much during a powered landing. And a heavy planet will always have an atmosphere for braking.

Pluto didn't.

For Pluto, the chemical jets to take us down and bring us back up were too heavy to carry all that way. We needed a highly maneuverable Nerva-type atomic rocket motor using hydrogen for reaction mass.

And we had it. But we didn't trust it.

Jerome Glass and I went down, leaving Sammy Cross in orbit. He griped about that, of course. He'd started that back at the Cape and kept it up for a year and a half. But someone had to stay. Someone had to be aboard the Earth-return vehicle, to fix anything that went wrong, to relay communications to Earth, and to fire the bombs that would solve Pluto's one genuine mystery.

We never did solve that one. Where *does* Pluto get all that mass? The planet's a dozen times as dense as it has any right to be. We could have solved that with the bombs, the same way they solved the mystery of the makeup of the Earth, sometime in the last century. They mapped the patterns of earthquake ripples moving through the Earth's bulk. But those ripples were from natural causes, like the Krakatoa eruption. On Pluto the bombs would have done it better.

A bright star-sun blazes suddenly between two fangs of mountain. I wonder if they'll know the answers, when my vigil ends.

The sky jumps and steadies, and—

I'm looking east, out over the plain where we landed the ship. The plain and the mountains behind seem to be sinking like Atlantis: an illusion created by the flowing stars. We slide endlessly down the black sky, Jerome and I and the mired ship.

The Nerva-K behaved perfectly. We hovered for several minutes to melt our way through various layers of frozen gases and get ourselves something solid to land on. Condensing volatiles steamed around us and boiled below, so that we settled in a soft white glow of fog lit by the hydrogen flame.

Black wet ground appeared below the curve of the landing skirt. I let the ship drop carefully, carefully . . . and we touched.

It took us an hour to check the ship and get ready to go outside. But who would be first? This was no idle matter. Pluto would be the solar system's last outpost for most of future history, and the statue to the first man on Pluto would probably remain untarnished forever.

Jerome won the toss. All for the sake of a turning coin, Jerome's would be the first name in the history books. I remember the grin I forced! I wish I could force one now. He was laughing and talking of marble statues as he went through the lock.

There's irony in that, if you like that sort of thing.

I was screwing down my helmet when Jerome started shouting obscenities into the helmet mike. I cut the checklist short and followed him out.

One look told it all.

The black wet dirt beneath our landing skirt had been dirty ice, water ice mixed haphazardly with lighter gases and ordinary rock. The heat draining out of the Nerva jet had melted that ice. The rocks within the ice had sunk, and so had the landing vehicle, so that when the water froze again it was halfway up the hull. Our landing craft was sunk solid in the ice.

We could have done some exploring before we tried to move the ship. When we called Sammy he suggested doing just that. But Sammy was up there in the Earth-return vehicle, and we were down here with our landing vehicle mired in the ice of another world.

We were terrified. Until we got clear we would be good for nothing, and we both knew it.

I wonder why I can't remember the fear.

We did have one chance. The landing vehicle was designed to move about on Pluto's surface; and so she had a skirt instead of landing jacks. Half a gravity of thrust would have given us a ground efffect, safer and cheaper than using the ship like a ballistic missile. The landing skirt must have trapped gas underneath when the ship sank, leaving the Nerva-K engine in a bubble cavity.

We could melt our way out.

I know we were as careful as two terrified men could be. The heat rose in the Nerva-K, agonizingly slow. In flight there would have been a coolant effect as cold hydrogen fuel ran through the pile. We couldn't use that. But the environment of the motor was terribly cold. The two factors might compensate, or—

Suddenly dials went wild. Something had cracked from the savage temperature differential. Jerome used the damper rods without effect. Maybe they'd melted.

Maybe wiring had cracked, or resistors had become superconductors in the cold. Maybe the pile—but it doesn't matter now.

I wonder why I can't remember the fear.

Sunlight—

And a logy, dreamy feeling. I'm conscious again. The same stars rise in formation over the same dark mountains.

Something heavy is nosing up against me. I feel its weight against my back and the backs of my legs. What is it? Why am I not terrified?

It slides around in front of me, questing. It looks like a huge amoeba, shapeless and translucent, with darker bodies showing within it. I'd guess it's about my own weight.

Life on Pluto! But how? Superfluids? Helium II contaminated by complex molecules? In that case the beast had best get moving; it will need shade come sunrise. Sunside temperature on Pluto is all of 50° Absolute.

No, come back! It's leaving, flowing down toward the splash crater. Did my thoughts send it away? Nonsense. It probably didn't like the taste of me. It must be terribly slow, that I can watch it move. The beast is still visible, blurred because I can't look directly at it, moving downhill toward the landing vehicle and the tiny statue to the first man to die on Pluto.

After the fiasco with the Nerva-K, one of us had to go down and see how much damage had been done. That meant tunneling down with the flame of a jet backpack, then crawling under the landing skirt. We didn't talk about the implications. We were probably dead. The man who went down into the bubble cavity was even more probably dead; but what of it? Dead is dead.

I feel no guilt. I'd have gone myself if I'd lost the toss.

The Nerva-K had spewed fused bits of the fission pile all over the bubble cavity. We were trapped for good. Rather, I was trapped, and Jerome was dead. The bubble cavity was a hell of radiation.

Jerome had been swearing softly as he went in. He came out perfectly silent. He'd used up all the good words on lighter matters, I think.

I remember I was crying, partly from grief and partly from fear. I remember that I kept my voice steady in spite of it. Jerome never knew. What he guessed is his own affair. He told me the situation, he told me good-bye, and then he strode out onto the ice and took off his helmet. A fuzzy white ball engulfed his head, exploded outward, then settled to the ground in microscopic snowflakes.

But all that seems infinitely remote. Jerome stands out there with his helmet clutched in his hands: a statue to himself, the first man on Pluto. A frost of recon-densed moisture conceals his espression.

Sunrise. I hope the amoeba—

That was wild. The sun stood poised for an instant, a white point-source between twin peaks. Then it streaked upward—and the spinning sky jolted to a stop. No won-der I didn't catch it before. It happened so fast.

A horrible thought. What has happened to me could have happened to Jerome! I wonder—

There was Sammy in the Earth-return vehicle, but he couldn't get down to me. I couldn't get up. The life sys-tem was in good order, but sooner or later I would freeze to death or run out of air.

I stayed with the landing vehicle about thirty hours, taking ice and soil samples, analyzing them, delivering the data to Sammy via laser beam; delivering also high-minded last messages, and feeling sorry for myself. On my trips outside I kept passing Jerome's statue. For a corpse, and one which has not been prettified by the post-surgical skills of an embalmer, he looks damn good. His frost-dusted skin is indistinguishable from marble, and his eyes are lifted toward the stars in poi-gnant yearning. Each time I passed him I wondered how I would look when my turn came.

"You've got to find an oxygen layer," Sammy kept saying.

"Why?"

"To keep you alive! Sooner or later they'll send a rescue ship. You can't give up now!"

I'd already given up. There was oxygen, but there was no such layer as Sammy kept hoping for. There were

veins of oxygen mixed with other things, like veins of
gold ore in rock. Too little, too finely distributed.

"Then use the water ice! That's only poetic justice,
isn't it? You can get the oxygen out by electrolysis!"

But a rescue ship would take years. They'd have to
build it from scratch, and redesign the landing vehicle
too. Electrolysis takes power, and heat takes power. I
had only the batteries.

Sooner or later I'd run out of power. Sammy couldn't
see this. He was more desperate than I was. I didn't run
out of last messages; I stopped sending them because
they were driving Sammy crazy.

I passed Jerome's statue one time too many, and an
idea came.

This is what comes of not wanting to die.

In Nevada, three billion miles from here, half a million corpses lie frozen in vaults surrounded by liquid
nitrogen. Half a million dead men wait for an earthy
resurrection, on the day medical science discovers how
to unfreeze them safely, how to cure what was killing
each one of them, how to cure the additional damage done
by ice crystals breaking cell walls all through their brains
and bodies.

Half a million fools? But what choice did they have?
They were dying.

I was dying.

A man can stay conscious for tens of seconds in vacuum. If I moved fast, I could get out of my suit in that
time. Without that insulation to protect me, Pluto's
black night would suck warmth from my body in seconds. At 50° Absolute, I'd stay in frozen storage until
one version or another of the Day of Resurrection.

Sunlight—

—And stars. No sign of the big blob that found me so
singularly tasteless yesterday. But I could be looking in
the wrong direction.

I hope it got to cover.

I'm looking east, out over the splash plain. In my pe-
ripheral vision the ship looks unchanged and undamaged.

My suit lies beside me on the ice. I stand on a peak of
black rock, poised in my silvered underwear, looking

eternally out at the horizon. Before the cold touched my brain I found a last moment in which to assume a heroic stance. Go east, young man. Wouldn't you know I'd get my directions mixed? But the fog of my breathing-air hid everything, and I was moving in terrible haste.

Sammy Cross must be on his way home now. He'll tell them where I am.

Stars pour up from behind the mountains. The mountains and the splash plain and Jerome and I sink endlessly beneath the sky.

My corpse must be the coldest in history. Even the hopeful dead of Earth are only stored at liquid nitrogen temperatures. Pluto's night makes that look torrid, after the 50° Absolute heat of day seeps away into space.

A superconductor is what I am. Sunlight raises the temperature too high, switching me off like a damned machine at every dawn. But at night my nervous system becomes a superconductor. Currents flow; thoughts flow; sensations flow. Sluggishly. The one hundred and fifty-three hours of Pluto's rotation flash by in what feels like fifteen minutes. At that rate I can wait it out.

I stand as a statue and a viewpoint. No wonder I can't get emotional about anything. Water is a rock here, and my glands are contoured ice within me. But I feel sensations: the pull of gravity, the pain in my ears, the tug of vacuum over every square inch of my body. The vacuum will not boil my blood. But the tensions are frozen into the ice of me, and my nerves tell me so. I feel the wind whistling from my lips, like an exhalation of cigarette smoke.

This is what comes of not wanting to die. What a joke if I got my wish!

Do you suppose they'll find me? Pluto's small for a planet. For a place to get lost in, a small planet is all too large. But there's the ship.

Though it seems to be covered with frost. Vaporized gases recondensed on the hull. Gray-white on gray-white, a lump on a dish of refrozen ice. I could stand here forever waiting for them to pick my ship from its surroundings.

Stop that.

Sunlight—

Stars rolling up the sky. The same patterns, endlessly rolling up from the same points. Does Jerome's corpse live the same half-life I live now? He should have stripped, as I did. My God! I wish I'd thought to wipe the ice from his eyes!

I wish that superfluid blob would come back.

Damn. It's *cold*.

Eye of an Octopus

IT WAS A well.

Henry Bedrosian and Christopher Luden bent over the lip, peering down into the jet darkness. Their balloon-tired motorcycle lay forgotten on the talcum sand, fine pink sand that stretched endlessly away to the flat horizon, borrowing its color from the sky. The sky was the color of blood. It might have been a flaming Kansas sunset, but the tiny sun was still at the zenith. The translucent hewn stone of the well-mouth stood like a blasphemy in the poisonous wilderness that was Mars.

It stood four feet above the sand, roughly circular, perhaps three yards across. The weathered stones were upright blocks, a foot tall by five inches wide by perhaps a foot thick. Whatever the material of those stones, they seemed to glow with a faintly blue inner light.

"It's so human!" said Henry Bedrosian. His voice held a touch of bewildered frustration, echoed by his dark, chisel-nosed face.

Chris Luden knew what he meant. "It's natural. A well's like a lever or a wheel. There aren't many changes you can make, because it's too simple. Did you notice the shape of the bricks?"

"Yes. Odd. But they could still be man made."

"In this air? Breathing nitric oxide, drinking red fuming nitric acid? But—" Chris drew a deep breath. "Why complain? It's life, Harry! We've discovered intelligent life!"

"We've got to tell Abe."

"Right."

But it was a long moment before either moved. They

stood leaning over the well, vivid green pressure suits against pink sand and dark red horizon, peering down into the blur of darkness at the bottom. Then they turned and mounted the Marsmobile.

The landing vehicle stood like an upright steel ball-point pen. Its bottom half was three spreading legs, a restarting solid rocket, and a spacious cargo hold, two-thirds empty now. The upper half was the return-to-orbit stage. Far away across the crescent dunes was a white patch, the jettisoned drag chute.

The Marsmobile, a glorified two-seater motorcycle with big round tires and a number of special modifications, putt-putted up to a landing leg and stopped. Henry got off and climbed to the cabin to call Abe Cooper in the orbiter. Chris Luden mounted to the cargo hold and rummaged through a disorganized hash of necessities until he had a long coil of thin line, a metal bucket, and a heavy rock hammer, all treated to resist the corrosive atmosphere. He dropped the objects next to the Marmobile and climbed down. "Now we'll see," he told himself.

Henry descended the ladder. "Abe's having kittens," he reported. "He says if we don't call him every five minutes he'll come down after us. He wants to know, how old is the well?"

"So do I." Chris brandished the hammer. "We'll knock a chip off and analyze it. Let's go."

The well was a mile and a half from the ship, and not of a conspicuous color. Probably they would have lost it if they hadn't left a flag to mark it.

"Let's see how deep it is first," said Luden. He put the hammer in the bucket for a weight, tied a line to the handle and let it fall. In the eery silence of the Martian desert they waited, listening . . . The rope was nearly gone when the bucket struck something. In a moment the ghost of a splash came floating up from the depths. Henry marked the line so they could measure how deep it had gone. It looked about three hundred feet. They hauled it up.

The bucket was half full of a cloudy, slightly oily fluid.

Chris handed it to his partner. "Harry, you want to take this back and analyze it?"

Henry's dark face grinned around the pointed beard. "I'll match you for it. We both know what it's gonna be."

"Sure, but it has to be done. Even." They matched fingers. Henry lost. He rode back to the ship, the bucket dangling from one hand, fluid slopping over the edge.

The stone which formed the well might have been quartz, or even some kind of unveined marble. It had been too badly weathered, too finely scored and polished and etched by the patient sand grains, to tell what it was. Chris Luden picked a likely looking block and brought the hammer down hard on what seemed to be a crack. He did it three times.

The hammer was ruined.

Luden shifted the hammer this way and that to examine the uneven, dulled edge and flattened corners. His blue eyes held a puzzled look. He knew the government might have quibbled about the weight of a tool for the Mars Project, but never the cost or quality. Here on Mars that hammer was worth tens of thousands of dollars. It *must* be made of some hard, durable steel alloy. Then—

He cocked his head in his helmet, tasting a strange idea . . .

"Harry!"

"Yeah?"

"How you doing?"

"I'm just coming in the airlock. Give me five minutes to find out that this stuff is nitric acid."

"Okay, but do me a favor. Have you got your ring?"

"The diamond horseshoe? Sure."

"Bring it back with you, outside your suit. Outside, that is."

"Now wait a minute, Chris. That's a valuable ring. Why not use your own?"

"I should have though of that! I'll just take off my pressure suit and— Uh! Can't seem to get my helmet unfastened—"

"Stop! Stop! I get the point." There was a click as Henry's radio went off.

Luden sat down to wait.

The sun was sliding toward the horizon. They had landed shortly before sunset yesterday, so they knew how suddenly the desert could turn from pink to midnight black, and how little light the insignificant moons gave. But sundown was four hours away.

The dunes all faced the same way, perfect crescents, as regular as if hand-made. Something must shape the winds here, causing them to blow always in one direction, like Earth's trade winds. And the dunes would crawl across the sands, slower than snails, following the winds.

How old were the stones against his back? If they were really—a strange and silly thought, but Chris wouldn't have volunteered for the Mars Project if he were not half a romantic—if they were really diamond, they must be terribly old, to be so worn by mere sand. Far older than the pyramids, and revered ancestor to the Sphinx. Maybe the race that carved those stones had since perished. Science-fiction writers often assumed an extinct Martian race. Why, perhaps the well had originally held water—

"Hello, Chris?"

"Here."

"It's dirty nitric acid, not too strong. Next time you'll believe me."

"Harry, they didn't send us here to make astute guesses. They did all the guessing when they built the ship. We came to find out for sure, right? Right."

"See you in ten minutes." Click.

Luden let his eyes drift back across the desert. It was a moment before he realized what had caught his eye. One of the dunes was irregular. The curves were wrong, asymmetrical. The normal crescent had left one sprawling, trailing arm. It stood out like a pear in a line of apples.

He had ten minutes, and the dune wasn't far. Luden got up and started walking.

He stood under the dune and looked back. The well was clearly visible. The distance was even shorter than he had thought. He had been deceived by the nearness of the horizon.

The lip of the dune was some fourteen feet high.

What had distorted it? An upthrusting spire of rock, perhaps, not quite high enough to show through the sand. They could find it with the sonar later.

It had to be under the one sprawling, twisted arm of sand.

"Chris! Where the hell are you? Chris?"

Chris jumped. He'd forgotten Henry. "Look due south of the well and you'll see me."

"Why don't you stay where you're put, you idiot? I thought you'd been buried by a sandstorm."

"Sorry, Harry. I got interested in something." Chris Luden was now standing on the twisted arm of sand. He sounded preoccupied. "Try scratching the blocks of the well with your ring."

"That's an *odd* thought," Henry laughed.

"Do it."

Silence. Luden felt the wind, looked down at the sand, tried to imagine what obstruction had dropped it here. Something not necessarily very large. It would not be beneath the dune; it would be on the windward side ... at the beginning of the arch ... there.

"I scratched it, Chris. There's a scratch all right. So that effectively takes—Ooops. Aaargh! Chris, you're doomed! Only death can save you from my wrath!"

"Why are you irritated with—"

"My diamond! It's ruined!"

"Relax. You could replace it a million times over with just one block from the well."

"Say, that's true. But we'll need the laser to cut it loose. They must have used diamond dust for the cement, too. And the fuel to get it back—"

"Harry, do me a favor. Bring—"

"That last favor cost me a three-thousand-dollar ring."

"Bring the Marsmobile out here. I want to do some digging."

"Be right there."

A minute later Henry stopped the machine alongside Chris's green suit. His smile showed that the scratches on his ring had not permanently scarred his psyche. "Where do we dig?"

"Right where I'm standing."

The Marsmobile was equipped with two down-thrusting compressed-air jets for getting over steep obstructions. A large tank under the vehicle's belly held the heavily compressed air, compressed directly from the thin Martian atmosphere by the motor. Henry turned on the jets and hovered over the spot where Chris had been standing, shifting his weight to keep the machine in place. Sand sprayed out in sheets. Chris ran to get out from under, and Henry grinned and doubled the thrust to send the fine grains showering over him. In half a minute the pressure became too low. Henry had to land. The Marsmobile shuddered and vibrated as its motor struggled to refill the pressure chamber.

"I hate to ask," said Henry, "but what's the point of all this?"

"There's something solid down there. I want to expose it."

"Okay, if you're sure we're in the right place. We've got six months of time to waste."

They wasted a few minutes silently watching the Marsmobile fill its pressure tank.

"Hey," said Henry. "You think we could stake a claim on this diamond mine?"

Chris Luden, sitting on the steep side of the dune, thoughtfully scratched the side of his helmet. "Why not? We haven't seen any live Martians, and it's for sure that nobody else has a claim. Sure, we'll file our claim; the worst they can do is disallow it."

"One thing. I didn't mention it before because I wanted you to see for yourself, but the heck with it. One of those blocks is covered solid with deep scratches."

"They all are."

"Not like these. These are *deep,* and they're all at forty-five degree angles, unless my imagination is fooling me. They're too fine to be sure, but I think it's some kind of writing."

And without waiting for an answer, Henry took off on the air jets. He was good at it. He was like a ballet dancer. You could see Henry shifting weight, but the scooter never seemed to move.

Something was emerging from the sand. Something not a rock.

Something like a piece of modern metal sculpture, with no use and no meaning but with a weird beauty nonetheless. Something that had been a machine and was now—nothing.

Henry Bedrosian balanced above the conical pit his jets had dug. The artifact was almost clear now. Something else showed beside it.

A mummy.

The Marsmobile settled on the last of its air. Chris plunged down the side of the pit as Henry climbed off.

The mummy was humanoid, about four feet long, with long arms, enormous fragile tapered fingers, and a traditionally oversized skull. No fine detail was visible; it had all been worn away. Chris couldn't even be sure how many fingers the—hominid—had had. One hand still held two; the other only one, plus a flattened opposable thumb. No toes showed on the feet. The thing lay face down.

The artifact, now uncovered, showed more detail. Yet the detail had no meaning. Thick bent metal bars, thin twisted wires, two enormous crumpled circles with something rotted clinging to what had been their rims —and then Henry's imagination clicked, the same visual knack that had gotten him A's in topology, and he said, "It's a bicycle."

"You've lost your mind."

"No, look. The wheels are too big, and—"

It was a fantastically distorted bicycle, with wheels eight feet across, a low, dwarf-sized saddle, and a system of gears to replace the chain. The gear ratio was very low. The saddle was almost against the rear wheel, and a tiller bar, now bent to scrap, had been fixed to the hub of the front wheel. Something had crumpled the bicycle like a crush-proof cigarette pack in a strong man's hand, and then nitric acid rust had done its worst to the metal.

"Okay, it's a bicycle," said Chris. "It's a Salvador Dali bicycle, but still a bicycle. They must have been a lot like us, hmmm? Bicycles, stone wells, writing—"

"Clothing."

"Where?"

"It must have been there. He's less worn around the torso, see? You can see the wrinkles in his skin. He must have been protected until his clothes rotted away."

"Maybe. He kind of ruins our lost race theory, doesn't he? He couldn't possibly be more than a couple of thousand years old. Hundreds would be more like it."

"Then he drank nitric acid after all. Well, that blows our diamond mine, partner. He's *got* to have living relatives."

"We can't count on their being too much like us. These things we've found—clothing, writing, wells—they're all things any intelligent being might be forced to invent. And parallel evolution might explain the biped shape."

"Parallel evolution?" Henry repeated.

"Like the eye of an octopus. It's nearly identical in structure to a human eye. Yet an octopus isn't remotely human. Most marsupials, you can't tell them from their mammal counterparts. Well, let's try to pick him up."

Any archaeologist would have shot them down in cold blood.

The mummy was as light and dry as cork, and showed no tendency to come apart in their hands. They strapped him gently over the luggage box and climbed on themselves. Chris drove back slowly and carefully.

Chris stood on the first rung of the ladder, adjusting the mummy's balance on his left shoulder. "We'll have to spray him with plastic before takeoff," he said. "Do we have any plastic spray?"

"I don't remember any. We'd better take lots of picture in case it does come apart."

"Right. There's a camera in the cabin." Chris started up, and Henry followed. They got the relic to the airlock without mishap.

"I've been thinking," said Henry. "That nitric acid wasn't dilute, exactly, but there was water in it. Maybe this guy's chemistry can extract the water from nitric acid."

"Good thought."

They put the mummy gently on a pile of blankets and began searching for the camera. After five frustrating minutes Chris deliberately banged his head against a wall. "I took it out to catch the sunset last night. It's in the cargo hold."

"Go get it."

Henry stood in the airlock, watching as Chris went down the ladder. After a moment in the cargo space Chris started up with the camera strap over his shoulder.

"I've been thinking too," said Chris, his voice seemingly dissociated from his climbing figure. "Diamond can't be *that* plentiful here, and carving it into blocks must have been real hard labor. Why diamond? And why write on a well?"

"Religious reasons? Maybe they worship water."

"That's what I was thinking."

"Of course you were. That plot's as old as Lowell."

Chris had reached the top. They squeezed into the airlock and waited for it to cycle.

The door opened. Both men had their helmets off by this time, and they both smelled it at once. Something chemical, something strong—

Thick, greasy smoke was pouring up from the ancient corpse.

Henry reacted first. He sprang for the double boiler in the small kitchen corner. The bottom half was still full of water; he snatched it up and threw the water over the smoldering Martian mummy while with his other hand he turned on the water faucet to get more.

The mummy went off like a napalm bomb.

Henry leaped away from the exploding flames and his head rammed something flat and very hard. He went down with his eyes full of leaping light. Immediately he sat up, knowing that something urgently needed doing but unable to remember what. He saw Chris, still in vacuum suit except for the helmet, run through the multicolored flames, pick the mummy up by the ankles and throw it into the airlock. Chris hit the "Cycle" button. The inner door swung shut.

Then Chris was bending over him. "Where does it hurt, Harry? Can you talk? Can you move?"

Henry sat up again. "I'm okay."

Chris expelled a gusty breath. Then he began to laugh.

Henry stood up a little shakily. His head ached. The fumes in the cabin weren't intolerable, and already the air plant was whining its eagerness to make the air pure and scentless. Red smoke from the open outer airlock door blew past a porthole, dying away. "What made him explode?" he wondered.

"The water," said Chris Luden. "What a wild chemistry he must have! I want to be there when we meet a live one."

"But what about the well? We *know* he used water."

"Yes he did. He sure as hell did. And did you know that an octopus eye is identical to a human eye?"

"Sure. But a well is a well, isn't it?"

"Not when it's a crematorium, Harry. What else could it be? There's no fire on Mars, but water must dissolve a body completely. And wouldn't I like to know what the morticians charge their customers for those cut diamond building blocks! The hardest substance known to Man or Martian! An everlasting monument to the dear departed!"

How the Heroes Die

ONLY SHEER RUTHLESSNESS could have taken him out of town alive. The mob behind Carter hadn't tried to guard the Marsbuggies, since Carter would have needed too much time to take a buggy through the vehicular airlock. They could have caught him there, and they knew it. Some were guarding the personnel lock, hoping he'd try for that. He might have; for if he could have closed the one door in their faces and opened the next, the safeties would have protected him while he went through the third and fourth and outside. On the Marsbuggy he was trapped in the bubble.

There was room to drive around in. Less than half the prefab houses had been erected so far. The rest of the bubbletown's floor was flat fused sand, empty but for scattered piles of foam-plastic walls and ceilings and floors. But they'd get him eventually. Already they were starting up another buggy.

They never expected him to run his vehicle through the bubble wall.

The Marsbuggy tilted, then righted itself. A blast of breathing-air roared out around him, picked up a cloud of fine sand, and hurled it explosively away into the thin, poisoned atmosphere. Carter grinned as he looked behind him. They would die now, all of them. He was the only one wearing a pressure suit. In an hour he could come back and repair the rip in the bubble. He'd have to dream up a fancy story to tell when the next ship came . . .

Carter frowned. What were they—

At least ten wind-harried men were wrestling with the

41

wall of a prefab house. As Carter watched, they picked the wall up off the fused sand, balanced it almost upright, and let go. The foam-plastic wall rose into the wind and slapped hard against the bubble, over the ten-foot rip.

Carter stopped his buggy to see what would happen.

Nobody was dead. The air was not shrieking away but leaking away. Slowly, methodically, a line of men climbed into their suits and filed through the personnel lock to repair the bubble.

A buggy entered the vehicular lock. The third and last was starting to life. Carter turned his buggy and was off.

Top speed for a Marsbuggy is about twenty-five miles per hour. The buggy rides on three wide balloon-tired wheels, each mounted at the end of a five-foot arm. What those wheels can't go over, the buggy can generally hop over on the compressed-air jet mounted underneath. The motor and the compressor are both powered by a Litton battery holding a tenth as much energy as the original Hiroshima bomb.

Carter had been careful, as careful as he had had time for. He was carrying a full load of oxygen, twelve four-hour tanks in the air bin behind him, and an extra tank rested against his knees. His batteries were nearly full; he would be out of air long before his power ran low. When the other buggies gave up he could circle round and return to the bubble in the time his extra tank would give him.

His own buggy and the two behind him were the only such vehicles on Mars. At twenty-five miles per hour he fled, and at twenty-five miles per hour they followed. The closest was half a mile behind.

Carter turned on his radio.

He found the middle of a conversation. "—Can't afford it. One of you will have to come back. We could lose two of the buggies, but not all three."

That was Shute, the bubbletown's research director and sole military man. The next voice, deep and sarcastic, belonged to Rufus Doolittle, the biochemist. "What'll we do, flip a coin?"

"Let me go," the third voice said tightly. "I've got a stake in this."

Carter felt apprehension touch the nape of his neck.

"Okay, Alf. Good luck," said Rufus. "Good hunting," he added maliciously, as if he knew Carter were listening.

"You concentrate on getting the bubble fixed. I'll see that Carter doesn't come back."

Behind Carter, the rearmost buggy swung in a wide loop toward town. The other came on. And it was driven by the linguist, Alf Harness.

Most of the bubble's dozen men were busy repairing the ten-foot rip with heaters and plastic sheeting. It would be a long job but an easy one, for by Shute's orders the bubble had been deflated. The trasparent plastic had fallen in folds across the prefab houses, forming a series of interconnected tents. One could move about underneath with little difficulty.

Lieutenant-Major Michael Shute watched the men at work and decided they had things under control. He walked away like a soldier on parade, stooping as little as possible as he moved beneath the dropping folds.

He stopped and watched Gondot operating the air-maker. Gondot noticed him and spoke without looking up.

"Mayor, why'd you let Alf chase Carter alone?"

Shute accepted his nickname. "We couldn't lose both tractors."

"Why not just post them on guard duty for two days?"

"And what if Carter got through the guard? He must be determined to wreck the dome. He'd catch us with out pants down. Even if some of us got into suits, could we stand another rip in the bubble?"

Gondot reached to scratch his short beard. His finger-tips rapped helmet plastic and he looked annoyed. "Maybe not. I can fill the bubble anytime you're ready, but then the airmarker'll be empty. We'll be almost out of tanked air by the time they finish mending that rip. Another'd finish us."

Shute nodded and turned away. All the air anyone could use—tons of nitrogen and oxygen—was right outside; but it was in the form of nitrogen dioxide gas. The airmaker could convert it three times as fast as men could use it. But if Carter tore the dome again, that would be too slow.

But Carter wouldn't. Alf would see to that. The emergency was over—this time.

And so Lieutenant-Major Shute could go back to worrying about the emergency's underlying causes.

His report on those causes had been finished a month ago. He had reread it several times since, and always it had seemed complete and to the point. Yet he had the feeling it could be written better. He ought to make it as effective as possible. What he had to say could only be said once, and then his career would be over and his voice silenced.

Cousins had sold some fiction once, writing as a hobby. Perhaps he would help. But Shute was reluctant to involve anyone else in what amounted to his own rebellion.

Yet—he'd have to rewrite that report now, or at least add to it. Lew Harness was dead, murdered. John Carter would be dead within two days. All Shute's responsibility. All pertinent.

The decision wasn't urgent. It would be a month before Earth was in reach of the bubbletown's sending station.

Most of the asteroids spend most of their time between Mars and Jupiter, and it often happens that one of them crosses a planet where theretofore it had crossed only an orbit. There are asteroid craters all over Mars. Old eroded ones, sharp new ones, big ones, little ones, ragged and smooth ones. The bubbletown was at the center of a large, fairly recent crater four miles across: an enormous, poorly cast ashtray discarded on the reddish sand.

The buggies ran over cracked glass, avoiding the occasional tilted blocks, running uphill toward the broken rim. A sky the color of blood surrounded a tiny, brilliant sun set precisely at the zenith.

Inevitably Alf was getting closer. When they crossed the rim and started downhill they would pull apart. It was going to be a long chase.

Now was the time for regrets, if there ever was such a time. But Carter wasn't the type, and he had nothing to be ashamed of anyway. Lew Harness had needed to die; had as much as *asked* to die. Carter was only puzzzled that his death should have provoked so violent a reaction. Could thay *all* be—the way Lew had been? Unlikely. If he'd stayed and explained—

They'd have torn him apart. Those vulpine faces, with the distended nostrils and the bared teeth!

And now he was being chased by one man. But that man was Lew's brother.

Here was the rim, and Alf was still well behind. Carter slowed as he went over, knowing that the way down would be rougher. He was just going over the edge when a rock ten yards away exploded in white fire.

Alf had a flare pistol.

Carter just stopped himself from scrambling out of the buggy to hide in the rocks. The buggy lurched downward and, like it or not, Carter had to forget his terror to keep the vehicle upright.

The rubble around the crater's rim slowed him still further. Carter angled the buggy for the nearest rise of sloping sand. As he reached it, Alf came over the rim, a quarter-mile behind. His silhouette hesitated there against the bloody sky, and another flare exploded, blinding bright and terrifyingly close.

Then Carter was on the straightaway, rolling down sloping sand to a perfectly flat horizon.

The radio said, "Gonna be a long one, Jack."

Carter pushed to transmit. "Right. How many flares do you have left?"

"Don't worry about it."

"I won't. Not the way you're throwing them away."

Alf didn't answer. Carter left the radio band open, knowing that ultimately Alf must talk to the man he needed to kill.

The crater which was home dropped behind and was gone. Endless flat desert rose before the buggies, flowed under the oversized wheels and dropped behind. Gentle crescent dunes patterned the sand, but they were no barrier to a buggy. Once there was a Martian well. It stood all alone on the sand, a weathered cylindrical wall seven feet high and ten in circumference, made of cut diamond blocks. The wells, and the slanting script written deep into their "dedication blocks," were reponsible for the town's presence on Mars. Since the only Martian ever found—a mummy centuries dead, at least—had exploded at the first contact with water, it was generally assumed that the wells were crematoriums. But it wasn't certain. Nothing was certain about Mars.

The radio maintained an eerie silence. Hours rolled past; the sun slid toward the deep red horizon, and still Alf did not speak. It was as if Alf had said everything there was to say to Jack Carter. And that was wrong! Alf should have needed to justify himself!

It was Carter who sighed and gave up. "You can't catch me, Alf."

"No, but I can stay behind you as long as I need to."

"You can stay behind me just twenty-four hours. You've got forty-eight hours of air. I don't believe you'll kill yourself just to kill me."

"Don't count on it. But I won't need to. Noon tomorrow, you'll be chasing me. You need to breathe, just like I do."

"Watch this," said Carter. The O-tank resting against his knee was empty. He tipped it over the side and watched it roll away.

"I had an extra tank," he said. He smiled in relief at his release from that damning weight. "I can live four hours longer than you can. Want to turn back, Alf?"

"No."

"He's not worth it, Alf. He was nothing but a queer."

"Does that mean he's got to die?"

"It does if the son of a bitch propositions me. Maybe you're a little that way yourself?"

"No. And Lew wasn't queer till he came here. They should have sent half men, half women."

"Amen."

"You know, lots of people get a little sick to their stomachs about homosexuals. I do myself, and it hurt to see it happening to Lew. But there's only one type who goes looking for 'em so he can beat up on 'em."

Carter frowned.

"Latents. Guys who think they might turn queer themselves if you gave 'em the opportunity. They can't stand queers around because queers are temptation."

"You're just returning the compliment."

"Maybe."

"Anyway, the town has enough problems without—things like that going on. This whole project could have been wrecked by someone like your brother."

"How bad do we need killers?"

"Pretty badly, this time." Suddenly Carter knew that he was now his own defense attorney. If he could convince Alf that he shouldn't be executed, he could convince the rest of them. If he couldn't—then he must destroy the bubble, or die. He went on talking as persuasively as he knew how.

"You see, Alf, the town has two purposes. One is to find out if we can live in an environment as hostile as this one. The other is to contact the Martians. Now there are just fifteen of us in town—"

"Twelve. Thirteen when I get back."

"Fourteen if we both do. Okay. Each of us is more or less necessary to the functioning of the town. But I'm needed in both fields. I'm the ecologist, Alf. I not only have to keep the town from dying from some sort of imbalance, I also have to figure out how the Martians live, what they live on, how Martian life forms depend on each other. You see?"

"Sure. How 'bout Lew? Was he necessary?"

"We can get along without him. He was the radio man. At least a couple of us have training enough to take over communications."

"You make me so happy. Doesn't the same go for you?"

Carrter thought hard and fast. Yes, Gondot in particular could keep the town's life-support system going with little help. But—"Not with the Martian ecology. There isn't—"

"There isn't any Martian ecology. Jack, has anyone

ever found *any* life on Mars besides that man-shaped mummy? You can't be an ecologist without something to make deductions from. You've got nothing to investigate. So what good are you?"

Carter kept talking. He was still arguing as the sun dropped into the sea of sand and darkness closed down with a snap. But he knew now it was no use. Alf's mind was closed.

By sunset the bubble was taut, and the tortured scream of incoming breathing-air had dropped to a tired sigh. Lieutenant-Major Shute unfastened the clamps at his shoulders and lifted his helmet, ready to jam it down fast if the air was too thin. It wasn't. He set the helmet down and signaled thumbs-up to the men watching him.

Ritual. Those dozen men had known the air would be safe. But rituals had grown fast where men worked in space, and the most rigid was that the man in charge fastened his helmet last and unfastened it first. Now suits were being removed. Men moved about their duties. Some moved toward the kitchen to clean up the vacuum-induced havoc so Hurley could get dinner.

Shute stopped Lee Cousins as he went by. "Lee, could I see you a minute?"

"Sure, Mayor." Shute was "the Mayor" to all bubble-town.

"I want your help as a writer," said Shute. "I'm going to send in a quite controversial report when we get within range of Earth, and I'd like you to help me make it convincing."

"Fine. Let's see it."

The ten streetlamps came on, dispelling the darkness which had fallen so suddenly. Shute led the way to his prefab bungalow, unlocked the safe, and handed Cousins the manuscript. Cousins hefted it. "Big," he said. "Might pay to cut it."

"By all means, if you can find anything unnecessary."

"I'll bet I can," Cousins grinned. He dropped on the bed and began to read.

Ten minutes later he asked, "Just what is the incidence of homosexuality in the Navy?"

"I haven't the faintest idea."

"Then it's not powerful evidence. You might quote a limerick to show that the problem's proverbial. I know a few."

"Good."

A little later Cousins said, "A lot of schools in England *are* coeducational. More every year."

"I know. But the present problem is among men who graduated from boys' schools when they were much younger."

"Make that clearer. Incidentally, was your high-school coeducational?"

"No."

"Any queers?"

"A few. At least one in every class. The seniors used to use paddles on the ones they suspected."

"Did it help?"

"No. Of course not."

"Okay. You've got two sets of circumstances under which a high rate of homosexuality occurs. In both cases you've got three conditions: a reasonable amount of leisure, no women, and a disciplinary pecking order. You need a third example."

"I couldn't think of one."

"The Nazi organization."

"Oh?"

"I'll give you details." Cousins went on reading. He finished the report and put it aside. "This'll cause merry hell," he said.

"I know."

"The worst thing about it is your threat to give the whole thing to the newspapers. If I were you I'd leave that out."

"If you were me you wouldn't," said Shute. "Everyone who had anything to do with WARGOD knew they were risking everything that's happened. They preferred to let us take that risk rather than risk public opinion themselves. There are hundreds of Decency Leagues in the United States. Maybe thousands, I don't know. But they'll all come down on the government like harpies if anyone tried to send a mixed crew to Mars or anywhere else in space. The only way I can make the government act is to give them a greater threat."

"You win. This is a greater threat."

"Did you find anything else to cut out?"

"Oh, hell yes. I'll go through this again with a red pencil. You talk too much, and use too many words that are too long, and you generalize. You'll have to give details or you'll lose impact."

"I'll be ruining some reputations."

"Can't be helped. We've got to have women on Mars, and right now. Rufe and Timmy are building up to a real spitting fight. Rufe thanks he caused Lew's death by leaving him. Timmy keeps taunting him with it."

"All right," said Shute. He stood up. He had been sitting erect throughout the discussion, as if sitting at attention. "Are the buggies still in radio range?"

"They can't hear us, but we can hear them. Timmy's working the radio."

"Good. I'll keep him on it until they go out of range. Shall we get dinner?"

Phobos rose where the sun had set, a scatttering of moving dots of light, like a crescent of dim stars. It grew brighter as it rose: a new moon becoming a half-moon in hours. Then it was too high to look at. Carter had to keep his eyes on the triangle of desert lit by his headlights. The headlight beams were the color of earthly sunlight, but to Carter's Mars-adapted eyes they turned everything blue.

He had chosen his course well. The desert ahead was flat for more than seven hundred miles. There would be no low hills rising suddenly before him to trap him into jet-jumping in faint moonlight or waiting for Alf to come down on him. Alf's turnover point would come at high noon tomorrow, and then Carter would have won.

For Alf would turn back toward the bubble, and Carter would go on into the desert. When Alf was safely over the horizon, Carter would turn left or right, go on for an hour, and then follow a course parallel to Alf's. He would be in sight of the bubble an hour later than Alf, with three hours in which to plan.

Then would come the hardest part. Certainly there would be someone on guard. Carter would have to charge past the guard—who might be armed with a flare pistol—tear the bubble open, and somehow confiscate the supply of O-tanks. Ripping the bubble open would probably kill everyone inside, but there would be men in suits outside. He would have to load some of the O-tanks on his buggy and open the stopcocks of the rest, all before anyone reached him.

What bothered him was the idea of charging a flare pistol . . . But perhaps he could just aim the buggy and jump out. He would have to see.

His eyelids were getting heavy, and his hands were cramped. But he dare not slow down, and he dared not sleep.

Several times he had thought of smashing the come-hither in his suit radio. With that thing constantly beeping, Alf could find him anytime he pleased. But Alf could find him anyway. His headlights were always behind, never catching up, never dropping away. If he ever got our of Alf's sight, that come-hither would have to go. But there was no point in letting Alf know that. Not yet.

Stars dropped into the black western horizon. Phobos rose again, brighter this time, and again became too high to watch. Deimos now showed above the steady shine of Alf's headlights.

Suddenly it was day, and there were thin black shadows pointing to a yellow horizon. Stars still glowed in a red-black sky. There was a crater ahead, a glass dish set in the desert, not too big to circle around. Carter angled left. The buggy behind him also angled. If he kept turning like this, Alf couldn't help but gain on him. Carter sucked water and nutrient solution from the nipples in his helmet, and concentrated on steering. His eyes felt gritty, and his mouth belonged to a Martian mummy.

"Morning," said Alf.

"Morning. Get plenty of sleep?"

"Not enough. I only slept about six hours, in snatches. I kept worrying you'd turn off and lose me."

For a moment Carter went hot and cold. Then he know that Alf was needling him. He'd no more slept than Carter had.

"Look to your right," said Alf.

To their right was the crater wall. And—Carter

looked again to be sure—there was a silhouette on the rim, a man-shaped shadow against the red sky. With one hand it balanced something tall and thin.

"A Martian," Carter said softly. Without thinking he turned his buggy to climb the wall. Two flares exploded in front of him, a second apart, and he frantically jammed the tiller bar hard left.

"God damn it, Alf! That was a *Martian!* We've got to go *after* it!"

The silhouette was gone. No doubt the Martian had run for its life when it saw the flares.

Alf said nothing. Nothing at all. And Carter rode on, past the crater, with a murderous fury building in him.

It was eleven o'clock. The tips of a range of hills were pushing above the western horizon.

"I'm just curious," Alf said, "but what would you have said to that Martian?"

Carter's voice was tight and bitter. "Does it matter?"

"Yah. The best you could have done was scare him. When we get in touch with the Martians, we'll do it just the way we planned."

Carter ground his teeth. Even without the accident of Lew Harness' death, there was no telling how long the translation plan would take. It involved three steps: sending pictures of the writings on the crematory wells and other artifacts to Earth, so that computers could translate the language; writing messages in that language to leave near the wells where Martians would find them; and then waiting for the Martians to make a move. But there was no reason to believe that the script on the wells wasn't from more than one language, or from the same language as it had changed over thousands of years. There was no reason to assume the Martians would be interested in strange beings living in a glorified balloon, regardless of whether the invaders knew how to write. And could the Martians read their own ancestors' script?

An idea . . . "You're a linguist," said Carter.

No answer.

"Alf, we've talked about whether the town needed Lew, and we've talked about whether the town needs me. How about you? Without you we'd *never* get the well-script translated."

"I doubt that. The Cal Tech computers are doing most of the work, and anyhow I left notes. But so what?"

"If you keep chasing me you'll force me to kill you. Can the town afford to lose you?"

"You can't do it. But I'll make you a deal if you want. It's eleven now. Give me two of your O-tanks, and we'll go back to town. We'll stop two hours from town, leave your buggy, and you'll ride the rest of the way tied up in the air bin. Then you can stand trial."

"You think they'll let me off?"

"Not after the way you ripped the bubble open on your way out. That was a blunder, Jack."

"Why don't you just take one tank?" If Alf did that, Carter would get back with two hours to spare. He knew, now, that he would have to wreck the bubble. He had no alternative. But Alf would be right behind him with the flare gun . . .

"No deal. I wouldn't feel safe if I didn't know you'd run out of air two hours before we got back. You want me to feel safe, don't you?"

It was better the other way. Let Alf turn back in an hour. Let Alf be in the bubble when Carter returned to tear it open.

"Carter turned him down," said Timmy. He hunched over the radio, holding his earphones with both hands, listening with every nerve for voices which had almost died into the distance.

"He's planning something," Gondot said uneasily.

"Naurally," said Shute. "He wants to lose Alf, return to the bubble, and wreck it. What other hope has he?"

"But he'd die too," said Timmy.

"Not necessarily. If he killed us all, he could mend the new rip while he lived on the O-tanks we've got left. I think he could keep the bubble in good enough repair to keep one man alive."

"My *Lord!* What can we do?"

"Relax, Timmy. It's simple math." It was easy for

Lieutenant-Major Shute to keep his voice light, and he
didn't want Timmy to start a panic. "If Alf turns back at
noon, Carter can't get here before noon tomorrow. At
four he'll be out of air. We'll just keep everyone in suits
for four hours." Privately he wondered if twelve men
could repair even a small rip before they used up the
bottled air. It would be one tank every twenty minutes
. . . but perhaps they wouldn't be tested.

"Five minutes of twelve," said Carter. "Turn back,
Alf. You'll only get home with ten minutes to spare."

The linguist chuckled. A quarter mile behind, the
blue dot of his buggy didn't move.

"You can't fight mathematics, Alf. Turn back."

"Too late."

"In five minutes it will be."

"I started this trip short of an O-tank. I should have
turned two hours ago."

Carter had to wet his lips from the water nipple before he answered. "You're lying. Will you stop bugging
me? Stop it!"

Alf laughed. "Watch me turn back."

His buggy came on.

It was noon, and the chase would not end. At twenty-five miles per, two Marsbuggies a quarter of a mile
apart moved serenely through an orange desert. Chemical stains of green rose ahead and fell behind. Crescent
dunes drifted by, as regular as waves on an ocean. The
ghostly path of a meteorite touched the northern horizon
in a momentary white flash. The hills were higher now,
humps of smooth rock like animals sleeping beyond the
horizon. The sun burned small and bright in a sky red-
dened by nitrogen dioxide and, near the horizon, blackened by its thinness to the color of bloody India ink.

Had the chase really started at noon? Exactly noon?
But it was twelve-thirty now, and he was *sure* that was
too late.

Alf had doomed himself—to doom Carter.

But he *wouldn't.*

"Great minds think alike," he told the radio.

"Really?" Alf's tone said he couldn't have cared less.

"You took an extra tank. Just like me."

"No I didn't, Jack."

"You must have. If there's one thing I'm sure of in life, it's that *you* are *not* the type to kill yourself. All right, Alf, I quit. Let's go back.

"Let's not."

"We'd have three hours to chase that Martian."

A flare exploded behind his buggy. Carter sighed raggedly. At two o'clock both buggies would turn back to bubbletown, where Carter would probably be executed.

But suppose I turn back now?

That's easy. Alf will shoot me with the flare gun.

He might miss. If I let him choose my course, I'll die for certain.

Carter sweated and cursed himself, but he couldn't do it. He couldn't deliberately turn into Alf's gun.

At two o'clock the base of the range came over the horizon. The hills were incredibly clear, almost as clear as they would have been on the Moon. But they were horribly weathered, and the sea of sand lapped around them as if eager to finish them off, to drag them down.

Carter rode with his eyes turned behind. His watch hands moved on, minute to minute, and Carter watched in disbelief as Alf's vehicle continued to follow. As the time approached and reached two-thirty, Carter's disbelief faded. It didn't matter, now, how much oxygen Alf had. They had passed Carter's turnover point.

"You've killed me," he said.

No answer.

"I killed Lew in a fistfight. What you've done to me is much worse. You're killing me by slow torture. You're a demon, Alf."

"Fistfight my aunt's purple asterisk. You hit Lew in the throat and watched him drown in his own blood. Don't tell *me* you didn't know what you were doing. Everybody in town knows you know karate."

"He died in minutes. I'll need a whole day!"

"You don't like that? Turn around and rush my gun. It's right here waiting."

"We could get back to the crater in time to search for that Martian. That's why I came to Mars. To learn what's here. So did you, Alf. Come on, let's turn back."

"You first."

But he couldn't. He *couldn't*. Karate can defeat any hand-to-hand weapon but a quaterstaff, and Carter had quarterstaff training too. But he couldn't charge a flare gun! Not even if Alf meant to turn back. And Alf didn't.

A faint whine vibrated through the bubble. The sandstorm was at the height of its fury, which made it about as dangerous as an enraged caterpillar. At worst it was an annoyance. The shrill, barely audible whine could get on one's nerves, and the darkness made streetlamps necessary. Tomorrow the bubble would be covered a tenth of an inch deep in fine, Moon-dry silt. Inside the bubble it would be darker than night until someone blew the silt away with an O-tank.

To Shute the storm was depressing. Here on Mars was Lieutenant-Major Shute, Boy Hero, facing terrifying dangers on the frontiers of human exploration! A sandstorm that wouldn't have harmed an infant. Nobody here faced a single danger that he had not brought with him.

Would it be like this forever? Men traveling enormous distances to face themselves?

There had been little work done since noon today. Shute had given up on that. On a stack of walls sat Timmy, practically surrounding the buggy-pickup radio, surrounded in turn by the bubble's population.

Timmy stood up as Shute approached the group. "They're gone," he announced, sounding very tired. He turned off the radio. The men looked at each other, and some got to their feet.

"Tim! How'd you lose them?"

Timmy noticed him. "They're too far away, Mayor."

"They never turned around?"

"They never did. They just kept going out into the desert. Alf must have gone insane. Carter's not worth dying for."

Shute thought, *But he was once.* Carter had been one of the best: tough, fearless, bright, enthusiastic. Shute had watched him deteriorate under the boredom and the close quarters aboard ship. He had seemed to recover when they reached Mars, when all of them suddenly had work to do. Then, yesterday morning—murder.

Alf. It was hard to lose Alf. Lew had been little loss, but Alf—

Cousins dropped into step beside him. "I've got that red-pencil work done."

"Thanks, Lee. I'll have to do it all over now."

"Don't do it over. Write an addendum. Show how and why three men died. Then you can say, 'I told you so.'"

"You think so?"

"My professional judgment. When's the funeral?"

"Day after tomorrow. That's Sunday. I thought it would be appropriate."

"You can say all three services at once. Good timing."

To all bubbletown, Jack Carter and Alf Harness were dead. But they still breathed—

The mountains came toward them: the only fixed points in an ocean of sand. Alf was closer now, something less than four hundred yards behind. At five o'clock Carter reached the base of the mountains.

They were too high to go over on the air jet. He could see spots where he might have landed the buggy while the pump filled the jet tank for another hop. But for what?

Better to wait for Alf.

Suddenly Carter knew that that was the one thing in the world Alf wanted. To roll up alongside in his buggy. To watch Carter's face until he was sure Carter knew exactly what was to come. And then to blast Carter down in flames from ten feet away, and watch while a bright magnesium-oxidizer flare burned through his suit and skin and vitals.

The hills were low and shallow. Even from yards away he might have been looking at the smooth flank of a sleeping beast—except that this beast was not breathing. Carter took a deep breath, noticing how stale the air had become despite the purifier unit, and turned on the compressed-air jet.

The air of Mars is terribly thin, but it can be compressed; and a rocket will work anywhere, even a compressed-air rocket. Carter went up, leaning as far back in the cabin as he could to compensate for the loss of weight in the O-tanks behind him, to put as little work as possible on gyroscopes meant to spin only in emergencies. He rose fast, and he tilted the buggy to send it skating along the thirty-degree slope of the hill. There were flat places along the slope, but not many. He should reach the first one easily . . .

A flare exploded in his eyes. Carter clenched his teeth and fought the urge to look behind. He tilted the buggy backward to slow him down. The jet pressure was dropping.

He came down like a feather two hundred feet above the desert. When he turned off the jet he could hear the gyros whining. He turned the stabilizer off and let them run down. Now there was only the chugging of the compressor, vibrating through his suit.

Alf was out of his buggy, standing at the base of the mountains, looking up.

"Come on," said Carter. "What are you waiting for?"

"Go on over if you want to."

"What's the matter? Are your gyros fouled?"

"Your brain is fouled, Carter. Go on over." Alf raised one arm stiffly out. The hand showed flame, and Carter ducked instinctively.

The compressor had almost stopped, which meant the tank was nearly full. But Carter would be a fool to take off before it was completely full. You got the greatest acceleration from an air jet during the first seconds of flight. The rest of the flight you got just enough pressure to keep you going.

But—Alf was getting into his buggy. Now the buggy was rising.

Carter turned on his jet and went up.

He came down hard, three hundred feet high, and only then dared to look down. He heard Alf's nasty laugh, and he saw that Alf was still at the foot of the mountains. It had been a bluff!

But *why* wasn't Alf coming after him?

The third hop took him to the top. The first downhill hop was the first he'd ever made, and it almost killed him. He had to do his decelerating on the last remnants of pressure in the jet tank! He waited until his hands stopped shaking, then continued the rest of the way on the wheels. There was no sign of Alf as he reached the foot of the range and started out into the desert.

Already the sun was about to go. Faint bluish stars in a red-black sky outlined the yellow hills behind him. Still no sign of Alf.

Alf spoke in his ear, gently, almost kindly. "You'll just have to come back, Jack."

"Don't hold your breath."

"I'd rather not have to. That's why I'm telling you this. Look at your watch."

It was about six-thirty.

"Did you look? Now count it up. I started with forty-four hours of air. You started with fifty-two. That gave us ninety-six breathing hours between us. Together we've used up sixty-one hours. That leaves thirty-five between us.

"Now, I stopped moving an hour ago. From where I am it's almost thirty hours back to base. Sometime in the next two and a half hours, you've got to get my air and stop me from breathing. Or I've got to do the same for you."

It made sense. Finally, everything made sense. "Alf, are you listening? Listen," said Carter, and he opened his radio panel and, moving by touch, found a wire he'd located long ago. He jerked it loose. His radio crackled deafeningly, then stopped.

"Did you hear that, Alf? I just jerked my come-hither loose. Now you couldn't find me even if you wanted to."

"I wouldn't have it any other way."

Then Carter realized what he'd done. There was now no possibility of Alf finding him. After all the miles and hours of the chase, now it was Carter chasing Alf. All Alf had to do was wait.

The dark fell on the west like a heavy curtain.

Carter went south, and he went immediately. It would take him an hour or more to cross the range. He would have to leapfrog to the top with only his headlights to guide him. His motor would not take him uphill over such a slope. He could use the wheels going down, with luck, but he would have to do so in total darkness. Deimos would not have risen; Phobos was not bright enough to help.

It had gone exactly as Alf had planned. Chase Carter to the range. If he attacks there, take his tanks and go home. If he makes it, show him why he has to come back. Time it so he has to come back in darkness. If by some miracle he makes it this time—well, there's always the flare gun.

Carter could give him only one surprise. He would cross six miles south of where he was expected, and approach Alf's buggy from the *southeast*.

Or was Alf expecting that too?

It didn't matter. Carter was beyond free will.

The first jump was like jumping blindfolded from a ship's airlock. He'd pointed the headlights straight down, and as he went up he watched the circle of light expand and dim. He angled east. First he wasn't moving at all. Then the slope slid toward him, far too fast. He back-angled. Nothing seemed to happen. The pressure under him died slowly, but it was dying, and the slope was a wavering blur surrounded by dark.

It came up, clarifying fast.

The landing jarred him from coccyx to cranium. He held himself rigid, waiting for the buggy to tumble end-for-end down the hill. But though the buggy was tilted at a horrifying angle, it stayed.

Carter sagged and buried his helmet in his arms. Two enormous hanging tears, swollen to pinballs in the low gravity, dropped onto his faceplate and spread. For the first time he regretted all of it. Killing Lew, when a kick to the kneecap would have put him out of action and taught him a permanent, memorable lesson. Snatching the buggy instead of surrendering himself for trial. Driving through the bubble—and making every man on Mars his mortal enemy. Hanging around to watch what would happen—when, perhaps, he could have run beyond the horizon before Alf came out the vehicular airlock. He clenched his fists and pressed them against his faceplate, remembering his attitude of mild interest as he sat watching Alf's buggy roll into the lock.

Time to go. Carter readied himself for another jump. This one would be horrible. He'd be taking off with the buggy canted thirty degrees backward . . .

Wait a minute.

There was something wrong with that picture of Alf's buggy as it rolled toward the lock surrounded by trotting men. Definitely something wrong there. But what?

It would come to him. He gripped the jet throttle and readied his other hand to flip on the gyros the moment he was airborne.

—Alf had planned so carefully. How had he come away with one O-tank too few?

And—if he really had everything planned, *how did Alf expect to get Carter's tanks if Carter crashed?*

Suppose Carter crashed his buggy against a hill, right now, on his second jump. How would Alf know? He wouldn't, not until nine o'clock came and Carter hadn't shown up. Then he'd know Carter had crashed somewhere. But it would be too late!

Unless Alf had lied.

That was it, that was what was wrong with his picture of Alf in the vehicular airlock. Put one O-tank in the air bin and it would stand out like a sore thumb. Fill the air bin and then remove one tank, and the hole in the hexagonal array would show like Sammy Davis III on the Berlin Nazis football team! There had been no such hole.

Let Carter crash now, and Alf would know it with four hours in which to search for his buggy.

Carter swung his headlights up to normal position, then moved the buggy backward in a dead-slow half circle. The buggy swayed but didn't topple. Now he could move down behind his headlights . . .

Nine o'clock. If Carter was wrong then he was dead now. Even now Alf might be unfastening his helmet, his eyes blank with the ultimate despair, still wonderng where Carter had got to. But if he was right . . .

Then Alf was nodding to himself, not smiling, merely confirming a guess. Now he was deciding whether to wait another five minutes on the chance that Carter was late, or to start searching now. Carter sat in his dark cabin at the foot of the black mountains, his left hand clutching a wrench, his eyes riveted on the luminous needle of the direction finder.

The wrench had been the heaviest in his toolbox. He'd found nothing sharper than a screwdriver, and that wouldn't have penetrated suit fabric.

The needle pointed straight toward Alf.

And it wasn't moving.

Alf had decided to wait.

How long would he wait?

Carter caught himself whispering, not loudly. *Move, idiot. You've got to search both sides of the range. Both sides and the top. Move. Move!*

Ye gods! Had he shut off his radio? Yes, the switch was down.

Move.

The needle moved. It jerked once, infinitesimally, and was quiet.

It was quiet a long time—seven or eight minutes. Then it jerked in the opposite direction. Alf was searching the wrong side of the hills!

And then Carter saw the flaw in his own plan. Alf must now assume he was dead. And if he, Carter, was dead, then he wasn't using air. Alf had two hours extra, but he thought he had four!

The needle twitched and moved—a good distance. Carter sighed and closed his eyes. Alf was coming over. He had sensibly decided to search this side first; for if Carter was on this side, dead, then Alf would have to cross the range again to reach home.

Twitch.

Twitch. He must be at the top.

Then the long, slow, steady movement down.

Headlights. Very faint, to the north. Would Alf turn north?

He turned south. Perfect. The headlights grew brighter . . . and Carter waited, with his buggy buried to the windshield in the sand at the base of the range.

Alf still had the flare gun. Despite all his certainty that Carter was dead, he was probably riding with the gun in his hand. But he was using his headlights, and he was going slowly, perhaps fifteen miles per hour.

He would pass . . . twenty yards west . . .

Carter gripped the wrench. *Here he comes.*

There was light in his eyes. *Don't see me.* And then

there wasn't. Carter swarmed out of the buggy and down the slopping sand. The headlights moved away, and Carter was after them, leaping as a Moonie leaps, both feet pushing at once into the sand, a second spent in flying, legs straddled and feet reaching forward for the landing and another leap.

One last enormous kangaroo jump—and he was on the O-tanks, falling on knees and forearms with feet lifted high so the metal wouldn't clang. One arm landed on nothing at all where empty O-tanks were missing. His body tried to roll off onto the sand. He wouldn't let it.

The transparent bubble of Alf's helmet was before him. The head inside swept back and forth, sweeping the triangle created by the headlights.

Carter crept forward. He poised himself over Alf's head, raised the wrench high, and brought it down with all his strength.

Cracks starred out in the plastic. Alf looked up with his eyes and mouth all wide open, his amazement unalloyed by rage or terror. Carter brought the weight down again.

There were more cracks, longer cracks. Alf winced and—finally—brought up the flare gun. Carter's muscles froze for an instant as he looked into its hellish mouth. Then he struck for what he knew must be the last time.

The wrench smashed through transparent plastic and scalp and skull. Carter knelt on the O-tanks for a moment, looking at the unpleasant thing he'd done. Then he lifted the body out by the shoulders, tumbled it over the side, and climbed into the cabin to stop the buggy.

It took him a few minutes to find his own buggy where he'd buried it in the sand. It took longer to uncover it. That was all right. He had plenty of time. If he crossed the range by twelve-thirty he would reach bubbletown on the last of his air.

There would be little room for finesse. On the other hand, he would be arriving an hour before dawn. They'd never see him. They would have stopped expecting him, or Alf, at noon tomorrow—even assuming they didn't know Alf had refused to turn back.

The bubble would be empty of air before anyone could get into a suit.

Later he could repair and fill the bubble. In a month Earth would hear of the disaster: how a meteorite had touched down at a corner of the dome, how John Carter had been outside at the time, the only man in a suit. They'd take him home and he could spend the rest of his life trying to forget.

He knew which tanks were his empties. Like every man in town, he had his own method of arranging them in the air bin. He dumped six and stopped. It was a shame to throw away empties. The tanks were too hard to replace.

He didn't know Alf's arrangement scheme. He'd have to test Alf's empties individually.

Already Alf had thrown some away. (To leave space for Carter's tanks?) One by one, Carter turned the valve of each tank. If it hissed, he put it in his own air bin. If it didn't, he dropped it.

One of them hissed. Just one.

Five O-tanks. He couldn't possibly make a thirty-hour trip on five O-tanks.

Somewhere, Alf had left three O-tanks where he could find them again. Just on the off chance: just in case something went terribly wrong for Alf, and Carter captured his buggy, Carter still wouldn't go home alive.

Alf must have left the tanks where he could find them easily. He must have left them near here; for he had never been out of Carter's sight until Carter crossed the range, and furthermore he'd kept just one tank to reach them. The tanks were nearby, and Carter had just two hours to find them.

In fact, he realized, they must be on the other side of the range. Alf hadn't stopped anywhere on this side.

But he could have left them on the hillside during his jumps to the top . . .

In a sudden frenzy of hurry, Carter jumped into his buggy and took it up. The headlights showed his progress to the top and over.

The first red rays of sunlight found Lee Cousins and Rufe Doolittle already outside the bubble. They were digging a grave. Cousins dug in stoic silence. In a mixture of pity and disgust he endured Rufe's constant compulsive flow of words.

". . . first man to be buried on another planet. Do you think Lew would have liked that? No, he'd hate it. He'd say it wasn't worth dying for. He wanted to go home. He would have, too, on the next ship . . ."

The sand came up in loose, dry shovelfuls. Practice was needed to keep it on the shovel. It tried to flow like a viscous liquid.

"I tried to tell the Mayor he'd have liked a well burial. The Mayor wouldn't listen. He said the Martians might not—hey!"

Cousins' eyes jerked up, and the movement caught them—a steadily moving fleck on the crater wall. Martian! was his first thought. What else could he be moving out there? And then he saw that it was a buggy.

To Lee Cousins it was like a corpse rising from its grave. The buggy moved like a blind thing down the tilted blocks of old glass, touched the drifted sand in the crater floor, all while he stood immobile. At the corner of his eye he saw Doolittle's shovel flying wide as Doolittle ran for the bubble.

The buggy only grazed the sand, then began reclimbing the crater. Cousins' paralysis left him and he ran for the town's remaining buggy.

The ghost was moving at half speed. He caught it a mile beyond the crater rim. Carter was in the cockpit. His helmet was in his lap clutched in a rigid death-grip.

Cousins reported. "He must have aimed the buggy along his direction finder when he felt his air going. Give him credit," he added, and lifted a shovelful from the second grave. "He did that much. He sent back the buggy."

Just after dawn a small biped form came around a hill to the east. It walked directly to the sprawled body of Alf Harness, picked up a foot in both delicate-looking hands, and began to tug the corpse across the sand, looking rather like an ant tugging a heavy bread crumb. In the twenty minutes it needed to reach Alf's buggy the figure never stopped to rest.

Dropping its prize, the Martian climbed the pile of empty O-tanks and peered into the air bin, then down at the body. But there was no way such a small, weak being could lift such a mass.

The Martian seemed to remember something. It scrambled down the O-tanks and crawled under the buggy's belly.

Minutes later it came out, dragging a length of nylon line. It tied each end of the line to one of Alf's ankles, then dropped the loop over the buggy's trailer-attachment knob.

For a time the figure stood motionless above Alf's broken helmet, contemplating its work. Alf's head might take a beating, riding that way; but as a specimen Alf's head was useless. Wherever nitrogen dioxide gas had touched moisture, red fuming nitric acid had formed. By now the rest of the body was dry and hard, fairly well preserved.

The figure climbed into the buggy. A little fumbling, surprisingly little, and the buggy was rolling. Twenty yards away it stopped with a jerk. The Martian climbed out and walked back. It knelt beside the three O-tanks which had been tied beneath the buggy with the borrowed nylon line, and it opened the stopcocks of each in turn. It leapt back in horrified haste when the noxious gas began hissing out.

Minutes later the buggy was moving south. The O-tanks hissed for a time, then were quiet.

The Jigsaw Man

Transplant technology, through two hundred years of development, had come into its own . . . and raised its own problems. The Belt escaped the most drastic social effects. Earth did not.

LN

In A.D. 1900, Karl Landsteiner classified human blood into four types: A, B, AB, and O, according to incompatibilities. For the first time it became possible to give a shock patient a transfusion with some hope that it wouldn't kill him.

The movement to abolish the death penalty was barely getting started, and already it was doomed.

Vh83uOAGn7 was his telephone number and his driving license number and his social security number and the number of his draft card and his medical record. Two of these had been revoked, and the others had ceased to matter, except for his medical record. His name was Warren Lewis Knowles. He was going to die.

The trial was a day away, but the verdict was no less certain for that. Lew was guilty. If anyone had doubted it, the persecution had ironclad proof. By eighteen tomorrow Lew would be condemned to death. Broxton would appeal the case on some grounds or other. The appeal would be denied.

The cell was comfortable, small, and padded. This was no slur on the prisoner's sanity, though insanity was no longer an excuse for breaking the law. Three of the walls were mere bars. The fourth wall, the outside wall, was cement padded and painted a restful shade of green. But the bars which separated him from the corridor, and from the morose old man on his left, and from the big, moronic-looking teenager on his right—the bars were four inches thick and eight inches apart, padded in silicone plastics. For the fourth time that day Lew took a clenched fistful of the plastic and tried to rip it away. It felt like a sponge rubber pillow, with a rigid core the thickness of a pencil, and it wouldn't rip. When he let go it snapped back to a perfect cylinder.

"It's not fair," he said.

The teenager didn't move. For all of the ten hours Lew had been in his cell, the kid had been sitting on the edge of his bunk with his lank black hair falling in his eyes and his five o'clock shadow getting gradually darker. He moved his long, hairy arms only at mealtimes, and the rest of him not at all.

The old man looked up at the sound of Lew's voice. He spoke with bitter sarcasm. "You framed?"

"No, I—"

"At least you're honest. What'd you do?"

Lew told him. He couldn't keep the hurt innocence out of his voice. The old man smiled derisively, nodding as if he'd expected just that.

"Stupidity. Stupidity's always been a capital crime. If you *had* to get yourself executed, why not for something important? See the kid on the other side of you?"

"Sure," Lew said without looking.

"He's an organlegger."

Lew felt the shock freezing in his face. He braced himself for another look into the next cell—and every nerve in his body jumped. The kid was looking at him. With his dull dark eyes barely visible under his mop of hair, he regarded Lew as a butcher might consider a badly aged side of beef.

Lew edged closer to the bars betwen his cell and the old man's. His voice was a hoarse whisper. "How many did he kill?"

"None."

"?"

"He was the snatch man. He'd find someone out alone at night, drug him and take him home to the doc that ran the ring. It was the doc that did all the killing. If Bernie'd brought home a dead donor, the doc would have skinned *him* down."

The old man sat with Lew almost directly behind him. He had twisted himself around to talk to Lew, but now he seemed to be losing interest. His hands, hidden from Lew by his bony back, were in constant nervous motion.

"How many did he snatch?"

"Four. Then he got caught. He's not very bright, Bernie."

"What did you do to get put here?"

The old man didn't answer. He ignored Lew completely, his shoulders twitching as he moved his hands. Lew shrugged and dropped back in his bunk.

It was nineteen o'clock of a Thursday night.

The ring had included three snatch men. Bernie had not yet been tried. Another was dead; he had escaped over the edge of a pedwalk when he felt the mercy bullet enter his arm. The third was being wheeled into the hospital next door to the courthouse.

Officially he was still alive. He had been sentenced; his appeal had been denied; but he was still alive as they moved him, drugged, into the operating room.

The interns lifted him from the table and inserted a mouthpiece so he could breathe when they dropped him into freezing liquid. They lowered him without a splash, and as his body temperature went down they dribbled something else into his veins. About half a pint of it. His temperature dropped toward freezing, his heartbeats were further and further apart. Finally his heart stopped. But it could have been started again. Men had been reprieved at this point. Officially the organlegger was still alive.

The doctor was a line of machines with a conveyor belt running through them. When the organlegger's body temperature reached a certain point, the belt started.

The first machine made a series of incisions in his chest. Skillfully and mechanically, the doctor performed a cardiectomy.

The organlegger was officially dead.

His heart went into storage immediately. His skin followed, most of it in one piece, all of it still living. The doctor took him apart with exquisite care, like disassembling a flexible, fragile, tremendously complex jigsaw puzzle. The brain was flashburned and the ashes saved for urn burial; but all the rest of the body, in slabs and small blobs and parchment-thin layers and lengths of tubing, went into storage in the hospital's organ banks. Any one of these units could be packed in a travel case at a moment's notice and flown to anywhere in the world in not much more than an hour. If the odds broke right, if the right people came down with the right diseases at the right time, the organlegger might save more lives than he had taken.

Which was the whole point.

Lying on his back, staring up at the ceiling television set, Lew suddenly began to shiver. He had not had the energy to put the sound plug in his ear, and the silent motion of the cartoon figures had suddenly become horrid. He turned the set off, and that didn't help either.

Bit by bit they would take him apart and store him away. He'd never seen an organ storage bank, but his uncle had owned a butcher-shop . . .

"Hey!" he yelled.

The kid's eyes came up, the only living part of him. The old man twisted round to look over his shoulder. At the end of the hall the guard looked up once, then went back to reading.

The fear was in Lew's belly; it pounded in his throat. "How can you stand it?"

The kid's eyes dropped to the floor. The old man said, "Stand what?"

"Don't you know what they're going to *do* to us?"

"Not to me. They won't take me apart like a hog."

Instantly Lew was at the bars. "Why not?"

The old man's voice had become very low. "Because there's a bomb where my right thighbone used to be. I'm gonna blow myself up. What they find, they'll never use."

The hope the old man had raised washed away, leaving bitterness. "Nuts. How could you put a bomb in your leg?"

"Take the bone out, bore a hole lengthwise through it, build the bomb in the hole, get all the organic material out of the bone so it won't rot, put the bone back in. 'Course your red corpuscle count goes down afterward. What I wanted to ask you. You want to join me?"

"Join you?"

"Hunch up against the bars. This thing'll take care of both of us."

Lew had backed up against the opposite set of bars.

"Your choice," said the old man. "I never told you what I was here for, did I? I was the doc. Bernie made his snatches for me."

Lew had backed up against the opposite set of bars. He felt them touch his shoulders and turned to find the kid looking dully into his eyes from two feet away. Organleggers! He was surrounded by professional killers!

"I know what it's like," the old man continued. "They won't do that to me. Well. If you're sure you don't want a clean death, go lie down behind your bunk. It's thick enough."

The bunk was a mattress and a set of springs mounted into a cement block which was an integral part of the cement floor. Lew curled himself into fetal position with his hands over his eyes.

He was sure he didn't want to die *now*.

Nothing happened.

After a while he opened his eyes, took his hands away and looked around.

The kid was looking at him. For the first time there was a sour grin plastered on his face. In the corridor the guard, who was always in a chair by the exit, was standing outside the bars looking down at him. He seemed concerned.

Lew felt the flush rising in his neck and nose and ears. The old man had been playing with him. He moved to get up . . .

And a hammer came down on the world.

The guard lay broken against the bars of the cell across the corridor. The lank-haired youngster was picking himself up from behind his bunk, shaking his head. Somebody groaned; and the groan rose to a scream. The air was full of cement dust.

Lew got up.

Blood lay like red oil on every surface that faced the explosion. Try as he might, and he didn't try very hard, Lew could find no other trace of the old man.

Except for the hole in the wall.

He must have been standing . . . right . . . there.

The hole would be big enough to crawl through, if Lew could reach it. But it was in the old man's cell. The silicone plastic sheathing on the bars between the cells had been ripped away, leaving only pencil-thick lengths of metal.

Lew tried to squeeze through.

The bars were humming, vibrating, though there was no sound. As Lew noticed the vibration he also found that he was becoming sleepy. He jammed his body between the bars, caught in a war between his rising panic and the sonic stunners which might have gone on automatically.

The bars wouldn't give. But his body did; and the bars were slippery with . . . He was through. He poked his head through the hole in the wall and looked down.

Way down. Far enough to make him dizzy.

The Topeka County courthouse was a small skyscraper, and Lew's cell must have been near the top. He looked down a smooth concrete slab studded with windows set flush with the sides. There would be no way to reach those windows, no way to open them, no way to break them.

The stunner was sapping his will. He would have been unconscious by now if his head had been in the cell with the rest of him. He had to force himself to turn and look up.

He was *at* the top. The edge of the roof was only a few feet above his eyes. He couldn't reach that far, not without . . .

He began to crawl out of the hole.

Win or lose, they wouldn't get him for the organ banks. The vehicular traffic level would smash every useful part of him. He sat on the lip of the hole, with his legs straight out inside the cell for balance, pushing his chest flat against the wall. When he had his balance he stretched his arms toward the roof. No good.

So he got one leg under him, keeping the other stiffly out, and *lunged*.

His hands closed over the edge as he started to fall back. He yelped with surprise, but it was too late. The top of the courthouse was moving! It had dragged him out of the hole before he could let go. He hung on, swinging slowly back and forth over empty space as the motion carried him away.

The top of the courthouse was a pedwalk.

He couldn't climb up, not without purchase for his feet. He didn't have the strength. The pedwalk was moving toward another building, about the same height. He could reach it if he only hung on.

And the windows in that building were different. They weren't made to open, not in those days of smog and air conditioning, but there were ledges. Perhaps the glass would break.

Perhaps it wouldn't.

The pull on his arms was agony. It would be so easy to let go . . . No. He had committed no crime worth dying for. He refused to die.

Over the decades of the twentieth century the movement continued to gain momentum. Loosely organized, international in scope, its members had only one goal: to replace execution with imprisonment and rehabilitation in every state and nation they could reach. They argued that killing a man for his crime teaches him nothing, that it serves as no deterrent to others who might commit the same crime; that death is irreversible, where as an innocent man may be released from prison if his innocence can be proved. Killing a man serves no good purpose, they said, unless for society's vengeance. Vengeance, they said, is unworthy of an enlightened society.

Perhaps they were right.

In 1940 Karl Landsteiner and Alexander S. Wiener made public their report on the Rh factor in human blood.

By mid-century most convicted killers were getting life imprisonment or less. Many were later returned to society, some "rehabilitated," others not. The death penalty had been passed for kidnapping in some states, but it was hard to persuade a jury to enforce it. Similarly with murder charges. A man wanted for burglary in Canada and murder in California fought extradition to Canada; he had less chance of being convicted in California. Many states had abolished the death penalty. France had none.

Rehabilitation of criminals was a major goal of the science/art of psychology.

But—

Blood banks were world-wide.

Already men and women with kidney diseases had been saved by a kidney transplanted from an identical twin. Not all kidney patients had identical twins. A doctor in Paris used transplants from close relatives, classifying up to a hundred points of incompatibility to judge in advance how successful the transplant would be.

Eye transplants were common. An eye donor could wait until he died before he saved another man's sight.

Human bone could *always* be transplanted, provided the bone was first cleaned of organic matter.

So matters stood in mid-century.

By 1990 it was possible to store any living human organ for any reasonable length of time. Transplants had become routine, helped along by the "scalpel of infinite thinness," the laser. The dying regularly willed their remains to organ banks. The mortuary lobbies couldn't stop it. But such gifts from the dead were not always useful.

In 1993 Vermont passed the first of the organ bank laws. Vermont had always had the death penalty. Now a condemned man could know that his death would save lives. It was no longer true that an execution served no good purpose. Not in Vermont.

Nor, later, in California. Or Washington. Georgia, Pakistan, England, Switzerland, France, Rhodesia . . .

The pedwalk was moving at ten miles per hour. Below, unnoticed by pedestrians who had quit work late and night owls who were just beginning their rounds, Lewis Knowles hung from the moving strip and watched the ledge go by beneath his dangling feet. The ledge was no more than two feet wide, a good four feet beneath his stretching toes.

He dropped.

As his feet struck he caught the edge of a window casement. Momentum jerked at him, but he didn't fall. After a long moment he breathed again.

He couldn't know what building this was, but it was not deserted. At twenty-one hundred at night, all the windows were ablaze. He tried to stay back out of the light as he peered in.

The window was an office. Empty.

He'd need something to wrap around his hand to break that window. But all he was wearing was a pair of shoesocks and a prison jumper. Well, he couldn't be more conspicuous than he was now. He took off the jumper, wrapped part of it around his hand, and struck.

He almost broke his hand.

Well . . . they'd let him keep his jewelry, his wristwatch and diamond ring. He drew a circle on the glass with the ring, pushing down hard, and struck again with the other hand. It *had* to be glass; if it was plastic he was doomed.

The glass popped out in a near-perfect circle.

He had to do it six times before the hole was big enough for him.

He smiled as he stepped inside, still holding his jumper. Now all he needed was an elevator. The cops would have picked him up in an instant if they'd caught him on the street in a prison jumper, but if he hid the jumper here he'd be safe. Who would suspect a licensed nudist?

Except that he didn't have a license. Or a nudist's shoulder pouch to put it in.

Or a shave.

That was very bad. Never had there been a nudist as hairy as this. Not just a five o'clock shadow, but a full beard all over, so to speak. Where could he get a razor?

He tried the desk drawers. Many businessmen kept

spare razors. He stopped when he was halfway through. Not because he'd found a razor, but because he knew where he was. The papers on the desk made it all too obvious.

A hospital.

He was still clutching the jumper. He dropped it in the wastebasket, covered it tidily with papers, and more or less collapsed into the chair behind the desk.

A hospital. He *would* pick a hospital. And *this* hospital, the one which had been built right next to the Topeka County courthouse, for good and sufficient reason.

But he hadn't picked it, not really. It had picked him. Had he ever in his life made a decision except on the instigation of others? Friends had borrowed his money for keeps, men had stolen his girls, he had avoided promotion by his knack for being ignored. Shirley had bullied him into marrying her, then left him four years later for a friend who wouldn't be bullied.

Even now, at the possible end of his life, it was the same. An aging body snatcher had given him his escape. An engineer had built the cell bars wide enough apart to let a small man squeeze between them. Another had put a pedwalk along two convenient roofs. And here he was.

The worst of it was that here he had no chance of masquerading as a nudist. Hospital gowns and masks would be the minimum. Even nudists had to wear clothing sometime.

The closet?

There was nothing in the closet but a spiffy green hat and a perfectly transparent rain poncho.

He could run for it. If he could find a razor he'd be safe once he reached the street. He bit at a knuckle, wishing he knew where the elevator was. Have to trust to luck. He began searching the drawers again.

He had his hand on a black leather razor case when the door opened. A beefy man in a hospital gown breezed in. The intern (there were no human doctors in hospitals) was halfway to the desk before he noticed Lew crouching over an open drawer. He stopped walking. His mouth fell open.

Lew closed it with the fist which still gripped the razor case. The man's teeth came together with a sharp click. His knees were buckling as Lew brushed past him and out the door.

The elevator was just down the hall, with the doors standing open. And nobody coming. Lew stepped in and punched O. He shaved as the elevator dropped. The razor cut fast and close, if a trifle noisily. He was working on his chest as the door opened.

A skinny technician stood directly in front of him, her mouth and eyes set in the utterly blank expression of those who wait for elevators. She brushed past him with a muttered apology, hardly noticing him. Lew stepped out fast. The doors were closing before he realized that he was on the wrong floor.

That damned tech! She'd stopped the elevator before it reached bottom.

He turned and stabbed the Down button. Then what he'd seen in the one cursory glance came back to him, and his head whipped around for another look.

The whole vast room was filled with glass tanks, ceiling height, arranged in a labyrinth like the bookcases in a library. In the tanks was a display more lewd than anything in Belsen. Why, those things had been *men* and *women!* No, he wouldn't look. He refused to look at anything but the elevator door. *What was taking that elevator so long?*

He heard a siren.

The hard tile floor began to vibrate against his bare feet. He felt a numbness in his muscles, a lethargy in his soul.

The elevator arrived . . . too late. He blocked the doors open with a chair. Most buildings didn't have stairs: only alternate elevators. They'd have to use the alternate elevator to reach him now. Well, where was it? . . . He wouldn't have time to find it. He was beginning to feel really sleepy. They must have several sonic projectors focused on this one room. Where one beam passed the interns would feel mildly relaxed, a little clumsy. But where the beams intersected, here, there would be unconsciousness. But not yet.

He had something to do first.

By the time they broke in they'd have something to kill him for.

The tanks were faced in plastic, not glass: a very special kind of plastic. To avoid provoking defense reactions in all the myriads of body parts which might be stored touching it, the plastic had to have unique characteristics. No engineer could have been expected to make it shatterproof too!

It shattered very satisfactorily.

Later Lew wondered how he managed to stay up as long as he did. The soothing hypersonic murmur of the stun beams kept pulling at him, pulling him down to a floor which seemed softer every moment. The chair he wielded became heavier and heavier. But as long as he could lift it, he smashed. He was knee deep in nutritive storage fluid, and there were dying things brushing against his ankles with every move; but his work was barely a third done when the silent siren song became too much for him.

He fell.

And after all that they never even mentioned the smashed organ banks!

Sitting in the courtroom, listening to the drone of courtroom ritual, Lew sought Mr. Broxton's ear to ask the question. Mr. Broxton smiled at him. "Why should they want to bring that up? They think they've got enough on you as it is. If you beat *this* rap, then they'll persecute you for wanton destruction of valuable medical resources. But they're sure you won't."

"And you?"

"I'm afraid they're right. But we'll try. Now, Hennessey's about to read the charges. Can you manage to look hurt and indignant?"

"Sure."

"Good."

The prosecution read the charges, his voice sounding like the voice of doom coming from under a thin blond mustache. Warren Lewis Knowles looked hurt and indignant. But he no longer felt that way. He had done something worth dying for.

The cause of it all was the organ banks. With good doctors and a sufficient flow of material in the organ banks, any taxpayer could hope to live indefinitely.

What voter would vote against eternal life? The death penalty was his immortality, and he would vote the death penalty for any crime at all.

Lewis Knowles had struck back.

"The state will prove that the said Warren Lewis Knowles did, in the space of two years, willfully drive through a total of six red traffic lights. During that same period the same Warren Knowles exceeded local speed limits no less than ten times, once by as much as fifteen miles per hour. His record had never been good. We will produce records of his arrest in 2082 on a charge of drunk driving, a charge which he was acquitted only through—"

"Objection!"

"Sustained. If he was acquitted, Counselor, the Court must assume him not guilty."

At the Bottom of a Hole

After more than a century of space travel, Man's understanding of his own solar system was nearly complete. So he moved on to industrial development.

The next hundred years saw the evolution of a civilization in space. For reasons of economy the Belters concentrated on the wealth of the asteroids. With fusion-driven ships they could have mined the planets; but their techniques were more universally applicable in free fall and among the falling mountains. Only Mercury was rich enough to attract the Belt miners.

For a time Earth was the center of the space industries. But the lifestyles of Belter and flatlander were so different that a split was inevitable. The flatland phobia—the inability to tolerate even an orbital flight—was common on Earth, and remained so. And there were Belters who would never go anywhere near a planet.

Between Earth and the Belt there was economic wrestling, but never war. The cultures needed each other. And they were held together by a common bond: the conquest of the stars. The ramrobots—the unmanned Bussard ramjet probes—were launched during the mid twenty-first century.

By 2100 AD, five nearby solar systems held budding colonies: the worlds were Jinx, Wunderland, We Made It, Plateau, and Down. None of these worlds was entirely Earthlike. Those who programed the ramrobots had used insufficient imagination. Some results are detailed in *A Gift From Earth* and the *Neutron Star* collection, and in this book in the story "The Borderland of Sol."

On Earth, three species of cetacean had been recognized as intelligent and admitted to the United Nations. Their lawsuit against the former whaling nations had not been resolved, and in fact never was. The cetaceans enjoyed the legal gymnastics too much ever to end it.

Mankind's first meeting with extraterrestrial intelligence came in 2106—though Kzanol had been on Earth for longer than humanity—and is chronicled in *World of Ptavvs*.   *LN*

TWELVE STORIES BELOW the roof gardens were citrus groves, grazing pastures, and truck farms. They curved out from the base of the hotel in neat little squares, curved out and up, and up, and up and over. Five miles overhead was the fusion sunlight tube, running down the radius of the slightly bulging cylinder that was Farmer's Asteroid. Five miles above the sunlight tube, the sky was a patchwork of small squares, split by a central wedding ring of lake and by tributary rivers, a sky alive with the tiny red glints of self-guided tractors.

Lucas Garner was half-daydreaming, letting his eyes rove the solid sky. At the Belt government's invitation he had entered a bubbleworld for the first time, combining a vacation from United Nations business with a chance at a brand new experience—a rare thing for a man seventeen decades old. He found it pleasantly kooky to look up into a curved sky of fused rock and imported topsoil.

"There's nothing immoral about smuggling," said Lit Shaeffer.

The surface overhead was dotted with hotels, as if the bubbleworld were turning to city. Garner knew it wasn't. Those hotels, and the scattered hotels in the other bubbleworld, served every Belter's occasional need for an Earthlike environment. Belters don't need houses. A Belter's home is the inside of his pressure suit.

Garner returned his attention to his host. "You mean smuggling's like picking pockets on Earth?"

"That's just what I don't mean," Shaeffer said. The Belter reached into his coverall pocket, pulled out something flat and black, and laid it on the table. "I'll want to play that in a minute. Garner, picking pockets is legal on Earth. Has to be, the way you crowd together. You couldn't enforce a law against picking pockets. In the Belt smuggling is against the law, but it isn't immoral. It's like a flatlander forgetting to feed the parking meter. There's no loss of self-respect. If you get caught you pay the fine and forget it."

"Oh."

"If a man wants to send his earnings through Ceres, that's up to him. It costs him a straight thirty percent. If he thinks he can get past the goldskins, that too is his choice. But if we catch him we'll confiscate his cargo, and everybody will be laughing at him. Nobody pities an inept smuggler."

"Is that what Muller tried to do?"

"Yah. He had a valuable cargo, twenty kilos of pure north magnetic poles. The temptation was too much for him. He tried to get past us, and we picked him up on radar. Then he did something stupid. He tried to whip around a hole.

"He must have been on course for Luna when we found him. Ceres was behind him with the radar. Our ships were ahead of him, matching course at two gee. His mining ship wouldn't throw more than point five gee, so eventually they'd pull alongside him no matter what he did. Then he noticed Mars was just ahead of him."

"The hole." Garner knew enough Belters to have learned a little of their slang.

"The very one. His first instinct must have been to change course. Belters learn to avoid gravity wells. A man can get killed half a dozen ways coming too close to a hole. A good autopilot will get him safely around it, or program an in-and-out spin, or even land him at the bottom, God forbid. But miners don't carry good autopilots. They carry cheap autopilots, and they stay clear of holes."

"You're leading up to something," Garner said regretfully. "Business?"

"You're too old to fool."

Sometimes Garner believed that himself. Sometime between the First World War and the blowing of the second bubbleworld, Garner had learned to read faces as accurately as men read print. Often it saved time—and in Garner's view his time was worth saving.

"Go on," he said.

"Muller's second thought was to use the hole. An in-and-out spin would change his course more then he could hope to do with the motor. He could time it so Mars would hide him from Ceres when he curved out. He could damn near touch the surface, too. Mars' atmosphere is as thin as a flatlander's dreams."

"Thanks a lot. Lit, isn't Mars UN property?"

"Only because we never wanted it."

Then Muller had been trespassing. "Go on. What happened to Muller?"

"I'll let him tell it. This is his log." Lit Shaeffer did something to the flat box, and a man's voice spoke.

April 20, 2112

The sky is flat, the land is flat, and they meet in a circle at infinity. No star shows but the big one, a little bigger than it shows through most of the Belt, but dimmed to red, like the sky.

It's the bottom of a hole, and I must have been crazy to risk it. But I'm *here*. I got down alive. I didn't expect to, not there at the end.

It was one crazy landing.

Imagine a universe half of which has been replaced by an ocher abstraction, too distant and far too big to show meaningful detail, moving past you at a hell of a clip. A strange, singing sound comes through the walls, like nothing you've ever heard before, like the sound of the wings of the angel of death. The walls are getting warm. You can hear the thermosystem whining even above the shriek of air whipping around the hull. Then, because you don't have enough problems, the ship shakes itself like a mortally wounded dinosaur.

That was my fuel tanks tearing loose. All at once and nothing first, the four of them sheered their mooring bars and went spinning down ahead of me, cherry red.

That faced me with two bad choices. I had to decide fast. If I finished the hyperbola I'd be heading into space on an unknown course with what fuel was left in my inboard cooling tank. My lifesystem wouldn't keep me alive more than two weeks. There wasn't much chance I could get anywhere in that time, with so little fuel, and I'd seen to it the goldskins couldn't come to *me*.

But the fuel in the cooling tank would get me down. Even the ships of Earth use only a little of their fuel getting in and out of their pet gravity well. Most of it gets burned getting them from place to place fast. And Mars is lighter than Earth.

But what then? I'd still have two weeks to live.

I remembered the old Lacis Solis base, deserted seventy years ago. Surely I could get the old lifesystems working well enough to support one màn. I might even find enough water to turn some into hydrogen by electrolysis. It was a better risk than heading out into nowhere.

Right or wrong, I went down.

The stars are gone, and the land around me makes no sense. Now I know why they call planet dwellers "flatlanders." I feel like a gnat on a table.

I'm sitting here shaking, afraid to step outside.

Beneath a red-black sky is a sea of dust punctuated by scattered, badly cast glass ashtrays. The smallest, just outside the port, are a few inches in diameter. The largest are miles across. As I came down the deep-radar showed me fragments of much larger craters deep under the dust. The dust is soft and fine, almost like quicksand. I came down like a feather, but the ship is buried to halfway up the lifesystem.

I set down just beyond the lip of one of the largest craters, the one which houses the ancient flatlander base. From above the base looked like a huge transparent raincoat discarded on the cracked bottom.

It's a weird place. But I'll have to go out sometime; how else can I use the base lifesystem?

My Uncle Bat used to tell me stupidity carries the death penalty.

I'll go outside tomorrow.

April 21, 2112

My clock says it's morning. The Sun's around on the other side of the planet, leaving the sky no longer bloody. It looks almost like space if you remember to look away from gravity, though the stars are dim, as if seen through fogged plastic. A big star has come over the horizon, brightening and dimming like a spinning rock. Must be Phobos, since it came from the sunset region.

I'm going out.

Later:

A sort of concave glass shell surrounds the ship where the fusion flame splashed down. The ship's lifesystem, the half that shows above the dust, rests in the center like a frog on a lilypad in Confinement Asteroid. The splashdown shell is all a spiderweb of cracks, but it's firm enough to walk on.

Not so the dust.

The dust is like thick oil. The moment I stepped onto it I started to sink. I had to swim to where the crater rim slopes out like the shore of an island. It was hard work. Fortunately the splashdown shell reaches to the crater rock at one point, so I won't have to do *that* again.

It's queer, this dust. I doubt you could find its like anywhere in the system. It's meteor debris, condensed from vaporized rock. On Earth dust this fine would be washed down to the sea by rain and turned to sedimentary rock, natural cement. On the Moon there would be vacuum cementing, the bugaboo of the Belt's microminiaturization industries. But here, there's just enough "air" to be absorbed by the dust surface . . . to prevent vacuum cementing . . . and not nearly enough to stop a meteorite. Result: it won't cement, nohow. So it behaves like viscous fluid. Probably the only rigid surfaces are the meteor craters and mountain ranges.

Going up the crater lip was rough. It's all cracked, tilted blocks of volcanic glass. The edges are almost sharp. This crater must be geologically recent. At the bottom, half-submerged in a shallow lake of dust, is bubbletown. I can walk okay in this gravity; it's something less than my ship's gee max. But I almost broke my ankles a couple of times getting down over those tilted, slippery, dust-covered blocks. As a whole the crater is a smashed ashtray pieced loosely together like an impromptu jigsaw puzzle.

The bubble covers the base like a deflated tent, with the airmaking machinery just outside. The airmaker is in a great cube of black metal, blackened by seventy years of Martian atmosphere. It's huge. It must have been a bitch to lift. How they moved that mass from Earth to Mars with only chemical and ion rockets, I'll never know. Also *why?* What was on Mars that they wanted?

If ever there was a useless world, this is it. It's not close to Earth, like the Moon. The gravity's inconveniently high. There are no natural resources. Lose your suit pressure and it'd be a race against time, whether you died of blowout or of red fuming nitrogen dioxide eating your lungs.

The wells?

Somewhere on Mars there are wells. The first expedition found one in the 1990s. A mummified *something* was nearby. It exploded when it touched water, so nobody ever knew more about it, including just how old it was.

Did they expect to find live Martians? If so, so what?

Outside the bubble are two two-seater Marsbuggies. They have an enormous wheelbase and wide, broad wheels, probably wide enough to keep the buggy above the dust while it's moving. You'd have to be careful where you stopped. I won't be using them anyway.

The airmaker will work, I think, if I can connect it to the ship's power system. Its batteries are drained, and its fusion plant must be mainly lead by now. Thousands of tons of breathing-air are all about me, tied up in nitrogen dioxide, NO_2. The airmaker will release oxygen and nitrogen, and will also pick up what little water vapor there is. I'll pull hydrogen out of the water for fuel. But can I get the power? There may be cables in the base.

It's for sure I can't call for help. My antennas burned off coming down.

I looked through the bubble and saw a body, male, a few feet away. He'd died of blowout. Odds are I'll find a rip in the bubble when I get around to looking.

Wonder what happened here?

April 22, 2112

I went to sleep at first sunlight. Mars' rotation is just a fraction longer than a ship's day, which is convenient. I can work when the stars show and the dust doesn't, and that'll keep me sane. But I've had breakfast and done clean-ship chores, and still it'll be two hours before sundown. Am I a coward? I *can't* go out there in the light.

Near the sun the sky is like fresh blood, tinged by nitrogen dioxide. On the other side it's almost black. Not a sign of a star. The desert is flat, broken only by craters and by a regular pattern of crescent dunes so shallow that they can be seen only near the horizon. Something like a straight lunar mountain range angles away into the desert; but it's terribly eroded, like something that died a long time ago. Could it be the tilted lip of an ancient asteroid crater? The Gods must have hated Mars, to put it right in the middle of the Belt. This shattered, pulverized land is like a symbol of age and corruption. Erosion seems to live only at the bottom of holes.

Later:

Almost dawn. I can see red washing out the stars.

After sundown I entered the base through the airlock, which still stands. Ten bodies are sprawled in what must have been the village square. Another was halfway into a suit in the administration building, and the twelfth was a few feet from the bubble wall, where I saw him yesterday. A dozen bodies, and they all died of blowout: explosive decompression if you want to be technical.

The circular area under the bubble is only half full of buildings. The rest is a carefully fused sand floor. Other buildings lie in stacks of walls, ceilings, floors, ready to be put up. I suppose the base personnel expected others from Earth.

One of the buildings held electrical wiring. I've hooked a cable to the airmaker battery, and was able to adapt the other end to the contact on my fusion plant. There's a lot of sparking, but the airmaker works. I'm letting it fill the stack of empty O-tanks I found against a pile of walls. The nitrogen dioxide is draining into the bubble.

I know now what happened to the flatlander base.

Bubbletown died by murder. No question of it. When nitrogen dioxide started pouring into the bubble I saw dust blowing out from the edge of town. There was a rip. It was sharp-edged, as if cut by a knife. I can mend it if I can find a bubble repair kit. There must be one somewhere.

Meanwhile I'm getting oxygen and water. The oxygen tanks I can empty into the lifesystem as they fill. The ship takes it back out of the air and stores it. If I can find a way to get the water here I can just pour it into the john. Can I carry it here in the O-tanks?

April 23, 2112

Dawn.

The administration building is also a tape library. They kept a record of the base doings, very complete and so far very boring. It reads like ship's log sounds, but more gossipy and more detailed. Later I'll read it all the way through.

I found some bubble plastic and contact cement and used them to patch the rip. The bubble still wouldn't inflate. So I went out and found two more rips just like the first. I patched them and looked for more. Found three. When I got them fixed it was nearly sunup.

The O-tanks hold water, but I have to heat them to boil the water to get it out. That's hard work. Question: is it easier to do that or to repair the dome and do my electrolysis inside? How many rips are there?

I've found six. So how many killers were there? No more than three. I've accounted for twelve inside, and according to the log there were fifteen in the second expedition.

No sign of the goldskins. If they'd guessed I was here they'd have come by now. With several months' worth of air in my lifesystem, I'll be home free once I get out of this hole.

April 24, 2112

Two more rips in the bubble, a total of eight. They're about twenty feet apart, evenly spaced around the transparent plastic fabric. It looks like at least one man ran around the dome slashing at the fabric until it wasn't taut enough to cut. I mended the rips. When I left the bubble it was swelling with air.

I'm halfway through the town log, and nobody's seen a Martian yet. I was right, that's what they came for. Thus far they've found three more wells. Like the first, these are made of cut diamond building blocks, fairly large, very well worn, probably tens or hundreds of thousands of years old. Two of the four have dirty nitrogen dioxide at the bottoms. The others are dry. Each of the four has a "dedication block" covered with queer, partially eroded writing. From a partial analysis of the script, it seems that the wells were actually crematoriums: a deceased Martian would explode when he touched water in the nitrogen dioxide at the bottom. It figures. Martians wouldn't have fire.

I still wonder why they came, the men of the base. What could Martians do for them? If they wanted someone to talk to, someone not human, there were dolphins and killer whales right in their own oceans. The trouble they took! And the risks! Just to get from one hole to another!

April 24, 2112

Strange. For the first time since the landing, I did not return to the ship when the sky turned light. When I did start back the sun was up. It showed as I went over the rim. I stood there between a pair of sharp obsidian teeth, staring down at my ship.

It looked like the entrance to Confinement Asteroid.

Confinement is where they take women when they get pregnant: a bubble of rock ten miles long and five miles across, spinning on its axis to produce one gee of outward pull. The children have to stay there for the first year, and the law says they have to spend a month out of each year there until they're fifteen. I've a wife named Letty waiting there now, waiting for the year to pass so she can leave with our daughter Janice. Most miners, they pay the fatherhood fee in one lump sum if they've got the money; it's about sixty thousand commercials, so some have to pay in installments, and sometimes it's the woman who pays; but when they pay they forget about it and leave the women to raise the kids. But I've been thinking about Letty. And Janice. The monopoles in my hold would buy gifts for Letty, and raise Janice with enough left over so she could do some traveling, and *still* I'd have enough commercials left for more children. I'd have them with Letty, if she'd agree. I think she would.

How'd I get onto that? As I was saying before I was so rudely interrupted, my ship looks like the entrance to Confinement—or to Farmer's Asteroid, or any underground city. With the fuel tanks gone there's nothing left but the drive and the lifesystem and a small magnetically insulated cargo hold. Only the top half of the lifesystem shows above the sea of dust, a blunt steel bubble with a thick door, not streamlined like a ship of Earth. The heavy drive tube hangs from the bottom, far beneath the dust. I wonder how deep the dust is.

The splashdown shell will leave a rim of congealed glass around my lifesystem. I wonder if it'll affect my takeoff?

Anyway, I'm losing my fear of daylight.

Yesterday I thought the bubble was inflating. It wasn't. More rips were hidden under the pool of dust, and when the pressure built up the dust blew away and down went the bubble. I repaired four rips today before sunlight caught me.

One man couldn't have made all those slashes.

That fabric's *tough*. Would a knife go through it? Or would you need something else, like an electric carving knife or a laser?

April 25, 2112

I spent most of today reading the bubbletown log.

There *was* a murder. Tensions among fifteen men with no women around can grow pretty fierce. One day a man named Carter killed a man named Harness, then ran for his life in one of the Marsbuggies, chased by the victim's brother. Neither came back alive. They must have run out of air.

Three dead out of fifteen leaves twelve.

Since I counted twelve bodies, who's left to slash the dome?

Martians?

In the entire log I find no mention of a Martian being

seen. Bubbletown never ran across any Martian artifact, except the wells. If there are Martians, where are they? Where are their cities? Mars was subjected to all kinds of orbital reconnaissance in the early days. Even a city as small as bubbletown would have been seen.

Maybe there are no cities. But where do the diamond blocks come from? Diamonds as big as the well material don't form naturally. It takes a respectable technology to make them that big. Which implies cities—I think.

That mummy. Could it have been hundreds of thousands of years old? A man couldn't last that long on Mars, because the water in his body would react with the nitrogen dioxide around him. On the Moon, he could last millions of years. The mummified Martian's body chemistry was and is a complete mystery, barring the napalmlike explosion when water touched it. Perhaps it *was* that durable, and perhaps one of the pair who left to die returned to cut the dome instead, and perhaps I'm seeing goblins. This is the place for it. If I ever get out of here, you *try* and catch me near another hole.

April 26, 2112

The sun shows clear and bright above a sharp-edged horizon. I stand at the port looking out. Nothing seems strange anymore. I've lived here all my life. The gravity is settling in my bones; I no longer stumble as I go over the crater lip.

The oxygen in my tanks will take me anywhere. Give me hydrogen and you'll find me on Luna, selling my monopoles without benefit of a middleman. But it comes slowly. I can get hydrogen only by carrying water here in the base O-tanks and then electrolyzing it into the fuel-cooling tank, where it liquifies.

The desert is empty except for a strange rosy cloud that covers one arm of horizon. Dust? Probably. I heard the wind singing faintly through my helmet as I returned to the ship. Naturally the sound can't get through the hull.

The desert is empty.

I can't repair the bubble. Today I found four more rips before giving up. They must circle the bubble all the way round. One man couldn't have done it. Two men couldn't.

It looks like Martians. But where are they?

They could walk on the sand, if their feet were flat and broad and webbed . . . and there'd be no footprints. The dust hides everything. If there were cities here the dust must have covered them ages ago. The mummy wouldn't have shown webbing; it would have been worn away.

Now it's starlessly black outside. The thin wind must have little trouble lifting the dust. I doubt it will bury me. Anyway the ship would rise to the surface.

Gotta sleep.

April 27, 2112

It's oh-four-hundred by the clock, and I haven't slept at all. The sun is directly overhead, blinding bright in a clear red sky. No more dust storm.

The Martians exist. I'm sure of it. Nobody else was left to murder the base.

But why don't they show themselves?

I'm going to the base, and I'm taking the log with me.

I'm in the village square. Oddly enough, it was easier making the trip in sunlight. You can see what you're stepping on, even in shadow, because the sky diffuses the light a little, like indirect lighting in a dome city.

The crater lip looks down on me from all sides, splintered shards of volcanic glass. It's a wonder I haven't cut my suit open yet, making that trip twice a day.

Why did I come here? I don't know. My eyes feel rusty, and there's too much light. Mummies surround me, with faces twisted by anguish and despair, and with fluids dried on their mouths. Blowout is an ugly death. Ten mummies here, and one by the edge of town, and one in the admin building.

I can see all of the crater lip from here. The buildings are low bungalows, and the square is big. True, the deflated bubble distorts things a little, but not much.

So. The Martians came over the lip in a yelling swarm or a silent one, brandishing sharp things. Nobody would have heard them if they yelled.

But ten men were in a position to see them.

Eleven men. There's a guy at the edge . . . no, they might have come from the other direction. But still, ten men. And they just waited here? I don't believe it.

The twelfth man. He's half into a suit. What did he see that they didn't?

I'm going to go look at him.

By God, I was right. He's got two fingers on a zipper, and he's pulling down. He's not half into a suit, he's half out of it!

No more goblins.

But who cut the dome?

The hell with it. I'm sleepy.

April 28, 2112

A day and a half of log to catch up on.

My cooling tank is full, or nearly. I'm ready to try the might of the goldskins again. There's air enough to let me take my time, and less chance of a radar spotting me if I move slowly. Goodby, Mars, lovely paradise for the manic-depressive.

That's not funny. Consider the men in the base.

Item: it took a lot of knives to make those slits.

Item: everyone was inside.

Item: no Martians. They would have been seen.

Therefore the slits were made from inside. If someone was running around making holes in the bubble, why didn't someone stop him?

It looks like mass suicide. Facts are facts. They must have spread evenly out around the dome, slashed, and then walked to the town square against a driving wind of breathing-air roaring out behind them. Why? Ask 'em. The two who aren't in the square may have been dissenters; if so, it didn't help them.

Being stuck at the bottom of a hole is not good for a man. Look at the insanity records on Earth.

I am now going back to a minute-to-minute log.

1120

Ready to prime drive. The dust won't hurt the fusion tube, nothing could do that, but backblast might damage the rest of the ship. Have to risk it.

1124

The first shot of plutonium didn't explode. Priming again.

1130

The drive's dead. I can't understand it. My instruments swear the fusion shield is drawing power, and when I push the right button the hot uranium gas sprays in there. What's wrong?

Maybe a break in the primer line. How am I going to find out? The primer line's way down there under the dust.

1245

I've sprayed enough uranium into the fusion tube to make a pinch bomb. By now the dust must be hotter than Washington.

How am I going to repair the primer line? Lift the ship in my strong, capable hands? Swim down through the dust and do it by touch? I haven't anything that'll do a welding job under ten feet of fine dust.

I think I've had it.

Maybe there's a way to signal the goldskins. A big, black SOS spread on the dust . . . if I could find something black to spread around. Have to search the base again.

1900

Nothing in the town. Signaling devices in plenty, for suits and Marsbuggies and orbital ships, but only the laser was meant to reach into space. I can't fix a seventy-year-old comm laser with spit and wire and good intentions.

I'm going off minute-to-minute. There'll be no take-off.

April 29, 2112

I've been stupid.

Those ten suicides. What did they do with their knives after they were through cutting? Where did they get them in the first place? Kitchen knives won't cut bubble plastic. A laser might, but there can't be more than a couple of portable lasers in the base. I haven't found any.

And the airmaker's batteries were stone dead.

Maybe the Martians kill to steal power. They wouldn't have fire. Then they took my uranium for the same reason, slicing my primer line under the sand and running it into their own container.

But how would they get down there? Dive under the dust?

Oh.

I'm getting out of here.

I made it to the crater. God knows why they didn't stop me. Don't they care? They've *got* my primer fuel.

They're under the dust. They live there, safe from meteors and violent temperature changes, and they build their cities there too. Maybe they're heavier than the dust, so they can walk around on the bottom.

Why, there must be a whole ecology down there! Maybe one-celled plants on top, to get energy from the sun, to be driven down by currents in the dust and by dust storms, to feed intermediate stages of life. Why didn't anybody *look?* Oh, I wish I could *tell* someone!

I haven't time for this. The town O-tanks won't fit my suit valves, and I can't go back to the ship. Within the next twenty-four hours I've got to repair and inflate the bubble, or die of runout.

Later:

Done. I've got my suit off, and I'm scratching like a madman. There were just three slits left to patch, none at all along the edge of the bubble where I found the lone mummy. I patched those three and the bubble swelled up like instant city.

When enough water flows in I'll take a bath. But I'll take it in the square, where I can see the whole rim.

I wonder how long it would take a Martian to get over the rim and down here to the bubble?

Wondering won't help. I could still be seeing goblins.

April 30, 2112

The water feels wonderful. At least these early tourists took some luxuries with them.

I can see perfectly in all directions. Time has filmed the bubble a little, merely enough to be annoying. The sky is jet black, cut raggedly in half by the crater rim.

I've turned on all the base lights. They light the interior of the crater, dimly, but well enough so I'd see anything creeping down on me. Unfortunately they also dim out the stars.

The goblins can't get me while I'm awake.

But I'm getting sleepy.

Is that a ship? No, just a meteor. The sky's lousy with meteors. I've got nothing to do but talk to myself until something happens.

Later:

I strolled up to the rim to see if my ship was still there. The Martians might have dragged it into the dust. They hadn't, and there's no sign of tampering.

Am I seeing goblins? I could find out. All I'd have to do is peep into the base fusion plant. Either there's a pile there, mostly lead by now . . . or the pile was stolen seventy years ago. Either way the residual radiation would punish my curiosity.

I'm watching the sun rise through the bubble wall. It has a strange beauty, unlike anything I've seen in space. I've seen Saturn from an infinity of angles when I pulled monopoles in the rings, but it can't compare to this.

Now I know I'm crazy. It's a hole! I'm at the bottom of the lousy hole!

The sun writes a jagged white line along the crater rim. I can see the whole rim from here, no fear of that. No matter how fast they move, I can get into my suit before they get down to me.

It would be good to see my enemy.

Why did they come here, the fifteen men who lived and died here? I know why I'm here: for love of money. Them too? A hundred years ago the biggest diamonds men could make looked like coarse sand. They may have come after the diamond wells. But travel was fiendishly expensive then. Could they have made a profit?

Or did they think they could develop Mars the way they developed the asteroids? Ridiculous! But they didn't have my hindsight. And holes *can* be useful . . . like the raw lead deposits along Mercury's dawnside crescent. Pure lead, condensed from dayside vapor, free for the hauling. We'd be doing the same with Martian diamonds if it weren't so cheap to make them.

Here's the Sun. An anticlimax: I can't look into it, though it's dimmer than the rock miner's Sun. No more postcard scenery till—

Wups.

I'd never reach my suit. One move and the bubble will be a sieve. Just now they're as motionless as I am, staring at me without eyes. I wonder how they sense me? Their spears are poised and ready. Can they really puncture bubble fabric? But the Martians must know their own strength, and they've done this before.

All this time I've been waiting for them to swarm over the rim. They came out of the dust pool in the bottom of the crater. I should have realized the obsidian would be as badly cracked down there as elsewhere.

They *do* look like goblins.

For moments the silence was broken only by the twin humming of a nearby bumblebee and a distant tractor. Then Lit reached to turn off the log. He said, "We'd have saved him if he could have held out."

"You knew he was there?"

"Yah. The Deimos scope watched him land. We sent in a routine request for permission to land on UN property. Unfortunately flatlanders can't move as fast as a drugged snail, and we knew of no reason to hurry them up. A telescope would have tracked Muller if he'd tried to leave."

"Was he nuts?"

"Oh, the Martians were real enough. But we didn't know that until way too late. We saw the bubble inflate and stay that way for a while, and we saw it deflate all of a sudden. It looked like Muller'd had an accident. We broke the law and sent a ship down to get him if he was still alive. And that's why I'm telling you all this, Garner. As First Speaker for the Belt Political Section, I hereby confess that two Belt ships have trespassed on United Nations property."

"You had good reasons. Go on."

"You'd have been proud of him, Garner. He didn't run for his suit; he knew perfectly well it was too far away. Instead, he ran toward an O-tank full of water. The Martians must have slashed the moment he turned, but he reached the tank, stepped through one of the holes and turned the O-tank on the Martians. In the low pressure it was like using a fire hose. He got six before he fell."

"They burned?"

"They did. But not completely. There are some remains. We took three bodies, along with their spears, and left the others in situ. You want the corpses?"

"Damn right."

"Why?"

"What do you mean, Lit?"

"Why do you want them? We took three mummies and three spears as souvenirs. To you they're not souvenirs. It was a Belter who died down there."

"I'm sorry, Lit, but those bodies are important. We can find out what a Martian's made of before we go down. It could make all the difference."

"Go down." Lit made a rude noise. "Luke, why do you want to go down there? What could you possibly *want* from Mars? Revenge? A million tons of dust?"

"Abstract knowledge."

"For what?"

"Lit, you amaze me. Why did Earth go to space in the first place, if not for abstract knowledge?"

Words crowded over each other to reach Lit's mouth. They jammed in his throat, and he was speechless. He spread his hands, made frantic gestures, gulped twice, and said, "It's *obvious!*"

"Tell me slow. I'm a little dense."

"There's *everything* in space. Monopoles. Metal. Vacuum for the vacuum industries. A place to build cheap without all kinds of bracing girders. Free fall for people with weak hearts. Room to test things that might blow up. A place to learn physics where you can watch it happen. Controlled environments—"

"Was it all that obvious before we got here?"

"Of course it was!" Lit glared at his visitor. The glare took in Garner's withered legs, his drooping, mottled, hairless skin, the decades that showed in his eyes—and Lit remembered his visitor's age. ". . . Wasn't it?"

Intent to Deceive

A WAITER CAME to meet them as they landed. It crossed the restaurant like a chess pawn come to life, slid to a graceful stop on the carport balcony, hesitated long enough to be sure it had their attention, then moved inside at a slow walking pace.

The sound of its motion was a gentle whisper of breeze from under the lip of its ground-effect skirt. It guided them across the floor of the Red Planet, between and around occupied tables, empty tables, tables which displayed decorative meats and bowls of flowers, and other whispering robot waiters. At a table for two on the far side of the room, it deftly removed one chair to accommodate Lucas Garner's travel chair. Somehow it had recognized Luke as a paraplegic. It held the other chair for Lloyd Masney to sit down.

The murals on the restaurant walls were dull red and bright silver: a Ray Bradbury Mars, with the silver spires of an ancient Martian city nestling among red sands. A straight canal dwindled into the distance at both sides of the big room. Its silver waters actually crossed the floor and were in turn crossed by bridges. Attenuated, fragile Martians moved through the streets of the mural. Sometimes they looked curiously out at the customers, the human intruders in their make-believe world.

"Strange place," said Masney. He was a big, compact man with white hair and a bushy white moustache.

Luke didn't answer. When Masney glanced up he was startled by his friend's malevolent expression. "What's wrong?" he asked, and turned to follow Luke's eyes.

Luke was glaring his extreme distaste at a target which could only have been the robot waiter.

The waiter was a standard make. Below a blank spherical head was a body cylindrical for most of its length. The arms it had used to adjust Masney's chair for him had already vanished into panels in its torso, to join other specialized arms and hands and interior shelves for carrying food. Like all the other waiters, it had been painted in an abstract pattern of dull red and bright silver to match the murals. The last foot of the robot's cylindrical torso was a short, flaring skirt. Like Luke's travel chair, the waiter moved on a ground-effect air cushion.

"What's wrong?" Masney repeated.

"Nothing," said Luke. He picked up the menu.

The robot waited for their orders. Motionless, with all its arms retracted, it had become a pop-art barber pole.

"Come on, Luke. Why were you looking at the waiter like that?"

"I don't like robot waiters."

"Mph? Why not?"

"You grew up with 'em. I didn't. I've never got used to them."

"What's to get used to? They're waiters. They bring food."

"All right," said Luke, studying the menu.

He was old. It was not spinal injury that had cost him the use of his legs these past ten years. Too many spinal nerves had worn out with age. A goatee had once adorned his chin, but now his chin was as bald as his brows and scalp. His face, satanic in its wrinkled age, attracted instant attention, so that his every vagrant thought seemed exaggerated in his expression. The loose skin of his arms and shoulders half hid the muscles of a wrestler: the only part of him that seemed young.

"Every time I think I know you," said Masney, "you surprise me. You're a hundred and seventy-four now, aren't you?"

"You sent me a birthday card."

"Oh, I can count. But I can't *grasp* it. You're almost twice my age. How long ago did they invent robot waiters?"

"Waiters weren't invented. They evolved, like computers."

"When?"

"You were just learning to spell when the first all-automated restaurant opened in New York."

Masney smiled and shook his head gently. "All that time, and you never got used to them. Conservative, that's you."

Luke put the menu down. "If you must know, something happened to me once in connection with robot waiters. I had your job about then."

"Oh?" Lloyd Masney was Superintendent of Police for Greater Los Angeles. He'd taken his desk from Luke after Luke had resigned to become an Arm of the UN, forty years back.

"I was just getting used to the job; I'd only held it a couple of years. When was it? I can't remember; around 2025, I think. They were just introducing automated restaurants. They were just introducing a lot of things."

"Weren't they always?"

"Naturally, naturally. Quit interrupting. Around ten that morning I took a cigarette break. I had the habit of doing that every ten minutes. I was thinking about getting back to work when Dreamer Glass walked in. Old friend, Dreamer. I'd sent him up for a ten-year stretch for false advertising. He'd just got out and he was visiting some old friends."

"With a firegun?"

Luke's smile was a startling flash of new white teeth. "Oh, no. Dreamer was a nice guy. Little too much imagination, that's all. We put him away for telling television audiences that his brand of dishwashing liquid was good for the hands. We tested it, and it wasn't. I always thought he got too stiff a sentence, but—well, the Intent-to-Deceive laws were new then, and we had to bear down hard on the test cases so John Q would know we meant it."

"Nowadays he'd get the organ banks."

"We didn't put criminals in the organ banks in those days. I wish we'd never started.

"So Dreamer went to jail on my evidence. Five years later I was Superintendent. Another two years and he was out on parole. I was no busier than usual the day he showed up, so I dug out the guests' bottle, and we poured it in our coffee. And talked. Dreamer wanted me to fill him in on the last ten years. He'd been talking to other friends, so he knew something. But there were odd gaps that could have gotten him in trouble. He knew about the Jupiter probe, for instance, but he'd never heard of hard and soft plith.

"I wish I'd never mentioned robot restaurants.

"At first he thought I was talking about a bigger and better automat. Then when he got the idea, he was wild to see it.

"So I took him to lunch at the Herr Ober, which was a few blocks from the old Police Headquarters Building. Herr Ober was the first all-automated restaurant in Ellay. The only human beings involved were the maintenance crew, and they only showed up once a week. Everything else, from the kitchen to the hat-check girl, was machinery. I'd never eaten there—"

"Then how did you know so much about it?"

"We'd had to chase a man in there a month earlier. He'd picked up a kid for ransom, and he still had her for a hostage. At least, we thought he did. Another story. Before I could figure how to get at him, I'd had to study the Herr Ober top to bottom." Luke snorted. "Look at that metal idiot. He's still waiting for our order. You! Get us two Vurguuz martinis." The pop-art barber pole rose an inch from the floor and slid off. "Where was I?

"Oh, yeah. The place wasn't crowded, which was a break. We picked a table, and I showed Dreamer how to punch the summons button to call a waiter. We already called them waiters, but they didn't look anything like the ones here. They were nothing but double-decker serving trays on wheels, with senses and motors and a typewriter all packed into one end."

"Ran on wheels, too, I'll bet."

"Yah. Noisy. But in those days it was impressive. Dreamer was bug-eyed. When that animated tray came for our orders he just stared. I ordered for both of us.

"We downed our drinks and had another round.

Dreamer told me about the Advertisers' Club that some-how got formed in his cell block. The cigarette men could have controlled it to the eyes, there were so many of them, but they couldn't agree on anything. What they really wanted to do was form a convict's lobby in Washington."

The waiter appeared with the martinis.

"Anyway, we had our drinks and ordered. Identical meals, because Dreamer still wasn't capable of making a decision. He kept staring around, grinning.

"The waiter brought us shrimp cocktails. While we were eating, Dreamer tried to pump me on who might have the advertising concession on the robots. Not on the restaurant, but on all the automatic machinery. There he was, knowing nothing about computers, but all ready to go out and sell them. I tried to tell him he'd picked a good way to get back in Quentin, but he wouldn't listen.

"We finished the shrimp, and the waiter brought us two more shrimp cocktails. Dreamer said, 'What's this?'

" 'I must have typed wrong,' I told him. 'I wanted two lunches, but the damn thing is bringing us two lunches each.' "

"Dreamer laughed. 'I'll eat them both,' he said, and did. 'Ten years is a long time between shrimp cocktails,' he said.

"The waiter took our empty cups away and brought us two more shrimp cocktails.

" 'This is too much of a good thing,' said Dreamer. 'Where do I go to talk to the manager?'

" 'I told you, it's all automatic. The manager's a computer in the basement.'

" 'Does it have an audio circuit for complaints?'

" 'I think so.'

" 'Where do I find it?'

"I looked around, trying to remember. 'Over there. Past the payment counter. But I don't—'

"Dreamer got up. 'I'll be right back.' he said.

"He was, too. He came back within seconds, and he was shaking. 'I couldn't get out of the dining room,' he told me. 'The payment counter wouldn't let me by.

There was a barrier. I tried to give it some money, but nothing happened. When I tried to go over the barrier, I got an electric shock!'

" 'That's for deadbeats. It won't let you by until you pay for your lunch. You can't pay until you get a bill from the waiter.'

" 'Well, let's pay and get out. This place scares me.'

"So I pushed the summons button, and the waiter came. Before I could reach the typer it had given us two more shrimp cocktails and moved away.

" 'This is ridiculous,' said Dreamer. 'Look, suppose I get up and stand around at the other side of the table. That way you can reach the typer when it delivers the next round, because I'll be blocking it from leaving.'

"We tried it. The thing wouldn't come to our table until Dreamer sat down. Didn't recognize him standing up, maybe. Then it served two more shrimp cocktails, and Dreamer got up quick and moved behind it. I had my hands on the typer when it backed off and knocked Dreamer flat.

"He got so mad, he stood up and kicked the first waiter that came by. The waiter shocked him good, and while he was getting up the thing tossed him a printed message to the effect that robot waiters were expensive and delicate and he shouldn't do that."

"That's true," Masney said, deadpan. "He shouldn't."

"I'd have been helping him do it, but I wasn't sure what those machines would do next. So I stayed in my seat and planned what I'd do to the guy who invented robot waiters, if I ever got out of there to track him down.

"Dreamer got up shaking his head. Then he started trying to get help from the other diners. I could have told him that wouldn't work. Nobody wanted to get involved. In the big cities they never do. Finally one of the waiters shot a slip at him that told him to stop bothering the other diners, only it was more polite than that.

"He came back to our table, but this time he didn't sit down. He looked scared. 'Listen, Garner,' he said, 'I'm going to try the kitchen. You stay here. I'll bring help.' And he turned and started away.

"I yelled, 'Come back here! We'll be all right if—' But by that time he was out of earshot, heading for the kitchen door. I know he heard me shout. He just didn't want to be stopped.

"The door was only four feet tall, because it was built for robots. Dreamer ducked under it and was gone. I didn't dare go after him. If he made it, fine, I'd have help. I didn't think he would.

"There was one more thing I wanted to try. I pushed the summons button, and when the waiter came with two more shrimp cocktails I typed 'Phone' before it could get away."

"To phone Headquarters? You should have tried that earlier."

"Sure. But it didn't work. The waiter scooted off and brought me another shrimp cocktail.

"So I waited. By and by everyone disappeared, and I was alone in the Herr Ober. Whenever I got hungry enough I'd eat some crackers or a shrimp cocktail. The waiter kept bringing me more water and more shrimp cocktails, so that was all right.

"I left notes on some tables, so that when the dinner-time crowd showed up they'd be warned. But the waiters removed the notes as fast as I wrote them. Keeping things neat. I quit that and waited for rescue.

"Nobody came to rescue me. Dreamer never came back.

"Six o'clock, and the place filled up again. Along about nine, three couples at a nearby table started getting an endless supply of canapes Lorenzo. I watched them. Eventually they got so mad that the six of them circled the waiter and picked it up. The waiter spun its wheels madly, and then it shocked them and they dropped it. It fell on one man's foot. Everyone in the place panicked. When the dust cleared there were only the seven of us left.

"The others were trying to decide what to do about the guy with his foot under the waiter. They were afraid to touch the waiter, of course. It wouldn't have taken my order, because I wasn't at one of its tables, but I got one of the others to type an order for aspirin, and off it went.

"So I got the six of them back to their table and told them not to move. One of the girls had sleeping pills. I fed three to the guy with the smashed foot.

"And so we waited."

"I hate to ask," said Masney, "but what were you waiting for?"

"Closing time!"

"Oh, of course. Then what?"

"At two o'clock our waiters stopped bringing us shrimp cocktails and canapes Lorenzo and brought us our bills. You wouldn't *believe* what they charged me for all those shrimp cocktails . . . We paid our bills and left, carrying the guy with the smashed foot. We took him to a hospital, and then we got to a phone and called everybody in sight. Next day the Herr Ober was closed for repairs. It never reopened."

"What about Dreamer?"

"He's one reason the place never reopened. Never found him."

"He couldn't just disappear."

"Couldn't he?"

"Could he?"

"Sometimes I think he must have taken advantage of the publicity. Started life over somewhere else, with no prison record. And then I remember that he went into a fully automated kitchen, through a door that wasn't built for humans. That kitchen machinery could handle full-sized sides of beef. Dreamer obviously wasn't a robot. What would the kitchen machinery take him for?"

Masney thought about it.

It came to Masney as they were finishing desert.

"Mmb!" he said. "Mmmb!" And he swallowed frantically. "You fink! You were sent straight from Homicide branch to Superintendent. You never had anything to do with the Intent to Deceive Branch!"

"I thought you'd catch that."

"But why would you lie?"

"You kept bugging me about why I hated robot waiters. I had to say something."

"All right. You conned me. Now, why do you hate robot waiters?"

"I don't. You just happened to look up at the wrong time. I was thinking how silly our waiter looked in his ground-effect miniskirt."

Cloak of Anarchy

SQUARE IN THE middle of what used to be the San Diego Freeway, I leaned back against a huge, twisted oak. The old bark was rough and powdery against my bare back. There was dark green shade shot with tight parallel beams of white gold. Long grass tickled my legs.

Forty yards away across a wide strip of lawn was a clump of elms, and a small grandmotherly woman sitting on a green towel. She looked like she'd grown there. A stalk of grass protruded between her teeth. I felt we were kindred spirits, and once when I caught her eye I wiggled a forefinger at her, and she waved back.

In a minute now I'd have to be getting up. Jill was metting me at the Wilshire exits in half an hour. But I'd started walking at the Sunset Boulevard ramps, and I was tired. A minute more . . .

It was a good place to watch the world rotate.

A good day for it, too. No clouds at all. On this hot blue summer afternoon, King's Free Park was as crowded as it ever gets.

Someone at police headquarters had expected that. Twice the usual number of copseyes floated overhead, waiting. Gold dots against blue, basketball-sized, twelve feet up. Each a television eye and a sonic stunner, each a hookup to police headquarters, they were there to enforce the law of the Park.

No violence.

No hand to be raised against another—and no other laws whatever. Life was often entertaining in a Free Park.

North toward Sunset, a man carried a white rectangu-

111

lar sign, blank on both sides. He was parading back and forth in front of a square-jawed youth on a plastic box, who was trying to lecture him on the subject of fusion power and the heat pollution problem. Even this far away I could hear the conviction and the dedication in his voice.

South, a handful of yelling marksmen were throwing rocks at a copseye, directed by a gesticulating man with wild black hair. The golden basketball was dodging the rocks, but barely. Some cop was baiting them. I wondered where they had got the rocks. Rocks were scarce in King's Free Park.

The black-haired man looked familiar. I watched him and his horde chasing the copseye . . . then forgot them when a girl walked out of a clump of elms.

She was lovely. Long, perfect legs, deep red hair worn longer than shoulder length, the face of an arrogant angel, and a body so perfect that it seemed unreal, like an adolescent's daydream. Her walk showed training; possibly she was a model, or dancer. Her only garment was a cloak of glowing blue velvet.

It was fifteen yards long, that cloak. It trailed back from two big gold disks that were stuck somehow to the skin of her shoulders. It trailed back and back, floating at a height of five feet all the way, twisting and turning to trace her path through the trees. She seemed like the illustration in a book of fairy tales, bearing in mind that the original fairy tales were not intended for children.

Neither was she. You could hear neck vertebrae popping all over the Park. Even the rock-throwers had stopped to watch.

She could sense the attention, or hear it in a whisper of sighs. It was what she was here for. She strolled along with a condescending angel's smile on her angel's face, not overdoing the walk, but letting it flow. She turned, regardless of whether there were obstacles to avoid, so that fifteen yards of flowing cloak could follow the curve.

I smiled, watching her go. She was lovely from the back, with dimples.

The man who stepped up to her a little farther on was the same one who had led the rock-throwers. Wild black

hair and beard, hollow cheeks and deep-set eyes, a diffident smile and a diffident walk . . . Ron Cole. Of
course.

I didn't hear what he said to the girl in the cloak, but
I saw the result. He flinched, then turned abruptly and
walked away with his eyes on his feet.

I got up and moved to intercept him. "Don't take it
personal," I said.

He looked up, startled. His voice, when it came, was
bitter. "How should I take it?"

"She'd have turned any man off the same way. She's
to look at, not to touch."

"You know her?"

"Never saw her before in my life."

"Then—?"

"Her cloak. Now you *must* have noticed her cloak."

The tail end of her cloak was just passing us, its folds
rippling an improbably deep, rich blue. Ronald Cole
smiled as if it hurt his face. "Yah."

"All right. Now suppose you made a pass, and suppose the lady liked your looks and took you up on it.
What would she do next? Bearing in mind that she can't
stop walking even for a second."

He thought it over first, then asked, "Why not?"

"If she stops walking, she loses the whole effect. Her
cloak just hangs there like some kind of tail. It's supposed to wave. If she lies down, it's even worse. A cloak
floating at five feet, then swooping into a clump of bushes and bobbing frantically—" Ron laughed helplessly in
falsetto. I said, "See? Her audience would get the giggles. That's not what she's after."

He sobered. "But if she really wanted to, she wouldn't
care about . . . oh. Right. She must have spent a fortune to get that effect."

"Sure. She wouldn't ruin it for Jacques Casanova
himself." I thought unfriendly thoughts toward the girl
in the cloak. There are polite ways to turn down a pass.
Ronald Cole was easy to hurt.

I asked, "Where did you get the rocks?"

"Rocks? Oh, we found a place where the center di-
vider shows through. We knocked off some chunks of
concrete." Ron looked down the length of the Park just

as a kid bounced a missile off a golden ball. "They got one! Come on!"

The fastest commercial shipping that ever sailed was the clipper ship; yet the world stopped building them after just twenty-five years. Steam had come. Steam was faster, safer, more dependable and cheaper.

The freeways served America for almost fifty years. Then modern transportation systems cleaned the air and made traffic jams archaic and left the nation with an embarrassing problem. What to do with ten thousand miles of unsightly abandoned freeways?

King's Free Park had been part of the San Diego Freeway, the section between Sunset and the Santa Monica interchange. Decades ago the concrete had been covered with topsoil. The borders had been landscaped from the start. Now the Park was as thoroughly covered with green as the much older Griffith Free Park.

Within King's Free Park was an orderly approximation of anarchy. People were searched at the entrances. There were no weapons inside. The copseyes, floating overhead and out of reach, were the next best thing to no law at all.

There was only one law to enforce. All acts of attempted violence carried the same penalty for attacker and victim. Let anyone raise his hands against his neighbor, and one of the golden basketballs would stun them both. They would wake separately, with copseyes watching. It was usually enough.

Naturally people threw rocks at copseyes. It was a Free Park, wasn't it?

"They got one! Come on!" Ron tugged at my arm. The felled copseye was hidden, surrounded by those who had destroyed it. "I hope they don't kick it apart. I told them I need it intact, but that might not stop them."

"It's a Free Park. And they bagged it."

"With my missiles!"

"Who are they?"

"I don't know. They were playing baseball when I found them. I told them I needed a copseye. They said they'd get me one."

I remembered Ron quite well now. Ronald Cole was an artist and an inventor. It would have been two sources of income for another man, but Ron was different. He invented new art forms. With solder and wire and diffraction gratings and several makes of plastics kit, and an incredible collection of serendipitous junk, Ron Cole made things the like of which had never been seen on Earth.

The market for new art forms has always been low, but now and then he did make a sale. It was enough to keep him in raw materials, especially since many of his raw materials came from basements and attics. Rarely there came a *big* sale, and then, briefly, he would be rich.

There was this about him: he knew who I was, but he hadn't remembered my name. Ron Cole had better things to think about than what name belonged with whom. A name was only a tag and a conversational gambit. "Russel! How are you?" A signal. Ron had developed a substitute.

Into a momentary gap in the conversation he would say, "Look at this," and hold out—miracles.

Once it had been a clear plastic sphere, golf-ball size, balanced on a polished silver concavity. When the ball rolled around on the curved mirror, the reflections were *fantastic*.

Once it had been a twisting sea serpent engraved on a Michelob beer bottle, the lovely vase-shaped bottle of the early 1960s that was too big for standard refrigerators.

And once it had been two strips of dull silvery metal, unexpectedly heavy. "What's this?"

I'd held them in the palm of my hand. They were heavier than lead. Platinum? But nobody carries that much platinum around. Joking, I'd asked, "U-235?"

"Are they warm?" he'd asked apprehensively. I'd fought off an urge to throw them as far as I could and dive behind a couch.

But they *had* been platinum. I never did learn why Ron was carrying them about. Something that didn't pan out.

Within a semicircle of spectators, the felled copseye lay on the grass. It was intact, possibly because two cheerful, conspicuously large men were standing over it, waving everyone back.

"Good," said Ron. He knelt above the golden sphere, turned it with his long artist's fingers. To me he said, "Help me get it open."

"What for? What are you after?"

"I'll tell you in a minute. Help me get—Never mind." The hemispherical cover came off. For the first time ever, I looked into a copseye.

It was impressively simple. I picked out the stunner by its parabolic reflector, the cameras, and a toroidal coil that had to be part of the floater device. No power source. I guessed that the shell itself was a power beam antenna. With the cover cracked there would be no way for a damn fool to electrocute himself.

Ron knelt and studied the strange guts of the copseye. From his pocket he took something made of glass and metal. He suddenly remembered my existence and held it out to me, saying, "Look at this."

I took it, expecting a surprise, and I got it. It was an old hunting watch, a big wind-up watch on a chain, with a protective case. They were in common use a couple of hundred years ago. I looked at the face, said, "Fifteen minutes slow. You didn't repair the whole works, did you?"

"Oh, no." He clicked the back open for me.

The works looked modern. I guessed, "Battery and tuning fork?"

"That's what the guard thought. Of course that's what I made it from. But the hands don't move; I set them just before they searched me."

"Aah. What does it do?"

"If I work it right, I think it'll knock down every copseye in King's Free Park."

For a minute or so I was laughing too hard to speak. Ron watched me with his head on one side, clearly wondering if I thought he was joking.

I managed to say, "That ought to cause all *kinds* of excitement."

Ron nodded vigorously. "Of course it all depends on

whether they use the kind of circuits I think they use. Look for yourself; the copseyes aren't supposed to be foolproof. They're supposed to be cheap. If one gets knocked down, the taxes don't go up much. The other way is to make them expensive and foolproof, and frustrate a lot of people. People aren't supposed to be frustrated in a Free Park."

"So?"

"Well, there's a cheap way to make the circuitry for the power system. If they did it that way, I can blow the whole thing. We'll see." Ron pulled thin copper wire from the cuffs of his shirt.

"How long will this take?"

"Oh, half an hour—maybe more."

That decided me. "I've got to be going. I'm meeting Jill Hayes at the Wilshire exits. You've met her, a big blond girl, my height—"

But he wasn't listening. "Okay, see you," he muttered. He began placing the copper wire inside the copseye, with tweezers. I left.

Crowds tend to draw crowds. A few minutes after leaving Ron, I joined a semicircle of the curious to see what they were watching.

A balding, lantern-jawed individual was putting something together—an archaic machine, with blades and a small gasoline motor. The T-shaped wooden handle was brand new and unpainted. The metal parts were dull with the look of ancient rust recently removed.

The crowd speculated in half-whispers. What was it? Not part of a car; not an outboard motor, though it had blades; too small for a motor scooter, too big for a motor skateboard—

"Lawn mower," said the white-haired lady next to me. She was one of those small, birdlike people who shrivel and grow weightless as they age, and live forever. Her words meant nothing to me. I was about to ask, when—

The lantern-jawed man finished his work, and twisted something, and the motor started with a roar. Black smoke puffed out. In triumph he gripped the handles. Outside, it was a prison offense to build a working internal combustion machine. Here—

With the fire of dedication burning in his eyes, he wheeled his infernal machine across the grass. He left a path as flat as a rug. It was a Free Park, wasn't it?

The smell hit everyone at once: black dirt in the air, a stink of half-burned hydrocarbons attacking nose and eyes. I gasped and coughed. I'd never smelled anything like it.

The crowd roared and converged.

He squawked when they picked up his machine. Someone found a switch and stopped it. Two men confiscated the tool kit and went to work with screwdriver and hammer. The owner objected. He picked up a heavy pair of pliers and tried to commit murder.

A copseye zapped him and the man with the hammer, and they both hit the lawn without bouncing. The rest of them pulled the lawn mower apart and bent and broke the pieces.

"I'm half sorry they did that," said the old woman. "Sometimes I miss the sound of lawn mowers. My dad used to mow the lawn on Sunday mornings."

I said, "It's a Free Park."

"Then why can't he build anything he pleases?"

"He can. He did. Anything he's free to build, we're free to kick apart." And my mind finished, *Like Ron's rigged copseye.*

Ron was good with tools. It would not surprise me a bit if he knew enough about copseyes to knock out the whole system.

Maybe someone ought to stop him.

But knocking down copseyes wasn't illegal. It happened all the time. It was part of the freedom of the Park. If Ron could knock them all down at once, well—

Maybe someone ought to stop him.

I passed a flock of high school girls, all chittering like birds, all about sixteen. It might have been their first trip inside a Free Park. I looked back because they were so cute, and caught them staring in awe and wonder at the dragon on my back.

A few years and they'd be too blasé to notice. It had taken Jill almost half an hour to apply it this morning: a glorious red-and-gold dragon breathing flames across my shoulder, flames that seemed to glow by their own light.

Lower down were a princess and a knight in golden armor, the princess tied to a stake, the knight fleeing for his life. I smiled back at the girls, and two of them waved.

Short blond hair and golden skin, the tallest girl in sight, wearing not even a nudist's shoulder pouch: Jill Hayes stood squarely in front of the Wilshire entrance, visibly wondering where I was. It was five minutes after three.

There was this about living with a physical culture nut. Jill insisted on getting me into shape. The daily exercises were part of that, and so was this business of walking half the length of King's Free Park . . .

I'd balked at doing it briskly, though. Who walks briskly in a Free Park? There's too much to see. She'd given me an hour; I'd held out for three. It was a compromise, like the paper slacks I was wearing despite Jill's nudist beliefs.

Sooner or later she'd find someone with muscles, or I'd relapse into laziness, and we'd split. Meanwhile . . . we got along. It seemed only sensible to let her finish my training.

She spotted me, yelled, "Russel! Here!" in a voice that must have reached both ends of the Park.

In answer I lifted my arm, semaphore-style, slowly over my head and back down.

And every copseye in King's Free Park fell out of the sky, dead.

Jill looked about her at all the startled faces and all the golden bubbles resting in bushes and on the grass. She approached me somewhat uncertainly. She asked, "Did you do that?"

I said, "Yah. If I wave my arms again, they'll all go back up."

"I think you'd better do it," she said primly. Jill had a fine poker face. I waved my arm grandly over my head and down, but of course, the copseyes stayed where they had fallen.

Jill said, "I wonder what happened to them?"

"It was Ron Cole. You remember him. He's the one who engraved some old Michelob beer bottles for Steuben——"

"Oh, yes. But *how?*"

We went off to ask him.

A brawny college man howled and charged past us at a dead run. We saw him kick a copseye like a soccer ball. The golden cover split, but the man howled again and hopped up and down hugging his foot.

We passed dented golden shells and broken resonators and bent parabolic reflectors. One woman looked flushed and proud; she was wearing several of the copper toroids as bracelets. A kid was collecting the cameras. Maybe he thought he could sell them outside.

I never saw an intact copseye after the first minute.

They weren't all busy kicking copseyes apart. Jill stared at the conservatively dressed group carrying POPULATION BY COPULATION signs, and wanted to know if they were serious. Their grim-faced leader handed us pamphlets that spoke of the evil and the blasphemy of Man's attempts to alter himself through gene tampering and extrauterine growth experiments. If it was a put-on, it was a good one.

We passed seven little men, each three to four feet high, traveling with a single tall, pretty brunette. They wore medieval garb. We both stared; but I was the one who noticed the makeup and the use of UnTan. African pigmies, probably part of a UN-sponsored tourist group; and the girl must be their guide.

Ron Cole was not where I had left him.

"He must have decided that discretion is the better part of cowardice. May be right, too," I surmised. "Nobody's every knocked down *all* the copseyes before."

"It's not illegal, is it?"

"Not illegal, but excessive. They can bar him from the Park, at the very least."

Jill stretched in the sun. She was all golden, and *big*. She said, "I'm thirsty. Is there a fountain around?"

"Sure, unless someone's plugged it by now. It's a—"

"Free Park. Do you mean to tell me they don't even protect the *fountains?*"

"You make one exception, it's like a wedge. When someone ruins a fountain, they wait and fix it that night. That way . . . If I see someone trying to wreck a fountain, I'll generally throw a punch at him. A lot of us do.

After a guy's lost enough of his holiday to the copseye stunners, he'll get the idea, sooner or later."

The fountain was a solid cube of concrete with four spigots and a hand-sized metal button. It was hard to jam, hard to hurt. Ron Cole stood near it, looking lost.

He seemed glad to see me, but still lost. I introduced him— "You remember Jill Hayes." He said, "Certainly. Hello, Jill," and, having put her name to its intended purpose, promptly forgot it.

Jill said, "We thought you'd made a break for it."

"I did."

"Oh?"

"You know how complicated the exits are. They have to be, to keep anyone from getting in through an exit with—like a shotgun." Ron ran both hands through his hair, without making it any more or less neat. "Well, all the exits have stopped working. They must be on the same circuits as the copseyes. I wasn't expecting that."

"Then we're locked in," I said. That was irritating. But underneath the irritation was a funny feeling in the pit of my stomach. "How long do you think—"

"No telling. They'll have to get new copseyes in somehow. And repair the beamed power system, and figure out how I bollixed it, and fix it so it doesn't happen again. I suppose someone must have kicked my rigged copseye to pieces by now, but the police don't know that."

"Oh, they'll just send in some cops," said Jill.

"Look around you."

There were pieces of copseyes in all directions. Not one remained whole. A cop would have to be out of his mind to enter a Free Park.

Not to mention the damage to the spirit of the Park.

"I wish I'd brought a bag lunch," said Ron.

I saw the cloak off to my right: a ribbon of glowing blue velvet hovering at five feet, like a carpeted path in the air. I didn't yell, or point, or anything. For Ron it might be pushing the wrong buttons.

Ron didn't see it. "Actually I'm kind of glad this happened," he said animatedly. "I've always thought that anarchy ought to be a viable form of society."

Jill made polite sounds of encouragement.

"After all, anarchy is only the last word in free enter-prise. What can a government do for people that people can't do for themselves? Protection from other coun-tries? If all the other countries are anarchies, too, you don't need armies. Police, maybe; but what's wrong with privately owned police?"

"Fire departments used to work that way," Jill re-membered. "They were hired by the insurance compa-nies. They only protected houses that belonged to their own clients."

"Right! So you buy theft and murder insurance, and the insurance companies hire a police force. The client carries a credit card—"

"Suppose the robber steals the card, too?"

"He can't use it. He doesn't have the right retina prints."

"But if the client doesn't have the credit card, he can't sic the cops on the thief."

"Oh." A noticeable pause. "Well—"

Half-listening, for I had heard it all before, I looked for the endpoints of the cloak. I found empty space at one end and a lovely red-haired girl at the other. She was talking to two men as outré as herself.

One can get the impression that a Free Park is one gi-gantic costume party. It isn't. Not one person in ten wears anything but street clothes; but the costumes are what get noticed.

These guys were part bird.

Their eyebrows and eyelashes were tiny feathers, green on one, golden on the other. Larger feathers cov-ered their heads, blue and green and gold, and ran in a crest down their spines. They were bare to the waist, showing physiques Jill would find acceptable.

Ron was lecturing. "What does a government do for *anyone* except the people who run the government? Once there were private post offices, and they were cheaper than what we've got now. Anything the govern-ment takes over gets more expensive, *immediately*. There's no reason why private enterprise can't do any-thing a government—"

Jill gasped. She said, "Ooh! How lovely."

Ron turned to look.

As if on cue, the girl in the cloak slapped one of the feathered men hard across the mouth. She tried to hit the other one, but he caught her wrist. Then all three froze.

I said, "See? Nobody wins. She doesn't even like standing still. She—" and I realized why they weren't moving.

In a Free Park it's easy for a girl to turn down an offer. If the guy won't take No for an answer, he gets slapped. The stun beam gets him and the girl. When she wakes up, she walks away.

Simple.

The girl recovered first. She gasped and jerked her wrist loose and turned to run. One of the feathered men didn't bother to chase her; he simply took a double handful of the cloak.

This was getting serious.

The cloak jerked her sharply backward. She didn't hesitate. She reached for the big gold disks at her shoulders, ripped them loose and ran on. The feathered men chased her, laughing.

The redhead wasn't laughing. She was running all out. Two drops of blood ran down her shoulders. I thought of trying to stop the feathered men, decided in favor of it—but they were already past.

The cloak hung like a carpeted path in the air, empty at both ends.

Jill hugged herself uneasily. "Ron, just how does one go about hiring your private police force?"

"Well, you can't expect it to form spontaneously—"

"Let's try the entrances. Maybe we can get out."

It was slow to build. Everyone knew what a copseye did. Nobody thought it through. Two feathered men chasing a lovely nude? A pretty sight: and why interfere? If she didn't want to be chased, she need only . . . what? And nothing else had changed. The costumes, the people with causes, the people looking for causes, the people-watchers, and pranksters—

Blank Sign had joined the POPULATION BY COPULATION faction. His grass-stained pink street tunic jarred strangely with their conservative suits, but he showed no sign of mockery; his face was as preternaturally solemn as theirs. Nonetheless they did not seem glad of his company.

It was crowded near the Wilshire exits. I saw enough bewildered and frustrated faces to guess that they were closed. The little vestibule area was so packed that we didn't even try to find out what was wrong with the doors.

"I don't think we ought to stay here," Jill said uneasily.

I noticed the way she was hugging herself. "Are you cold?"

"No." She shivered. "But I wish I were dressed."

"How about a strip of that velvet cloak?"

"Good!"

We were too late. The cloak was gone.

It was a warm September day, near sunset. Clad only in paper slacks, I was not cold in the least. I said, "Take my slacks."

"No, hon, I'm the nudist." But Jill hugged herself with both arms.

"Here," said Ron, and handed her his sweater. She flashed him a grateful look, then, clearly embarrassed, she wrapped the sweater around her waist and knotted the sleeves.

Ron didn't get it at all. I asked him, "Do you know the difference between nude and naked?"

He shook his head.

"Nude is artistic. Naked is defenseless."

Nudity was popular in a Free Park. That night, nakedness was not. There must have been pieces of that cloak all over King's Free Park. I saw at least four that night: one worn as a kilt, two being used as crude sarongs, and one as a bandage.

On a normal day, the entrances to King's Free Park close at six. Those who want to stay, stay as long as they like. Usually there are not many, because there are no lights to be broken in a Free Park; but light does seep in from the city beyond. The copseyes float about, guided by infrared, but most of them are not manned.

Tonight would be different.

It was after sunset, but still light. A small and ancient lady came stumping toward us with a look of murder on her lined face. At first I thought it was meant for us; but that wasn't it. She was so mad she couldn't see straight.

She saw my feet and looked up. "Oh, it's you. The one who helped break the lawn mower," she said— which was unjust. "A Free Park, is it? A Free Park! Two men just took away my dinner!"

I spread my hands. "I'm sorry. I really am. If you still had it, we could try to talk you into sharing it."

She lost some of her mad; which brought her embarrassingly close to tears. "Then we're all hungry together. I brought it in a plastic bag. Next time I'll use something that isn't transparent, by d-damn!" She noticed Jill and her improvised sweater-skirt, and added, "I'm sorry, dear, I gave my towel to a girl who needed it even more."

"Thank you anyway."

"Please, may I stay with you people until the cops-eyes start working again? I don't feel safe, somehow. I'm Glenda Hawthorne."

We introduced ourselves. Glenda Hawthorne shook our hands. By now it was quite dark. We couldn't see the city beyond the high green hedges, but the change was startling when the lights of Westwood and Santa Monica flashed on.

The police were taking their own good time getting us some copseyes.

We reached the grassy field sometimes used by the Society for Creative Anachronism for their tournaments. They fight on foot with weighted and padded weapons designed to behave like swords, broad-axes, morning-stars, et cetera. The weapons are bugged so that they won't fall into the wrong hands. The field is big and flat and bare of trees, sloping upward at the edges.

On one of the slopes, something moved.

I stopped. It didn't move again, but it showed clearly in light reflected down from the white clouds. I made out something man-shaped and faintly pink, and a pale rectangle nearby.

I spoke low. "Stay here."

Jill said, "Don't be silly. There's nothing for anyone to hide under. Come on."

The blank sign was bent and marked with shoe prints. The man who had been carrying it looked up at us with pain in his eyes. Drying blood ran from his nose. With effort he whispered, "I think they dislocated my shoulder."

"Let me look." Jill bent over him. She probed him a bit, then set herself and pulled hard and steadily on his arm. Blank Sign yelled in pain and despair.

"That'll do it." Jill sounded satisfied. "How does it feel?"

"It doesn't hurt as much." He smiled, almost.

"What happened?"

"They started pushing me and kicking me to make me go away. I was *doing* it, I was walking away. I *was.* Then someone snatched away my sign—" He stopped for a moment, then went off at a tangent. "I wasn't hurting anyone with my sign. I'm a Psych Major. I'm writing a thesis on what people read into a blank sign. Like the blank sheets in the Rorschach tests."

"What kind of reactions do you get?"

"Usually hostile. But nothing like *that.*" Blank Sign sounded bewildered. "Wouldn't you think a Free Park is the one place you'd find freedom of speech?"

Jill wiped at his face with a tissue from Glenda Hawthorne's purse. She said, "Especially when you're not saying anything. Hey, Ron, tell us more about your government by anarchy."

Ron cleared his throat. "I hope you're not judging it by *this.* King's Free Park hasn't been an anarchy for more than a couple of hours. It needs time to develop."

Glenda Hawthorne and Blank Sign must have wondered what the hell he was talking about. I wished him joy in explaining it to them, and wondered if he would explain who had knocked down the copseyes.

This field would be a good place to spend the night. It was open, with no cover and no shadows, no way for anyone to sneak up on us.

And I was learning to think like a true paranoid.

We lay on wet grass, sometimes dozing, sometimes

talking. Two other groups no bigger than ours occupied the jousting field. They kept their distance, we kept ours. Now and then we heard voices, and knew that they were not asleep; not all at once, anyway.

Blank Sign dozed restlessly. His ribs were giving him trouble, though Jill said none of them were broken. Every so often he whimpered and tried to move and woke himself up. Then he had to hold himself still until he fell asleep again.

"Money," said Jill. "It takes a government to print money."

"But you could get IOUs printed. Standard denominations, printed for a fee and notarized. Backed by your good name."

Jill laughed softly. "Thought of everything, haven't you? You couldn't travel very far that way."

"Credit cards, then."

I had stopped believing in Ron's anarchy. I said, "Ron, remember the girl in the long blue cloak?"

A little gap of silence. "Yah?"

"Pretty, wasn't she? Fun to watch."

"Granted."

"If there weren't any laws to stop you from raping her, she'd be muffled to the ears in a long dress and carrying a tear gas pen. What fun would that be? I *like* the nude look. Look how fast it disappeared after the cops-eyes fell."

"Mm-m," said Ron.

The night was turning cold. Faraway voices; occasional distant shouts, came like thin gray threads in a black tapestry of silence. Mrs. Hawthorne spoke into that silence.

"What was that boy really saying with his blank sign?"

"He wasn't saying anything," said Jill.

"Now, just a minute, dear. I think he was, even if he didn't know it." Mrs. Hawthorne talked slowly, using the words to shape her thoughts. "Once there was an organization to protest the forced contraception bill. I was one of them. We carried signs for hours at a time. We printed leaflets. We stopped people passing so that we could talk to them. We gave up our time, we went to considerable trouble and expense, because we wanted to get our ideas across.

"Now, if a man had joined us with a blank sign, he would have been *saying* something.

"His sign says that he has no opinion. If he joins us, he says that we have no opinion either. He's saying our opinions aren't worth anything."

I said, "Tell him when he wakes up. He can put it in his notebook."

"But his notebook is *wrong*. He wouldn't push his blank sign in among people he agreed with, would he?"

"Maybe not."

"I . . . suppose I don't like people with no opinions." Mrs. Hawthorne stood up. She had been sitting tailor-fashion for some hours. "Do you know if there's a pop machine nearby?"

There wasn't, of course. No private company would risk getting their machines smashed once or twice a day. But she had reminded the rest of us that we were thirsty. Eventually we all got up and trooped away in the direction of the fountain.

All but Blank Sign.

I'd *liked* that blank sign gag. How odd, how ominous, that so basic a right as freedom of speech could depend on so slight a thing as a floating copseye.

I was thirsty.

The Park was bright by city lights, crossed by sharp-edged shadows. In such light it seems that one can see much more than he really can. I could see into every shadow; but, though there were stirrings all around us, I could see nobody until he moved. We four, sitting under an oak with our backs to the tremendous trunk, must be invisible from any distance.

We talked little. The Park was quiet except for occasional laughter from the fountain.

I couldn't forget my thirst. I could feel others being thirsty around me. The fountain was right out there in the open, a solid block of concrete with five men around it.

They were dressed alike, in paper shorts with big pockets. They looked alike: like first-string atheletes.

Maybe they belonged to the same order, or frat, or ROTC class.

They had taken over the fountain.

When someone came to get a drink, the tall ash-blond one would step forward with his arm held stiffly out, palm forward. He had a wide mouth and a grin that might otherwise have been infectious, and a deep, echoing voice. He would intone, "Go back. None may pass here but the immortal Cthulhu—" or something equally silly.

Trouble was, they weren't kidding. Or: they were kidding, but they wouldn't let anyone have a drink.

When we arrived, a girl dressed in a towel had been trying to talk some sense into them. It hadn't worked. It might even have boosted their egos: a lovely half-naked girl begging them for water. Eventually she'd given up and gone away.

In that light her hair might have been red. I hoped it was the girl in the cloak.

And a beefy man in a yellow business jumper had made the mistake of demanding his Rights. It was not a night for Rights. The blond kid had goaded him into screaming insults, a stream of unimaginative profanity, which ended when he tried to hit the blond kid. Then three of them had swarmed over him. The man had left crawling, moaning of police and lawsuits.

Why hadn't somebody done something?

I had watched it all from sitting position. I could list my own reasons. One: it was hard to face the fact that a copseye would not zap them both, any second now. Two: I didn't like the screaming fat man much. He talked dirty. Three: I'd been waiting for someone else to step in.

Mrs. Hawthorne said, "Ronald, what time is it?"

Ron may have been the only man in King's Free Park who knew the time. People generally left their valuables in lockers at the entrances. But years ago, when Ron was flush with money from the sale of the engraved beer bottles, he'd bought an implant-watch. He told time by one red mark and two red lines glowing beneath the skin of his wrist.

We had put the women between us, but I saw the motion as he glanced at his wrist. "Quarter of twelve."

"Don't you think they'll get bored and go away? It's been twenty minutes since anyone tried to get a drink," Mrs. Hawthorne said.

Jill shifted against me in the dark. "They can't be any more bored than we are. I think they'll get bored and stay anyway. Besides—" She stopped.

I said, "Besides that, we're thirsty *now*."

"Right."

"Ron, have you seen any sign of those rock throwers you collected? Especially the one who knocked down the copseye."

"No."

I wasn't surprised. In this darkness? "Do you remember his . . ." and I didn't even finish.

". . . Yes!" Ron said suddenly.

"You're kidding."

"No. His name was Bugeyes. You don't forget a name like that."

"I take it he had bulging eyes?"

"I didn't notice."

Well, it was worth a try. I stood and cupped my hands for a megaphone and shouted, *"Bugeyes!"*

One of the Water Monopoly shouted, "Let's keep the noise down out there!"

"Bugeyes!"

A chorus of remarks from the Water Monopoly. "Strange habits these peasants—" "Most of them are just thirsty. *This* character—"

From off to the side: "What do you want?"

"We want to talk to you! Stay where you are!" To Ron I said, "Come on." To Jill and Mrs. Hawthorne, "Stay here. Don't get involved."

We moved out into the open space between us and Bugeyes' voice.

Two of the five kids came immediately to intercept us. They must have been bored, all right, and looking for action.

We ran for it. We reached the shadows of the trees before those two reached us. They stopped, laughing like maniacs, and moved back to the fountain.

Ron and I, we lay on our bellies in the shadows of low bushes. Across too much shadowless grass, four men in paper shorts stood at parade rest at the four corners of the fountain. The fifth man watched for a victim.

A boy walked out between us into the moonlight. His eyes were shining, big, expressive eyes, maybe a bit too prominent. His hands were big, too—with knobby knuckles. One hand was full of acorns.

He pitched them rapidly, one at a time, overhand. First one, then another of the Water Monopoly twitched and looked in our direction. Bugeyes kept throwing.

Quite suddenly, two of them started toward us at a run. Bugeyes kept throwing until they were almost on him; then he threw his acorns in a handful and dived into the shadows.

The two of them ran between us. We let the first go by: the wide-mouthed blond spokesman, his expression low and murderous now. The other was short and broad-shouldered, an intimidating silhouette, seemingly all muscle. A tackle. I stood up in front of him, expecting him to stop in surprise; and he did, and I hit him in the mouth as hard as I could.

He stepped back in shock. Ron wrapped an arm around his throat.

He bucked. Instantly, Ron hung on. I did something I'd seen often enough on television: linked my fingers and brought both hands down on the back of his neck.

The blond spokesman should be back by now; and I turned, and he was. He was on me before I could get my hands up. We rolled on the ground, me with my arms pinned to my sides, him unable to use his hands without letting go. It was lousy planning for both of us. He was squeezing the breath out of me. Ron hovered over us, waiting for a chance to hit him.

Suddenly there were others, a lot of others. Three of them pulled the blond kid off me, and a beefy, bloody man in a yellow business jumper stepped forward and crowned him with a rock.

The blond kid went limp.

The man squared off and threw a straight left hook with the rock in his hand. The blond kid's head snapped back, fell forward.

I yelled, "Hey!" jumped forward, got hold of the arm that held the rock.

Someone hit me solidly in the side of the neck.

I dropped. It felt like all my strings had been cut. Someone was helping me to my feet—Ron—voices babbling in whispers, one shouting, "Get him—"

I couldn't see the blond kid. The other one, the tackle, was up and staggering away. Shadows came from between the trees to play pileup on him. The woods were alive, and it was just a *little* patch of woods. Full of angry, thirsty people.

Bugeyes reappeared, grinning widely. "Now what? Go somewhere else and try it again?"

"Oh, no. It's getting very vicious out tonight. Ron, we've got to stop them. They'll kill him!"

"It's a Free Park. Can you stand now?"

"Ron, they'll *kill* him!"

The rest of the Water Trust was charging to the rescue. One of them had a tree branch with the leaves stripped off. Behind them, shadows converged on the fountain.

We fled.

I had to stop after a dozen paces. My head was trying to explode. Ron looked back anxiously, but I waved him on. Behind me the man with the branch broke through the trees and ran toward me to do murder.

Behind him, all the noise suddenly stopped.

I braced myself for the blow.

And fainted.

He was lying across my legs, with the branch still in his hand. Jill and Ron were pulling at my shoulders. A pair of golden moons floated overhead.

I wriggled loose. I felt my head. It seemed intact.

Ron said, "The copseyes zapped him before he got to you."

"What about the others? Did they kill them?"

"I don't know." Ron ran his hands through his hair. "I was wrong. Anarchy isn't stable. It comes apart too easily."

"Well, don't do any more experiments. Okay?"

People were beginning to stand up. They streamed toward the exits, gathering momentum, beneath the yellow gaze of the copseyes.

The Warriors

The organ bank problem is basic to an understanding of this era, and of later eras on the colony worlds. It forms a background for the three tales of Gil the ARM, and for the society of Mount Lookitthat as detailed in *A Gift From Earth*.

Phssthpok the Pak was the second extraterrestrial to meet mankind. Though he had traveled all the way from the galactic core, he was hardly an alien; the Pak are related to humankind. Before his death he created the first of the protector-stage humans, from a Belt miner named Jack Brennan.

There followed a Golden Age—a period of peace and contentment for Earth and Belt—that lasted for two hundred and fifty years. In particular, breakthroughs in alloplasty and regeneration ended the organ bank problem. Probably all of this was due to subtle interventions by the super-intelligent being who now called himself the Brennan-monster. Brennan's story is chronicled in *Protector*.

Unfortunately Brennan was unable to anticipate the existence of the Kzinti . . .   *LN*

"I'M SURE THEY saw us coming," the Alien Technologies Officer persisted. "Do you see that ring, sir?"

The silvery image of the enemy ship almost filled the viewer. It showed as a broad, wide ring encircling a cylindrical axis, like a mechanical pencil floating inside a

135

platinum bracelet. A finned craft projected from the pointed end of the axial section. Angular letters ran down the axis, totally unlike the dots-and-commas of Kzinti script.

"Of course I see it," said the Captain.

"It was rotating when we first picked them up. It stopped when we got within two hundred thousand miles, and it hasn't moved since."

The Captain flicked his tail back and forth, gently, thoughtfully, like a pink lash. "You worry me," he commented. "If they know we're here, why haven't they tried to get away? Are they so sure they can beat us?" He whirled to face the A-T Officer. "Should *we* be running?"

"No, sir! I don't know why they're still here, but they can't have anything to be confident about. That's one of the most primitive spacecraft I've ever seen." He moved his claw about on the screen, pointing as he talked.

"The outer shell is an iron alloy. The rotating ring is a method of imitating gravity by using centripetal force. So they don't have the gravity planer. In fact they're probably using a reaction drive."

The Captain's catlike ears went up. "But we're light-years from the nearest star!"

"They must have a better reaction drive than we ever developed. We had the gravity planer before we needed one that good."

There was a buzzing sound from the big control board. "Enter," said the Captain.

The Weapons Officer fell up through the entrance hatch and came to attention. "Sir, we have all weapons trained on the enemy."

"Good." The Captain swung around. "A-T, how sure are you that they aren't a threat to us?"

The A-T Officer bared sharply pointed teeth. "I don't see how they could be, sir."

"Good. Weapons, keep all your guns ready to fire, but don't use them unless I give the order. I'll have the ears of the man who destroys that ship without orders. I want to take it intact."

"Yes, sir."

"Where's the Telepath?"

"He's on his way, sir. He was asleep."

"He's always asleep. Tell him to get his tail up here."

The Weapons Officer saluted, turned, and dropped through the exit hole.

"Captain?"

The A-T Officer was standing by the viewer, which now showed the ringed end of the alien ship. He pointed to the mirror-bright end of the axial cylinder. "It looks like that end was designed to project light. That would make it a photon drive, sir."

The Captain considered. "Could it be a signal device?"

"Urrrrr . . . Yes, sir."

"Then don't jump to conclusions."

Like a piece of toast, the Telepath popped up through the entrance hatch. He came to exaggerated attention. "Reporting as ordered, sir."

"You omitted to buzz for entrance."

"Sorry, sir." The lighted viewscreen caught the Telepath's eye and he padded over for a better look, forgetting that he was at attention. The A-T Officer winced, wishing he were somewhere else.

The Telepath's eyes were violent around the edges. His pink tail hung limp. As usual, he looked as if he were dying for lack of sleep. His fur was flattened along the side he slept on; he hadn't even bothered to brush it. The effect was as far from the ideal of a Conquest Warrior as one can get and still be a member of the Kzinti species. The wonder was that the Captain had not yet murdered him.

He never would, of course. Telepaths were too rare, too valuable, and—understandably—too emotionally unstable. The Captain always kept his temper with the Telepath. At times like this it was the innocent bystander who stood to lose his rank or his ears at the clank of a falling molecule.

"That's an enemy ship we've tracked down," the Captain was saying. "We'd like to get some information from them. Would you read their minds for us?"

"Yes, sir." The Telepath's voice showed his instant misery, but he knew better than to protest. He left the screen and sank into a chair. Slowly his ears folded into tight knots, his pupils contracted, and his ratlike tail went limp as flannel.

The world of the eleventh sense pushed in on him.

He caught the Captain's thought: ". . . sloppy civilian get of a sthondat . . ." and frantically tuned it out. He hated the Captain's mind. He found other minds aboard ship, isolated and blanked them out one by one. Now there were none left. There was only unconsciousness and chaos.

Chaos was not empty. Something was thinking strange and disturbing thoughts.

The Telepath forced himself to listen.

Steve Weaver floated bonelessly near a wall of the radio room. He was blond, blue-eyed, and big, and he could often be seen as he was now, relaxed but completely motionless, as if there were some very good reason why he shouldn't even blink. A streamer of smoke drifted from his left hand and crossed the room to bury itself in the air vent.

"That's that," Ann Harrison said wearily. She flicked four switches in the bank of radio controls. At each click a small light went out.

"You can't get them?"

"Right. I'll bet they don't even have a radio." Ann released her chair net and stretched out into a five-pointed star. "I've left the receiver on, with the volume up, in case they try to get us later. Man, that feels good!" Abruptly she curled into a tight ball. She had been crouched at the communications bank for more than an hour. Ann might have been Steve's twin; she was almost as tall as he was, had the same color hair and eyes, and the flat muscles of conscientious exercise showed beneath her blue falling jumper as she flexed.

Steve snapped his cigarette butt at the air conditioner, moving only his fingers. "Okay. What have they got?"

Ann looked startled. "*I* don't know."

"Think of it as a puzzle. They don't have a radio. How might they talk to each other? How can we check on our guesses? We assume they're trying to reach us, of course."

"Yes, of course."

"Think about it, Ann. Get Jim thinking about it, too." Jim Davis was her husband that year, and the ship's doctor full time. "You're the girl most likely to succeed. Have a smog stick?"

"Please."

Steve pushed his cigarette ration across the room. "Take a few. I've got to go."

The depleted package came whizzing back. "Thanks," said Ann.

"Let me know if anything happens, will you? Or if you think of anything."

"I will. And fear not, Steve, something's bound to turn up. They must be trying just as hard as we are."

Every compartment in the personnel ring opened into the narrow doughnut-shaped hall which ran round the ring's forward rim. Steve pushed himself into the hall, jockeyed to contact the floor, and pushed. From there it was easy going. The floor curved up to meet him, and he proceeded down the hall like a swimming frog. Of the twelve men and woman on the *Angel's Pencil,* Steve was best at this; for Steve was a Belter, and the others were all flatlanders, Earthborn.

Ann probably wouldn't think of anything, he guessed. It wasn't that she wasn't intelligent. She didn't have the curiosity, the sheer love of solving puzzles. Only he and Jim Davis—

He was going too fast, and not concentrating. He almost crashed into Sue Bhang as she appeared below the curve of the ceiling.

They managed to stop themselves against the walls. "Hi, jaywalker," said Sue.

"Hi, Sue. Where you headed?"

"Radio room. You?"

"I thought I'd check the drive systems again. Not that we're likely to need the drive, but it can't hurt to be certain."

"You'd go twitchy without something to do, wouldn't you?" She cocked her head to one side, as always when she had questions. "Steve, when are you going to rotate us again? I can't seem to get used to falling."

But she looked like she'd been born falling, he thought. Her small, slender form was meant for flying;

gravity should never have touched her. "When I'm sure we won't need the drive. We might as well stay ready 'til then. Besides, I'm hoping you'll change back to a skirt."

She laughed, pleased. "Then you can turn it off. I'm not changing, and we won't be moving. Abel says the other ship did two hundred gee when it matched courses with us. How many can the *Angel's Pencil* do?"

Steve looked awed. "Just point zero five. And I was thinking of chasing them! Well, maybe we can be the ones to open communications. I just came from the radio room, by the way. Ann can't get anything."

"Too bad."

"We'll just have to wait."

"Steve, you're always so impatient. Do Belters always move at a run? Come here." She took a handhold and pulled him over to one of the thick windows which lined the forward side of the corridor. "There they are," she said, pointing out.

The star was both duller and larger than those around it. Among points which glowed arc-lamp blue-white with the Doppler shift, the alien ship showed as a dull red disk.

"I looked at it through the telescope," said Steve. "There are lumps and ridges all over it. And there's a circle of green dots and commas painted on one side. Looked like writing."

"How long have we been waiting to meet them? Five hundred thousand years? Well, there they are. Relax. They won't go away." Sue gazed out the window, her whole attention on the dull red circle, her gleaming jet hair floating out around her head. "The first aliens. I wonder what they'll be like."

"It's anyone's guess. They must be pretty strong to take punishment like that, unless they have some kind of acceleration shield, but free fall doesn't bother them either. That ship isn't designed to spin." He was staring intently out at the stars, his big form characteristically motionless, his expression somber. Abruptly he said, "Sue, I'm worried."

"About what?"

"Suppose they're hostile?"

"Hostile?" She tasted the unfamiliar word, decided she didn't like it.

"After all, we know nothing about them. Suppose they want to fight? We'd—"

She gasped. Steve flinched before the horror in her face. "What—what put that idea in your head?"

"I'm sorry I shocked you, Sue."

"Oh, don't worry about that, but *why?* Did—shh."

Jim Davis had come into view. The *Angel's Pencil* had left Earth when he was twenty-seven; now he was a slightly paunchy thirty-eight, the oldest man on board, an amiable man with abnormally long, delicate fingers. His grandfather, with the same hands, had been a world-famous surgeon. Nowadays surgery was normally done by autodocs, and the arachnodactyls were to Davis merely an affliction. He bounced by, walking on magnetic sandals, looking like a comedian as he bobbed about the magnetic plates. "Hi, group," he called as he went by.

"Hello, Jim." Sue's voice was strained. She waited until he was out of sight before she spoke again.

Hoarsely she whispered, "Did you fight in the Belt?" She didn't really believe it; it was merely the worst thing she could think of.

Vehemently Steve snapped, "No!" Then, reluctantly, he added, "But it did happen occasionally." Quickly he tried to explain. "The trouble was that all the doctors, including the psychists, were at the big bases, like Ceres. It was the only way they could help the people who needed them—be where the miners could find them. But all the danger was out in the rocks.

"You noticed a habit of mine once. I never make gestures. All Belters have that trait. It's because on a small mining ship you could hit something waving your arms around. Something like the airlock button."

"Sometimes it's almost eerie. You don't move for minutes at a time."

"There's always tension out in the rocks. Sometimes a miner would see too much danger and boredom and frustration, too much cramping inside and too much room outside, and he wouldn't get to a psychist in time.

He'd pick a fight in a bar. I saw it happen once. The guy was using his hands like mallets."

Steve had been looking far into the past. Now he turned back to Sue. She looked white and sick, like a novice nurse standing up to her first really bad case. His ears began to turn red. "Sorry," he said miserably.

She felt like running; she was as embarrassed as he was. Instead she said, and tried to mean it, "It doesn't matter. So you think the people in the other ship might want to, uh, make war?"

He nodded.

"Did you have history-of-Earth courses?"

He smiled ruefully. "No, I couldn't qualify. Sometimes I wonder how many people do."

"About one in twelve."

"That's not many."

"People in general have trouble assimilating the facts of life about their ancestors. You probably know that there used to be wars before—hmmm—three hundred years ago, but do you know what a war is? Can you visualize one? Can you see a fusion electric point deliberately built to explode in the middle of the city? Do you know what a concentration camp is? A limited action? You probably think murder ended with war. Well, it didn't. The last murder occurred in twenty-one something, just a hundred and sixty years ago.

"Anyone who says human nature can't be changed is out of his head. To make it stick, he's got to define human nature—and he can't. Three things gave us our present peaceful civilization, and each one was a technological change." Sue's voice had taken on a dry, remote lecture-hall tone, like the voice on a teacher tape. "One was the development of psychistry beyond the alchemist stage. Another was the full development of land for food production. The third was the Fertility Restriction Laws and the annual contraceptive shots. They gave us room to breathe. Maybe Belt mining and the stellar colonies had something to do with it too; they gave us an inanimate enemy. Even the historians argue about that one.

"Here's the delicate point I'm trying to nail down." Sue rapped on the window. "Look at that spacecraft. It has enough power to move it around like a mail missile and enough fuel to move it up to our point eight light—right?"

"Right."

"—with plenty of power left for maneuvering. It's a better ship than ours. If they've had time to learn how to build a ship like that, they've had time to build up their own versions of psychistry, modern food production, contraception, economic theory, everything they need to abolish war. See?"

Steve had to smile at her earnestness. "Sure, Sue, it makes sense. But that guy in the bar came from our culture, and he was hostile enough. If we can't understand how he thinks, how can we guess about the mind of something whose very chemical makeup we can't guess at yet?"

"It's sentient. It builds tools."

"Right."

"And if Jim hears you talking like this, you'll be in psychistry treatment."

"That's the best argument you've given me," Steve grinned, and stroked her under the ear with two fingertips. He felt her go suddenly stiff, saw the pain in her face; and at the same time his own pain struck, a real tiger of a headache, as if his brain were trying to swell beyond his skull.

"I've got them, sir," the Telepath said blurrily. "Ask me anything."

The Captain hurried, knowing that the Telepath couldn't stand this for long. "How do they power their ship?"

"It's a light-pressure drive powered by incomplete hydrogen fusion. They use an electromagnetic ramscoop to get their own hydrogen from space."

"Clever . . . Can they get away from us?"

"No. Their drive is on idle, ready to go, but it won't help them. It's pitifully weak."

"What kind of weapons do they have?"

The Telepath remained silent for a long time. The others waited patiently for his answer. There was sound in the control dome, but it was the kind of sound one learns not to hear: the whine of heavy current, the muted purr of voices from below, the strange sound like continuously ripping cloth which came from the gravity motors.

"None at all, sir." The Kzin's voice became clearer; his hypnotic relaxation was broken by muscle twitches. He twisted as if in a nightmare. "Nothing aboard ship, not even a knife or a club. Wait, they've got cooking knives. But that's all they use them for. They don't fight."

"They don't fight?"

"No, sir. They don't expect us to fight, either. The idea has occurred to three of them, and each has dismissed it from his mind."

"But why?" the Captain asked, knowing the question was irrelevant, unable to hold it back.

"I don't know, sir. It's a science they use, or a religion. I don't understand," the Telepath whimpered. "I don't understand at all."

Which must be tough on him, the Captain thought. Completely alien thoughts . . . "What are they doing now?"

"Waiting for us to talk to them. They tried to talk to us, and they think we must be trying just as hard."

"But why?—never mind, it's not important. Can they be killed by heat?"

"Yes, sir."

"Break contact."

The Telepath shook his head violently. He looked like he'd been in a washing machine. The Captain touched a sensitized surface and bellowed, "Weapons Officer!"

"Here."

"Use the inductors on the enemy ship."

"But, sir! They're so slow! What if the alien attacks?"

"Don't argue with me, you—" Snarling, the Captain delivered an impassioned monologue on the virtues of unquestioning obedience. When he switched off, the Alien Technologies Officer was back at the viewer and the Telepath had gone to sleep.

The Captain purred happily, wishing that they were all this easy.

When the occupants had been killed by heat he would take the ship. He could tell everything he needed to know about their planet by examining their life-support system. He could locate it by tracing the ship's trajectory. Probably they hadn't even taken evasive action!

If they came from a Kzin-like world it would become a Kzin world. And he, as Conquest Leader, would command one percent of its wealth for the rest of his life! Truly, the future looked rich. No longer would he be called by his profession. He would bear a *name* . . .

"Incidental information," said A-T Officer. "The ship was generating one and twelve sixty-fourth gee before it stopped rotating."

"Little heavy," the Captain mused. "Might be too much air, but it should be easy to Kzinform it. A-T, we find the strangest life forms. Remember the Chunquen?"

"Both sexes were sentient. They fought constantly."

"And that funny religion on Altair One. They thought they could travel in time."

"Yes sir. When we landed the infantry they were all gone."

"They must have all committed suicide with disintegrators. But why? They knew we only wanted slaves. And I'm still trying to figure out how they got rid of the disintegrators afterward."

"Some beings," said the A-T Officer, "will do anything to keep their beliefs."

Eleven years beyond Pluto, eight years from her destination, the fourth colony ship to We Made It fell between the stars. Before her the stars were green-white and blue-white, blazing points against nascent black. Behind they were sparse, dying red embers. To the sides the constellations were strangely flattened. The universe was shorter than it had been.

For awhile Jim Davis was very busy. Everyone, including himself, had a throbbing blinding headache. To each patient Dr. Davis handed a tiny pink pill from the dispenser slot of the huge autodoc which covered the back wall of the infirmary. They milled outside the door waiting for the pills to take effect, looking like a full-fledged mob in the narrow corridor; and then someone thought it would be a good idea to go to the lounge, and everyone followed him. It was an unusually silent mob. Nobody felt like talking while the pain was with them. Even the sound of magnetic sandals was lost in the plastic pile rug.

Steve saw Jim Davis behind him. "Hey, Doc," he called softly. "How long before the pain stops?"

"Mine's gone away. You got your pills a little after I did, right?"

"Right. Thanks, Doc."

They didn't take pain well, these people. They were too unused to it.

In single file they walked or floated into the lounge. Low-pitched conversations started. People took couches, using the sticky plastic strips on their falling jumpers. Others stood or floated near walls. The lounge was big enough to hold them all in comfort.

Steve wriggled near the ceiling, trying to pull on his sandals.

"I hope they don't try that again," he heard Sue say. "It hurt."

"Try what?" Someone Steve didn't recognize, half-listening as he was.

"Whatever they tried. Telepathy, perhaps."

"No. I don't believe in telepathy. Could they have set up ultrasonic vibrations in the walls?"

Steve had his sandals on. He left the magnets turned off.

". . . a cold beer. Do you realize we'll never taste beer again?" Jim Davis' voice.

"I miss waterskiing." Ann Harrison sounded wistful. "The feel of a pusher unit shoving into the small of your back, the water beating against your feet, the sun . . ."

Steve pushed himself toward them. "Taboo subject," he called.

"We're on it anyway," Jim boomed cheerfully. "Unless you'd rather talk about the alien, which everyone else is doing. I'd rather drop it for the moment. What's your greatest regret at leaving Earth?"

"Only that I didn't stay long enough to really see it."

"Oh, of course." Jim suddenly remembered the drink-

ing bulb in his hand. He drank from it, hospitably
passed it to Steve.

"This waiting makes me restless," said Steve. "What
are they likely to try next? Shake the ship in Morse
code?"

Jim smiled. "Maybe they won't try anything next.
They may give up and leave."

"Oh, I hope not!" said Ann.

"Would that be so bad?"

Steve had a start. What was Jim thinking?

"Of course!" Ann protested. "We've got to find out
what they're like! And think of what they can teach us,
Jim!"

When conversation got controversial it was good
manners to change the subject. "Say," said Steve, "I
happened to notice the wall was warm when I pushed
off. Is that good or bad?"

"That's funny. It should be cold, if anything," said
Jim. "There's nothing out there but starlight. Except—"
A most peculiar expression flitted across his face. He
drew his feet up and touched the magnetic soles with his
fingertips.

"Eeeee! Jim! Jim!"

Steve tried to whirl around and got nowhere. That
was Sue! He switched on his shoes, thumped to the
floor, and went to help.

Sue was surrounded by bewildered people. They split
to let Jim Davis through, and he tried to lead her out of
the lounge. He looked frightened. Sue was moaning and
thrashing, paying no attention to his efforts.

Steve pushed through to her. "All the metal is heating
up," Davis shouted. "We've got to get her hearing aid
out."

"Infirmary," Sue shouted.

Four of them took Sue down the hall to the infirmary.
She was still crying and struggling feebly when they got
her in, but Jim was there ahead of them with a spray
hypo. He used it and she went to sleep.

The four watched anxiously as Jim went to work. The
autodoc would have taken precious time for diagnosis.
Jim operated by hand. He was able to do a fast job, for

the tiny instrument was buried just below the skin behind her ear. Still, the scalpel must have burned his fingers before he was done. Steve could feel the growing
warmth against the soles of his feet.

Did the aliens know what they were doing?

Did it matter? The ship was being attacked. His ship.

Steve slipped into the corridor and ran for the control room. Running on magnetic soles, he looked like a
terrified penguin, but he moved fast. He knew he might
be making a terrible mistake; the aliens might be trying
desperately to reach the *Angel's Pencil;* he would never
know. They had to be stopped before everyone was
roasted.

The shoes burned his feet. He whimpered with the
pain, but otherwise ignored it. The air burned in his
mouth and throat. Even his teeth were hot.

He had to wrap his shirt around his hands to open the
control-room door. The pain in his feet was unbearable;
he tore off his sandals and swam to the control board.
He kept his shirt over his hands to work the controls. A
twist of a large white knob turned the drive on full, and
he slipped into the pilot seat before the gentle light pressure could build up.

He turned to the rear-view telescope. It was aimed at
the solar system, for the drive could be used for messages at this distance. He set it for short range and began to turn the ship.

The enemy ship glowed in the high infrared.

"It will take longer to heat the crew-carrying section,"
reported the Alien Technologies Officer. "They'll have
temperature control there."

"That's all right. When you think they should all be
dead, wake up the Telepath and have him check." The
Captain continued to brush his fur, killing time. "You
know, if they hadn't been so completely helpless I
wouldn't have tried this slow method. I'd have cut the
ring free of the motor section first. Maybe I should have
done that anyway. Safer."

The A-T Officer wanted all the credit he could get.
"Sir, they couldn't have any big weapons. There isn't

room. With a reaction drive, the motor and the fuel tanks take up most of the available space."

The other ship began to turn away from its tormentor. Its drive end glowed red.

"They're trying to get away," the Captain said, as the glowing end swung toward them. "Are you sure they can't?"

"Yes sir. That light drive won't take them anywhere."

The Captain purred thoughtfully. "What would happen if the light hit our ship?"

"Just a bright light, I think. The lens is flat, so it must be emitting a very wide beam. They'd need a parabolic reflector to be dangerous. Unless—" His ears went straight up.

"Unless what?" The Captain spoke softly, demandingly.

"A laser. But that's all right, sir. They don't have any weapons."

The Captain sprang at the control board. "Stupid!" he spat. "They don't know weapons from sthondat blood. Weapons Officer! How could a telepath find out what they don't know? WEAPONS OFFICER!"

"Here, sir."

"Burn—"

An awful light shone in the control dome. The Captain burst into flame, then blew out as the air left through a glowing split in the dome.

Steve was lying on his back. The ship was spinning again, pressing him into what felt like his own bunk.

He opened his eyes.

Jim Davis crossed the room and stood over him. "You awake?"

Steve sat bolt upright, his eyes wide.

"Easy." Jim's gray eyes were concerned.

Steve blinked up at him. "What happened?" he asked, and discovered how hoarse he was.

Jim sat down in one of the chairs. "You tell me. We tried to get to the control room when the ship started moving. Why didn't you ring the strap-down? You turned off the drive just as Ann came through the door. Then you fainted."

"How about the other ship?" Steve tried to repress the urgency in his voice, and couldn't.

"Some of the others are over there now, examining the wreckage." Steve felt his heart stop. "I guess I was afraid from the start that alien ship was dangerous. I'm more psychist than emdee, and I qualified for history class, so maybe I know more than is good for me about human nature. Too much to think that beings with space travel will automatically be peaceful. I tried to think so, but they aren't. They've got things any self-respecting human being would be ashamed to have nightmares about. Bomb missiles, fusion bombs, lasers, that induction projector they used on us. And antimissiles. You know what that means? They've got enemies like themselves, Steve. Maybe nearby."

"So I killed them." The room seemed to swoop around him, but his voice came out miraculously steady.

"You saved the ship."

"It was an accident. I was trying to get us away."

"No, you weren't." Davis' accusation was as casual as if he were describing the chemical makeup of urea. "That ship was four hundred miles away. You would have had to sight on it with a telescope to hit it. You knew what you were doing, too, because you turned off the drive as soon as you'd burned through the ship."

Steve's back muscles would no longer support him. He flopped back to horizontal. "All right, you know," he told the ceiling. "Do the others?"

"I doubt it. Killing in self-defense is too far outside their experience. I think Sue's guessed."

"Oooo."

"If she has, she's taking it well," Davis said briskly. "Better than most of them will, when they find out the universe is full of warriors. This is the end of the world, Steve."

"What?"

"I'm being theatrical. But it is. Three hundred years of the peaceful life for everyone. They'll call it the Golden Age. No starvation, no war, no physical sickness other than senescence, no permanent mental sickness at all, even by our rigid standards. When someone over fourteen tries to use his fist on someone else we say he's sick, and we cure him. And now it's over. Peace isn't a stable condition, not for us. Maybe not for anything that lives."

"Can I see the ship from here?"

"Yes. It's just behind us."

Steve rolled out of bed, went to the window.

Someone had steered the ships much closer together. The Kzinti ship was a huge red sphere with ugly projections scattered at seeming random over the hull. The beam had sliced it into two unequal halves, sliced it like an ax through an egg. Steve watched, unable to turn aside, as the big half rotated to show its honeycombed interior.

"In a little while," said Jim, "the men will be coming back. They'll be frightened. Someone will probably insist that we arm ourselves against the next attacks, using weapons from the other ship. I'll have to agree with him.

"Maybe they'll think I'm sick myself. Maybe I am. But it's the kind of sickness we'll need." Jim looked desperately unhappy. "We're going to become an armed society. And of course we'll have to warn the Earth . . ."

The Borderland of Sol

The organ bank problem remained an important social factor for most of the colony worlds. On Jinx it was unimportant; there was too much empty land for felons to flee to. On Plateau it created a hideous social stratification, vestiges of which remained long after ramrobot packages ended the organ bank problem itself.

Sol had its own problems. The Kzinti had discovered and conquered Wunderland and were on their way to Earth.

For a time the situation was touchy. Sol held off the Kzinti by virtue of two accidents: the timely development of manned Bussard ramjets ("The Ethics of Madness") and the existence of giant laser cannon in the outer asteroids. These had been used to launch light-sail craft to Bussard ramjet speeds; now they were turned on the Kzinti. The Kzinti were amazed and hurt. Their telepaths had reported a species given over entirely to peace.

While Sol battled the Kzinti, an Outsider ship had arrived at We Made It. The Outsiders were interstellar traders, fragile, cold beings. They sold the secret of the faster-than-light drive to the human colony on We Made It. Two years later, a ship powered by the Outsider hyperdrive arrived in Sol system. The crew had not known of the war. They were amazed at their heroes' welcome.

It was the Outsiders' faster-than-light drive that ended the first Man–Kzin War. The second, third,

153

and fourth are hardly worth discussing. The Kzinti always had a tendency to attack before they were quite ready.

The hyperdrive also opened up known space. There were other intelligent species around: Grogs, Bandersnatchi, Pierson's Puppeteers, Kdatlyno. An interstellar, interspecies civilization developed . . . and tales of that time are told in *Neutron Star*, the other known space collection.

Beowulf Shaeffer was a child of that time. A wandering crashlander, he was generally too lazy to stay out of trouble, but bright enough to think his way out once he was in. It was he who discovered that the galactic core was exploding . . . that within twenty thousand years, humanity would have to move elsewhere.

The following is the fifth of the tales of Beowulf Shaeffer.   *LN*

THREE MONTHS ON Jinx, marooned.

I played tourist for the first couple of months. I never saw the high-pressure regions around the ocean because the only way down would have been with a safari of hunting tanks. But I traveled the habitable lands on either side of the sea, the East Band civilized, the West Band a developing frontier. I wandered the East End in a vacuum suit, toured the distilleries and other vacuum industries, and stared up into the orange vastness of Primary, Jinx's big twin brother.

I spent most of the second month between the Institute of Knowledge and the Camelot Hotel. Tourism had palled.

For me, that's unusual. I'm a born tourist. But—

Jinx's one point seven eight gravities put an unreasonable restriction on elegance and ingenuity in architectural design. The buildings in the habitable bands all look alike: squat and massive.

The East and West Ends, the vacuum regions, aren't that different from any industrialized moon. I never developed much of an interest in touring factories.

As for the ocean shorelines, the only vehicles that go

there go to hunt Bandersnatchi. The Bandersnatchi are freaks: enormous, intelligent white slugs the size of mountains. They hunt the tanks. There are rigid restrictions to the equipment the tanks can carry, covenants established between men and Bandersnatchi, so that the Bandersnatchi win about forty percent of the duels. I wanted no part of that.

And all my touring had to be done in three times the gravity of my home world.

I spent the third month in Sirius Mater, and most of that in the Camelot Hotel, which has gravity generators in most of the rooms. When I went out I rode a floating contour couch. I passed like an invalid among the Jinxians, who were amused. Or was that my imagination?

I was in a hall of the Institute of Knowledge when I came on Carlos Wu running his fingertips over a Kdatlyno touch-sculpture.

A dark, slender man with narrow shoulders and straight black hair, Carlos was lithe as a monkey in any normal gravity; but on Jinx he used a travel couch exactly like mine. He studied the busts with his head tilted to one side. And I studied the familiar back, sure it couldn't be him.

"Carlos, aren't you supposed to be on Earth?"

He jumped. But when the couch spun around he was grinning. "Bey! I might say the same for you."

I admitted it. "I was headed for Earth, but when all those ships started disappearing around Sol system the captain changed his mind and steered for Sirius. Nothing any of the passengers could do about it. What about you? How are Sharrol and the kids?"

"Sharrol's fine, the kids are fine, and they're all waiting for you to come home." His fingers were still trailing over the Lloobee touch-sculpture called *Heroes,* feeling the warm, fleshy textures. *Heroes* was a most unusual touch-sculpture; there were visual as well as textural effects. Carlos studied the two human busts, then said, "That's *your* face, isn't it?"

"Yah."

"Not that you ever looked that good in your life. How did a Kdatlyno come to pick Beowulf Shaeffer as a classic hero? Was it your name? And who's the other guy?"

"I'll tell you about it sometime. Carlos, what are you doing *here?*"

"I . . . left Earth a couple of weeks after Louis was born." He was embarrassed. Why? "I haven't been off Earth in ten years. I needed the break."

But he'd left just before I was supposed to get home. And . . . hadn't someone once said that Carlos Wu had a touch of the flatland phobia? I began to understand what was wrong. "Carlos, you did Sharrol and me a valuable favor."

He laughed without looking at me. "Men have killed other men for such favors. I thought it was . . . tactful . . . to be gone when you came home."

Now I knew. Carlos was here because the Fertility Board on Earth would not favor me with a parenthood license.

You can't really blame the Board for using any excuse at all to reduce the number of producing parents. I am an albino. Sharrol and I wanted each other; but we both wanted children, and Sharrol can't leave Earth. She has the flatland phobia, the fear of strange air and altered days and changed gravity and black sky beneath her feet.

The only solution we'd found had been to ask a good friend to help.

Carlos Wu is a registered genius with an incredible resistance to disease and injury. He carries an unlimited parenthood license, one of sixty-odd among Earth's eighteen billion people. He gets similar offers every week . . . but he is a good friend, and he'd agreed. In the last two years Sharrol and Carlos had had two children, who were now waiting on earth for me to become their father.

I felt only gratitude for what he'd done for us. "I forgive you your odd ideas on tact," I said magnanimously. "Now. As long as we're stuck on Jinx, may I show you around? I've met some interesting people."

"You always do." He hesitated, then, "I'm not actually stuck on Jinx. I've been offered a ride home. I may be able to get you in on it."

"Oh, really? I didn't think there were any ships going to Sol system these days. Or leaving."

"This ship belongs to a government man. Ever heard of a Sigmund Ausfaller?"

"That sounds vaguely . . . Wait! Stop! The last time I saw Sigmund Ausfaller, he had just put a bomb aboard my ship!"

Carlos blinked at me. "You're kidding."

"I'm not."

"Sigmund Ausfaller is in the Bureau of Alien Affairs. Bombing spacecraft isn't one of his functions."

"Maybe he was off duty," I said viciously.

"Well, it doesn't really sound like you'd want to share a spacecraft cabin with him. Maybe—"

But I'd thought of something else, and now there just wasn't any way out of it. "No, let's meet him. Where do we find him?"

"The bar of the Camelot," said Carlos.

Reclining luxuriously on our travel couches, we slid on air cushions through Sirius Mater. The orange trees that lined the walks were foreshortened by gravity; their trunks were thick cones, and the oranges on the branches were not much bigger than ping pong balls.

Their world had altered them, even as our worlds have altered you and me. And underground civilization and point six gravities have made of me a pale stick-figure of a man, tall and attenuated. The Jinxians we passed were short and wide, designed like bricks, men and women both. Among them the occasional offworlder seemed as shockingly different as a Kdatlyno or a Pierson's Puppeteer.

And so we came to the Camelot.

The Camelot is a low, two-story structure that sprawls like a cubistic octopus across several acres of downtown Sirius Mater. Most offworlders stay here, for the gravity control in the rooms and corridors and for access to the Institute of Knowledge, the finest museum and research complex in human space.

The Camelot Bar carries one Earth gravity throughout. We left our travel couches in the vestibule and walked in like men. Jinxians were walking in like bouncing rubber bricks, with big happy grins on their wide faces. Jinxians love low gravity. A good many migrate to other worlds.

We spotted Ausfaller easily: a rounded, moon-faced flatlander with thick, dark, wavy hair and a thin black mustache. He stood as we approached. "Beowulf Shaeffer!" he beamed. "How good to see you again! I believe it has been eight years or thereabouts. How have you been?"

"I lived," I told him.

Carlos rubbed his hands together briskly. "Sigmund! Why did you bomb Bey's ship?"

Ausfaller blinked in surprise. "Did he tell you it was his ship? It wasn't. He was thinking of stealing it. I reasoned that he would not steal a ship with a hidden time bomb aboard."

"But how did you come into it?" Carlos slid into the booth beside him. "You're not police. You're in the Extremely Foreign Relations Bureau."

"The ship belonged to General Products Corporation, which is owned by Pierson's Puppeteers, not human beings."

Carlos turned on me. "Bey! Shame on you."

"Dammit! They were trying to blackmail me into a suicide mission! And Ausfaller let them get away with it! And that's the least convincing exhibition of tact I've ever seen!"

"Good thing they soundproof these booths," said Carlos. "Let's order."

Soundproofing field or not, people were staring. I sat down. When our drinks came I drank deep. Why had I mentioned the bomb at all?

Ausfaller was saying, "Well, Carlos, have you changed your mind about coming with me?"

"Yes, if I can take a friend."

Ausfaller frowned, looked at me. "You wish to reach Earth too?"

I'd made up my mind. "I don't think so. In fact, I'd like to talk you out of taking Carlos."

Carlos said, "Hey!"

I overrode him. "Ausfaller, do you know who Carlos *is*? He had an unlimited parenthood license at the age of eighteen. Eighteen! I don't mind you risking your own life, in fact I love the idea. But his?"

"It's not that big a risk!" Carlos snapped.

"Yah? What has Ausfaller got that eight other ships didn't have?"

"Two things," Ausfaller said patiently. "One is that we will be incoming. Six of the eight ships that vanished were *leaving* Sol system. If there are pirates around Sol, they must find it much easier to locate an outgoing ship."

"They caught two incoming. Two ships, fifty crew-members and passengers, gone: Poof!"

"They would not take me so easily," Ausfaller boasted. "The *Hobo Kelly* is deceptive. It seems to be a cargo and passenger ship, but it is a warship, armed and capable of thirty gees acceleration. In normal space we can run from anything we can't fight. We are assuming pirates, are we not? Pirates would insist on robbing a ship before they destroy it."

I was intrigued. "Why? Why a disguised warship? Are you *hoping* you'll be attacked?"

"If there are actually pirates, yes, I hope to be attacked. But not when entering Sol system. We plan a substitution. A quite ordinary cargo craft will land on Earth, take on cargo of some value, and depart for Wunderland on a straight-line course. My ship will replace it before it has passed through the asteroids. So you see, there is no risk of losing Mr. Wu's precious genes."

Palms flat to the table, arms straight, Carlos stood looming over us. "Diffidently I raise the point that they are my futzy genes and I'll do what I futzy please with them! Bey, I've already had my share of children, and yours too!"

"Peace, Carlos. I didn't mean to step on any of your inalienable rights." I turned to Ausfaller. "I still don't see why these disappearing ships should interest the Extremely Foreign Relations Bureau."

"There were alien passengers aboard some of the ships."

"Oh."

"And we have wondered if the pirates themselves are aliens. Certainly they have a technique not known to humanity. Of six outgoing ships, five vanished after reporting that they were about to enter hyperdrive."

I whistled. "They can precipitate a ship out of hyperdrive? That's impossible. Isn't it? Carlos?"

Carlos' mouth twisted. "Not if it's being done. But I don't understand the principle. If the ships were just disappearing, that'd be different. Any ship does that if it goes too deep into a gravity well on hyperdrive."

"Then . . . maybe it isn't pirates at all. Carlos, could there be living beings in hyperspace, actually eating the ships?"

"For all of me, there could. I don't know everything, Bey, contrary to popular opinion." But after a minute he shook his head. "I don't buy it. I might buy an uncharted mass on the fringes of Sol system. Ships that came too near in hyperdrive would disappear."

"No," said Ausfaller. "No single mass could have caused all of the disappearances. Charter or not, a planet is bounded by gravity and inertia. We ran computer simulations. It would have taken at least three large masses, all unknown, all moving into heavy trade routes, simultaneously."

"How large? Mars size or better?"

"So you have been thinking about this too."

Carlos smiled. "Yah. It may sound impossible, but it isn't. It's only improbable. There are unbelievable amounts of garbage out there beyond Neptune. Four known planets and endless chunks of ice and stone and nickel-iron."

"Still, it is most improbable."

Carlos nodded. A silence fell.

I was still thinking about monsters in hyperspace. The lovely thing about that hypothesis was that you couldn't even estimate a probability. We knew too little.

Humanity has been using hyperdrive for almost four hundred years now. Few ships have disappeared in that time, except during wars. Now, eight ships in ten months, all around Sol system.

Suppose one hyperspace beast had discovered ships in this region, say during one of the Man–Kzin Wars? He'd gone to get his friends. Now they were preying around Sol system. The flow of ships around Sol is greater than that around any three colony stars. But if more monsters came, they'd surely have to move on to the other colonies.

I couldn't imagine a defense against such things. We might have to give up interstellar travel.

Ausfaller said, "I would be glad if you would change your mind and come with us, Mr. Shaeffer."

"Um? Are you sure you want me on the same ship with you?"

"Oh, emphatically! How else may I be sure that you have not hidden a bomb aboard?" Ausfaller laughed. "Also, we can use a qualified pilot. Finally, I would like the chance to pick your brain, Beowulf Shaeffer. You have an odd facility for doing my job for me."

"What do you mean by that?"

"General Products used blackmail in persuading you to do a close orbit around a neutron star. You learned something about their home world—we still do not know what it was—and blackmailed them back. We know that blackmail contracts are a normal part of Puppeteer business practice. You earned their respect. You have dealt with them since. You have dealt also with Outsider, without friction. But it was your handling of the Lloobee kidnapping that I found impressive."

Carlos was sitting at attention. I hadn't had a chance to tell him about that one yet. I grinned and said, "I'm proud of that myself."

"Well you should be. You did more than retrieve known space's top Kdatlyno touch-sculptor: you did it with honor, killing one of their number and leaving Lloobee free to pursue the others with publicity. Otherwise the Kdatlyno would have been annoyed."

Helping Sigmund Ausfaller had been the farthest thing from my thoughts for these past eight years; yet suddenly I felt damn good. Maybe it was the way Carlos was listening. It takes a lot to impress Carlos Wu.

Carlos said, "If you thought it was pirates, you'd come along, wouldn't you, Bey? After all, they probably can't *find* incoming ships."

"Sure."

"And you don't really believe in hyperspace monsters."

I hedged. "Not if I hear a better explanation. The thing is, I'm not sure I believe in supertechnological pirates either. What about those wandering masses?"

Carlos pursed his lips, said, "All right. The solar system has a good number of planets—at least a dozen so far discovered, four of them outside the major singularity around Sol."

"And not including Pluto?"

"No, we think of Pluto as a loose moon of Neptune. It runs *Neptune, Persephone, Caïna, Antenora, Ptolemea,* in order of distance from the sun. And the orbits aren't flat to the plane of the system. Persephone is tilted at a hundred and twenty degrees to the system, and retrograde. If they find another planet out there they'll call it *Judecca.*"

"Why?"

"Hell. The four innermost divisions of Dante's Hell. They form a great ice plain with sinners frozen into it."

"Stick to the point," said Ausfaller.

"Start with the cometary halo," Carlos told me. "It's very thin: about one comet per spherical volume of the Earth's orbit. Mass is denser going inward: a few planets, some inner comets, some chunks of ice and rock, all in skewed orbits and still spread pretty thin. Inside Neptune there are lots of planets and asteroids and more flattening of orbits to conform with Sol's rotation. Outside Neptune space is vast and empty. There *could* be uncharted planets. Singularities to swallow ships."

Ausfaller was indignant. "But for three to move into main trade lanes simultaneously?"

"It's not impossible, Sigmund."

"The probability—"

"Infinitesimal, right. Bey, it's damn near impossible. Any sane man would assume pirates."

It had been a long time since I had seen Sharrol. I was sore tempted. "Ausfaller, have you traced the sale of any of the loot? Have you gotten any ransom notes? *Convince me!*

Ausfaller threw back his head and laughed.

"What's funny?"

"We have hundreds of ransom notes. Any mental deficient can write a ransom note, and these disappearances have had a good deal of publicity. The demands were all fakes. I wish one or another had been genuine. A son of the Patriarch of Kzin was aboard *Wayfarer* when she disappeared. As for loot—hmm. There has been a fall in the black market prices of boosterspice and gem woods. Otherwise—" He shrugged. "There has been no sign of the Barr originals or the Midas Rock or any of the more conspicuous treasures aboard the missing ships."

"Then you don't know one way or another."

"No. Will you go with us?"

"I haven't decided yet. When are you leaving?"

They'd be taking off tomorrow morning from the East End. That gave me time to make up my mind.

After dinner I went back to my room, feeling depressed. Carlos was going, that was clear enough. Hardly my fault . . . but he was here on Jinx because he'd done me and Sharrol a large favor. If he was killed going home . . .

A tape from Sharrol was waiting in my room. There were pictures of the children, Tanya and Louis, and shots of the apartment she'd found us in the Twin Peaks arcology, and much more.

I ran through it three times. Then I called Ausfaller's room. It had been just too futzy long.

I circled Jinx once on the way out. I've always done that, even back when I was flying for Nakamura Lines; and no passenger has ever objected.

Jinx is the close moon of a gas giant planet more massive then Jupiter, and smaller than Jupiter because its core has been compressed to degenerate matter. A billion years ago Jinx and Primary were even closer, before tidal drag moved them apart. This same tidal force had earlier locked Jinx's rotation to Primary and forced the moon into an egg shape, a prolate spheroid. When the moon moved outward its shape became more nearly spherical; but the cold rock surface resisted change.

That is why the ocean of Jinx rings its waist, beneath an atmosphere too compressed and too hot to breathe; whereas the points nearest to and furthest from Primary, the East and West Ends, actually rise out of the atmosphere.

From space Jinx looks like God's Own Easter Egg: the Ends bone white tinged with yellow; then the brighter glare from rings of glittering ice fields at the limits of the atmosphere; then the varying blues of an Earthlike world, increasingly overlaid with the white frosting of cloud as the eyes move inward, until the waist of the planet/moon is girdled with pure white. The ocean never shows at all.

I took us once around, and out.

Sirius has its own share of floating miscellaneous matter cluttering the path to interstellar space. I stayed at the controls for most of five days, for that reason and because I wanted to get the feel of an unfamiliar ship.

Hobo Kelly was a belly-landing job, three hundred feet long, of triangular cross section. Beneath an up-tilted, forward-thrusting nose were big clamshell doors for cargo. She had adequate belly jets and a much larger fusion motor at the tail, and a line of windows indicating cabins. Certainly she looked harmless enough; and certainly there was deception involved. The cabin should have held forty or fifty, but there was room only for four. The rest of what should have been cabin space was only windows with holograph projections in them.

The drive ran sure and smooth up to a maximum at ten gravities: not a lot for a ship designed to haul massive cargo. The cabin gravity held without putting out more than a fraction of its power. When Jinx and Primary were invisible against the stars, when Sirius was so distant I could look directly at it, I turned to the hidden control panel Ausfaller had unlocked for me. Ausfaller woke up, found me doing that, and began showing me which did what.

He had a big X-ray laser and some smaller laser cannon set for different frequencies. He had four self-guided fusion bombs. He had a telescope so good that the ostensible ship's telescope was only a finder for it. He had deep-radar.

And none of it showed beyond the discolored hull.

Ausfaller was armed for Bandersnatchi. I felt mixed emotions. It seemed we could fight anything, and run from it too. But what kind of enemy was he expecting?

All through those four weeks in hyperdrive, while we drove through the Blind Spot at three days to the light-year, the topic of the ship eaters reared its disturbing head.

Oh, we spoke of other things: of music and art, and of the latest techniques in animation, the computer programs that let you make your own holo flicks almost for lunch money. We told stories. I told Carlos why the Kdatlyno Lloobee had made busts of me and Emil Horne. I spoke of the only time the Pierson's Puppeteers had ever paid off the guarantee on a General Products hull, after the supposedly indestructible hull had been destroyed by antimatter. Ausfaller had some good ones . . . a lot more stories that he was allowed to tell, I gathered, from the way he had to search his memory every time.

But we kept coming back to the ship eaters.

"It boils down to three possibilities," I decided. "Kzinti, Puppeteers, and Humans."

Carlos guffawed. "Puppeteers? Puppeteers wouldn't have the guts!"

"I threw them in because they might have some interest in manipulating the interstellar stock market. Look: our hypothetical pirates have set up an embargo, cutting Sol system off from the outside world. The Puppeteers have the capital to take advantage of what that does to the market. And they need money. For their migration."

"The Puppeteers are philosophical cowards."

"That's right. They wouldn't risk robbing the ships, or coming anywhere near them. Suppose they can make them disappear from a distance?"

Carlos wasn't laughing now. "That's easier than dropping them out of hyperspace to rob them. It wouldn't take more than a great big gravity generator . . . and we've never known the limits of Puppeteer technology."

Ausfaller asked, "You think this is possible?"

"Just barely. The same goes for the Kzinti. The Kzinti are ferocious enough. Trouble is, if we ever learned they were preying on our ships we'd raise pluperfect hell. The Kzinti know that, and they know we can beat them. Took them long enough, but they learned."

"So you think it's Humans," said Carlos.

"Yah. If it's pirates."

The piracy theory still looked shaky. Spectrum telescopes had not even found concentrations of ship's metals in the space where they have vanished. Would pirates steal the whole ship? If the hyperdrive motor were still intact after the attack, the rifled ship could be launched into infinity; but could pirates count on that happening eight times out of eight?

And none of the missing ships had called for help via hyperwave.

I'd never believed pirates. Space pirates have existed, but they died without successors. Intercepting a spacecraft was too difficult. They couldn't make it pay.

Ships fly themselves in hyperdrive. All a pilot need do is watch for green radial lines in the mass sensor. But he has to do that frequently, because the mass sensor is a psionic device; it must be watched by a mind, not another machine.

As the narrow green line that marked Sol grew longer, I became abnormally conscious of the debris around Sol system. I spent the last twelve hours of the flight at the controls, chain-smoking with my feet. I should add that I do that normally, when I want both hands free; but now I did it to annoy Ausfaller. I'd seen the way his eyes bugged the first time he saw me take a drag from a cigarette between my toes. Flatlanders are less than limber.

Carlos and Ausfaller shared the control room with me as we penetrated Sol's cometary halo. They were relieved to be nearing the end of a long trip. I was nervous. "Carlos, just how large a mass would it take to make us disappear?"

"Planet size, Mars and up. Beyond that it depends on how close you get and how dense it is. If it's dense enough it can be less massive and still flip you out of the universe. But you'd see it in the mass sensor."

"Only for an instant . . . and not then, if it's turned off. What if someone turned on a giant gravity generator as we went past?"

"For what? They couldn't rob the ship. Where's their profit?"

"Stocks."

But Ausfaller was shaking his head. "The expense of such an operation would be enormous. No group of pirates would have enough additional capital on hand to make it worthwhile. Of the Puppeteers I might believe it."

Hell, he was right. No Human that wealthy would need to turn pirate.

The long green line marking Sol was almost touching the surface of the mass sensor. I said, "Breakout in ten minutes."

And the ship lurched savagely.

"Strap down!" I yelled, and glanced at the hyperdrive monitors. The motor was drawing no power, and the rest of the dials were going bananas.

I activated the windows. I'd kept them turned off in hyperspace, lest my flatlander passengers go mad watching the Blind Spot. The screens came on and I saw stars. We were in normal space.

"Futz! They got us anyway." Carlos sounded neither frightened nor angry, but awed.

As I raised the hidden panel Ausfaller cried, "Wait!" I ignored him. I threw the red switch, and *Hobo Kelly* lurched again as her belly blew off.

Ausfaller began cursing in some dead flatlander language.

Now two-thirds of *Hobo Kelly* receded, slowly turning. What was left must show as what she was: a Number Two General Products hull, Puppeteer-built, a slender transparent spear three hundred feet long and twenty feet wide, with instruments of war clustered along what was now her belly. Screens that had been blank came to life. And I lit the main drive and ran it up to full power.

Ausfaller spoke in rage and venom. "Shaeffer, you idiot, you coward! We run without knowing what we run from. Now they know exactly what we are. What chance that they will follow us now? This ship was built for a specific purpose, and you have ruined it!"

"I've freed your special instruments," I pointed out.

"Why don't you see what you can find?" Meanwhile I could get us the futz out of here.

Ausfaller became very busy. I watched what he was getting on screens at my side of the control panel. Was anything chasing us? They'd find us hard to catch and harder to digest. They could hardly have been expecting a General Products hull. Since the Puppeteers stopped making them the price of used GP hulls has gone out of sight.

There *were* ships out there. Ausfaller got a closeup of them: three space tugs of the Belter type, shaped like thick saucers, equipped with oversized drives and powerful electromagnetic generators. Belters use them to tug nickel-iron asteroids to where somebody wants the ore. With those heavy drives they could probably catch us; but would they have adequate cabin gravity?

They weren't trying. They seemed to be neither following nor fleeing. And they looked harmless enough.

But Ausfaller was doing a job on them with his other instruments. I approved. *Hobo Kelly* had looked peaceful enough a moment ago. Now her belly bristled with weaponry. The tugs could be equally deceptive.

From behind me Carlos asked, "Bey? What happened?"

"How the futz would I know?"

"What do the instruments show?"

He must mean the hyperdrive complex. A couple of the indicators had gone wild; five more were dead. I said so. "And the drive's drawing no power at all. I've never heard of anything like this. Carlos, it's *still* theoretically impossible."

"I'm . . . not so sure of that. I want to look at the drive."

"The access tubes don't have cabin gravity."

Ausfaller had abandoned the receding tugs. He'd found what looked to be a large comet, a ball of frozen gasses a good distance to the side. I watched as he ran the deep-radar over it. No fleet of robber ships lurked behind it.

I asked, "Did you deep-radar the tugs?"

"Of course. We can examine the tapes in detail later.

I saw nothing. And nothing has attacked us since we left hyperspace."

I'd been driving us in a random direction. Now I turned us toward Sol, the brightest star in the heavens. Those lost ten minutes in hyperspace would add about three days to our voyage.

"If there was an enemy, you frightened him away. Shaeffer, this mission and this ship have cost my department an enormous sum, and we have learned nothing at all."

"Not quite nothing," said Carlos. "I still want to see the hyperdrive motor. Bey, would you run us down to one gee?"

"Yah. But . . . miracles make me nervous, Carlos."

"Join the club."

We crawled along an access tube just a little bigger than a big man's shoulders, between the hyperdrive motor housing and the surrounding fuel tankage. Carlos reached an inspection window. He looked in. He started to laugh.

I inquired as to what was so futzy funny.

Still chortling, Carlos moved on. I crawled after him and looked in.

There was no hyperdrive motor in the hyperdrive motor housing.

I went in through a repair hatch and stood in the cylindrical housing, looking about me. Nothing. Not even an exit hole. The superconducting cables and the mounts for the motor had been sheared so cleanly that the cut ends looked like little mirrors.

Ausfaller insisted on seeing for himself. Carlos and I waited in the control room. For awhile Carlos kept bursting into fits of giggles. Then he got a dreamy, faraway look that was even more annoying.

I wondered what was going on in his head, and reached the uncomfortable conclusion that I could never know. Some years ago I took IQ tests, hoping to get a parenthood license that way. I am not a genius.

I knew only that Carlos had thought of something I

hadn't, and he wasn't telling, and I was too proud to ask.

Ausfaller had no pride. He came back looking like he'd seen a ghost. "Gone! Where could it go? How could it happen?"

"That I can answer," Carlos said happily. "It takes an extremely high gravity gradient. The motor hit that, wrapped space around itself and took off at some higher level of hyperdrive, one we can't reach. By now it could be well on its way to the edge of the universe."

I said, "You're sure, huh? An hour ago there wasn't a theory to cover any of this."

"Well, I'm sure our motor's gone. Beyond that it gets a little hazy. But this is one well-established model of what happens when a ship hits a singularity. At a lower gravity gradient the motor would take the whole ship with it, then strew atoms of the ship along its path till there was nothing left but the hyperdrive field itself."

"Ugh."

Now Carlos burned with the love of an idea. "Sigmund, I want to use your hyperwave. I could still be wrong, but there are things we can check."

"If we are still within the singularity of some mass, the hyperwave will destroy itself."

"Yah. I think it's worth the risk."

We'd dropped out, or been knocked out, ten minutes short of the singularity around Sol. That added up to sixteen light-hours of normal space, plus almost five light-hours from the edge of the singularity inward to Earth. Fortunately hyperwave is instantaneous, and every civilized system keeps a hyperwave relay station just outside the singularity. Southworth Station would relay our message inward by laser, get the return message the same way and pass it on to us ten hours later.

We turned on the hyperwave and nothing exploded.

Ausfaller made his own call first, to Ceres, to get the registry of the tugs we'd spotted. Afterward Carlos called Elephant's computer setup in New York, using a code number Elephant doesn't give to many people. "I'll pay him back later. Maybe with a story to go with it," he gloated.

I listened as Carlos outlined his needs. He wanted full

records on a meteorite that had touched down in Tunguska, Siberia, USSR, Earth, in 1908 AD. He wanted a reprise on three models of the origin of the universe or lack of same: the Big Bang, the Cyclic Universe, the Steady State Universe. He wanted data on collapsars. He wanted names, career outlines, and addresses for the best known students of gravitational phenomena in Sol system. He was smiling when he clicked off.

I said, "You got me. I haven't the remotest idea what you're after."

Still smiling, Carlos got up and went to his cabin to catch some sleep.

I turned off the main thrust motor entirely. When we were deep in Sol system we could decelerate at thirty gravities. Meanwhile we were carrying a hefty velocity picked up on our way out of Sirius system.

Ausfaller stayed in the control room. Maybe his motive was the same as mine. No police ships out here. We could still be attacked.

He spent the time going through his pictures of the three mining tugs. We didn't talk, but I watched.

The tugs seemed ordinary enough. Telescopic photos showed no suspicious breaks in the hulls, no hatches for guns. In the deep-radar scan they showed like ghosts: we could pick out the massive force-field rings, the hollow, equally massive drive tubes, the lesser densities of fuel tank and life-support system. There were no gaps or shadows that shouldn't have been there.

By and by Ausfaller said, "Do you know what *Hobo Kelly* was worth?"

I said I could make a close estimate.

"It was worth my career. I thought to destroy a pirate fleet with *Hobo Kelly*. But my pilot fled. Fled! What have I now, to show for my expensive Trojan Horse?"

I suppressed the obvious answer, along with the plea that my first responsibility was Carlos' life. Ausfaller wouldn't buy that. Instead, "Carlos has something. I know him. He knows how it happened."

"Can you get it out of him?"

"I don't know." I could put it to Carlos that we'd be safer if we knew what was out to get us. But Carlos was a flatlander. It would color his attitudes.

"So," said Ausfaller. "We have only the unavailable knowledge in Carlos' skull."

A weapon beyond human technology had knocked me out of hyperspace. I'd run. Of *course* I'd run. Staying in the neighborhood would have been insane, said I to myself, said I. But, unreasonably, I still felt bad about it.

To Ausfaller I said, "What about the mining tugs? I can't understand what they're doing out here. In the Belt they use them to move nickle-iron asteroids to industrial sites."

"It is the same here. Most of what they find is useless: stony masses or balls of ice; but what little metal there is, is valuable. They must have it for building."

"For building what? What kind of people would live here? You might as well set up shop in interstellar space!"

"Precisely. There are no tourists, but there are research groups, here where space is flat and empty and temperatures are near absolute zero. I know that the Quicksliver Group was established here to study hyperspace phenomena. We do not understand hyperspace, even yet. Remember that we did not invent the hyperdrive; we bought it from an alien race. Then there is a gene-tailoring laboratory trying to develop a kind of tree that will grow on comets."

"You're kidding."

"But they are serious. A photosynthetic plant to use the chemicals present in all comets . . . it would be very valuable. The whole cometary halo could be seeded with oxygen-producing plants—" Ausfaller stopped abruptly, then, "Never mind. But all these groups need building materials. It is cheaper to build out here than to ship everything from Earth or the Belt. The presence of tugs is not suspicious."

"But there was noting else around us. Nothing at all."

Ausfaller nodded.

When Carlos came to join us many hours later, blinking sleep out of his eyes, I asked him, "Carlos, could the tugs have had anything to do with your theory?"

"I don't see how. I've got half an idea, and half an hour from now I could look like a halfwit. The theory I want isn't even in fashion any more. Now that we know what the quasars are, everyone seems to like the Steady State Hypothesis. You know how that works: the tension in completely empty space produces more hydrogen atoms, forever. The universe has no beginning and no end." He looked stubborn. "But if I'm right, then I know where the ships went to after being robbed. That's more than anyone else knows."

Ausfaller jumped on him. "Where are they? Are the passengers alive?"

"I'm sorry, Sigmund. They're all dead. There won't even be bodies to bury."

"What is it? What are we fighting?"

"A gravitational effect. A sharp warping of space. A planet wouldn't do that, and a battery of cabin gravity generators wouldn't do it; they couldn't produce that sharply bounded a field."

"A collapsar," Ausfaller suggested.

Carlos grinned at him. "That would do it, but there are other problems. A collapsar can't even form at less than around five solar masses. You'd think someone would have noticed something that big, this close to Sol."

"Then *what?*"

Carlos shook his head. We would wait.

The relay from Southworth Station gave us registration for three space tugs, used and of varying ages, all three purchased two years ago from IntraBelt Mining by the Sixth Congregational Church of Rodney.

"Rodney?"

But Carlos and Ausfaller were both chortling. "Belters do that sometimes," Carlos told me. "It's a way of saying it's nobody's business who's buying the ships."

"That's pretty funny, all right, but we still don't know who owns them."

"They may be honest Belters. They may not."

Hard on the heels of the first call came the data Carlos had asked for, playing directly into the shipboard computer. Carlos called up a list of names and phone numbers: Sol system's preeminent students of gravity and its effects, listed in alphabetical order.

An address caught my attention:

Julian Forward, #1192326 Southworth Station.

A hyperwave relay tag. He was out *here,* somewhere in the enormous gap between Neptune's orbit and the cometary belt, out here where the hyperwave relay could function. I looked for more Southworth Station numbers. They were there:

Launcelot Starkey, #1844719 Southworth Station.
Jill Luciano, #1844719 Southworth Station.
Mariana Wilton, #1844719 Southworth Station.

"These people," said Ausfaller. "You wish to discuss your theory with one of them?"

"That's right. Sigmund, isn't 1844719 the tag for the Quicksilver Group?"

"I think so. I also think that they are not within our reach, now that our hyperdrive is gone. The Quicksilver Group was established in distant orbit around Antenora, which is now on the other side of the sun. Carlos, has it occurred to you that one of these people may have built the ship-eating device?"

"What? . . . You're right. It would take someone who knew something about gravity. But I'd say the Quicksilver Group was beyond suspicion. With upwards of ten thousand people at work, how could anyone hide anything?"

"What about this Julian Forward?"

"Forward. Yah. I've always wanted to meet him."

"You know of him? Who is he?"

"He used to be with the Institute of Knowledge on Jinx. I haven't heard of him in years. He did some work on the gravity waves from the galactic core . . . work that turned out to be wrong. Sigmund, let's give him a call."

"And ask him what?"

"Why . . . ?" Then Carlos remembered the situation. "Oh. You think he might—Yah."

"How well do you know this man?"

"I know him by reputation. He's quite famous. I don't see how such a man could go in for mass murder."

"Earlier you said that we were looking for a man skilled in the study of gravitational phenomena."

"Granted."

Ausfaller sucked at his lower lip. Then, "Perhaps we can do no more than talk to him. He could be on the other side of the sun and still head a pirate fleet—"

"No. That he could not."

"Think again," said Ausfaller. "We are outside the singularity of Sol. A pirate fleet would surely include hyperdrive ships."

"If Julian Forward is the ship eater, he'll have to be nearby. The, uh, device won't move in hyperspace."

I said, "Carlos, what we don't know can kill us. Will you quit playing games—" But he was smiling, shaking his head. Futz. "All right, we can still check on Forward. Call him up and ask where he is! Is he likely to know you by reputation?"

"Sure. I'm famous too."

"Okay. If he's close enough, we might even beg him for a ride home. The way things stand we'll be at the mercy of any hyperdrive ship for as long as we're out here."

"I hope we are attacked," said Ausfaller. "We can outfight—"

"But we can't outrun. They can dodge, we can't."

"Peace, you two. First things first." Carlos sat down at the hyperwave controls and tapped out a number.

Suddenly Ausfaller said, "Can you contrive to keep my name out of this exchange? If necessary you can be the ship's owner."

Carlos looked around in surprise. Before he could answer, the screen lit. I saw ash-blond hair cut in a Belter crest, over a lean white face and an impersonal smile.

"Forward Station. Good evening."

"Good evening. This is Carlos Wu of Earth calling long distance. May I speak to Dr. Julian Forward, please?"

"I'll see if he's available." The screen went on HOLD.

In the interval Carlos burst out: "What kind of game are *you* playing now? How can I explain owning an armed, disguised warship?"

But I began to see what Ausfaller was getting at. I said, "You'd want to avoid explaining that, whatever the truth was. Maybe he won't ask. I—" I shut up, because we were facing Forward.

Julian Forward was a Jinxian, short and wide, with arms as thick as legs and legs as thick as pillars. His skin was almost as black as his hair: a Sirius suntan, probably maintained by sunlights. He perched on the edge of a massage chair. "Carlos Wu!" he said with flattering enthusiasm. "Are you the same Carlos Wu who solved the Sealeyham Limits Problem?"

Carlos said he was. They went into a discussion of mathematics—a possible application of Carlos' solution to another limits problem, I gathered. I glanced at Ausfaller—not obtrusively, because for Forward he wasn't supposed to exist—and saw him pensively studying his side view of Forward.

"Well," Forward said, "what can I do for you?"

"Julian Forward, meet Beowulf Shaeffer," said Carlos. I bowed. "Bey was giving me a lift home when our hyperdrive motor disappeared."

"Disappeared?"

I butted in, for verisimilitude. "Disappeared, futzy right. The hyperdrive motor casing is empty. The motor supports are sheared off. We're stuck out here with no hyperdrive and no idea how it happened."

"Almost true," Carlos said happily. "Dr. Forward, I do have some ideas as to what happened here. I'd like to discuss them with you."

"Where are you now?"

I pulled our position and velocity from the computer and flashed them to Forward Station. I wasn't sure it was a good idea; but Ausfaller had time to stop me, and he didn't.

"Fine," said Forward's image. "It looks like you can get here a lot faster than you can get to Earth. Forward Station is ahead of you, within twenty a.u. of your position. You can wait here for the next ferry. Better than going on in a crippled ship."

"Good! We'll work out a course and let you know when to expect us."

"I welcome the chance to meet Carlos Wu." Forward gave us his own coordinates and rang off.

Carlos turned. "All right, Bey. Now *you* own an armed and disguised warship. *You* figure out where you got it."

"We've got worse problems than that. Forward Station is exactly where the ship eater ought to be."

He nodded. But he was amused.

"So what's our next move? We can't run from hyperdrive ships. Not now. Is Forward likely to try to kill us?"

"If we don't reach Forward Station on schedule, he might send ships after us. We know too much. We've told him so," said Carlos. "The hyperdrive motor disappeared completely. I know half a dozen people who could figure out how it happened, knowing just that." He smiled suddenly. "That's assuming Forward's the ship eater. Wo don't know that. I think we have a splendid chance to find out, one way or the other."

"How? Just walk in?"

Ausfaller was nodding approvingly. "Dr. Forward expects you and Carlos to enter his web unsuspecting, leaving an empty ship. I think we can prepare a few surprises for him. For example, he may not have guessed that this is a General Products hull. And I will be aboard to fight."

True. Only antimatter could harm a GP hull . . . though things could go through it, like light and gravity and shock waves. "So you'll be in the indestructible hull," I said, "and we'll be helpless in the base. Very clever. I'd rather run for it myself. But then, you have your career to consider."

"I will not deny it. But there are ways in which I can prepare you."

Behind Ausfaller's cabin, behind what looked like an unbroken wall, was a room the size of a walk-in closet. Ausfaller seemed quite proud of it. He didn't show us everything in there, but I saw enough to cost me what remained of my first impression of Ausfaller. This man did not have the soul of a pudgy bureaucrat.

Behind a glass panel he kept a couple of dozen special-purpose weapons. A row of four clamps held three identical hand weapons, disposable rocket launchers for a fat slug that Ausfaller billed as a tiny atomic bomb. The fourth clamp was empty. There were laser rifles and pistols; a shotgun of peculiar design, with four inches of recoil shock absorber; throwing knives; an Olympic target pistol with a sculpted grip and room for just one .22 bullet.

I wondered what he was doing with a hobbyist's touch-sculpting setup. Maybe he could make sculptures to drive a Human or an alien mad. Maybe something less subtle: maybe they'd explode at the touch of the right fingerprints.

He had a compact automated tailor's shop. "I'm going to make you some new suits," he said. When Carlos asked why, he said, "You can keep secrets? So can I."

He asked us for our preference in styles. I played it straight, asking for a falling jumper in green and silver, with lots of pockets. It wasn't the best I've ever owned, but it fitted.

"I didn't ask for buttons," I told him.

"I hope you don't mind. Carlos, you will have buttons too."

Carlos chose a fiery red tunic with a green-and-gold dragon coiling across the back. The buttons carried his family monogram. Ausfaller stood before us, examining us in our new finery, with approval.

"Now, watch," he said. "Here I stand before you, unarmed——"

"Right."

"*Sure* you are."

Ausfaller grinned. He took the top and bottom buttons between his fingers and tugged hard. They came off. The material between them ripped open as if a thread had been strung between them.

Holding the buttons as if to keep an invisible thread taut, he moved them on either side of a crudely done plastic touch-sculpture. The sculpture fell apart.

"Sinclair molecule chain. It will cut through any normal matter, if you pull hard enough. You must be very careful. It will cut your fingers so easily that you will hardly notice they are gone. Notice that the buttons are large, to give an easy grip." He laid the buttons carefully on a table and set a heavy weight between them. "This third button down is a sonic grenade. Ten feet away it will kill. Thirty feet away it will stun."

I said, "Don't demonstrate."

"You may want to practice throwing dummy buttons at a target. This second button is Power Pill, the commercial stimulant. Break the button and take half when you need it. The entire dose may stop your heart."

"I never heard of Power Pill. How does it work on crashlanders?"

He was taken aback. "I don't know. Perhaps you had better restrict yourself to a quarter dose."

"Or avoid it entirely," I said.

"There is one more thing I will not demonstrate. Feel the material of your garments. You feel three layers of material? The middle layer is a nearly perfect mirror. It will reflect even X-rays. Now you can repel a laser blast, for at least the first second. The collar unrolls to a hood."

Carlos was nodding in satisfaction.

I guess it's true: all flatlanders think that way.

For a billion and a half years, humanity's ancestors had evolved to the conditions of one world: Earth. A flatlander grows up in an environment peculiarly suited to him. Instinctively he sees the whole universe the same way.

We know better, we who were born on other worlds. On We Made It there are the hellish winds of summer and winter. On Jinx, the gravity. On Plateau, the all-encircling cliff edge, and a drop of forty miles into unbearable heat and pressure. On Down, the red sunlight, and plants that will not grow without help from untraviolet lamps.

But flatlanders think the universe was made for their benefit. To them, danger is unreal.

"Earplugs," said Ausfaller, holding up a handful of soft plastic cylinders.

We inserted them. Ausfaller said, "Can you hear me?"

"Sure." "Yah." They didn't block our hearing at all.

"Transmitter and hearing aid, with sonic padding between. If you are blasted with sound, as by an explosion or a sonic stunner, the hearing aid will stop transmitting. If you go suddenly deaf you will know you are under attack."

To me, Ausfaller's elaborate precautions only spoke of what we might be walking into. I said nothing. If we ran for it our chances were even worse.

Back to the control room, where Ausfaller set up a relay to the Alien Affairs Bureau on Earth. He gave them a condensed version of what had happened to us, plus some cautious speculation. He invited Carlos to read his theories into the record.

Carlos declined. "I could still be wrong. Give me a chance to do some studying."

Ausfaller went grumpily to his bunk. He had been up too long, and it showed.

Carlos shook his head as Ausfaller disappeared into his cabin. "Paranoia. In his job I guess he has to be paranoid."

"You could use some of that yourself."

He didn't hear me. "Imagine suspecting an interstellar celebrity of being a space pirate!"

"He's in the right place at the right time."

"Hey, Bey, forget what I said. The, uh, ship-eating device has to be in the right place, but the pirates don't. They can just leave it loose and use hyperdrive ships to commute to their base."

That was something to keep in mind. Compared to the inner system this volume within the cometary halo was enormous; but to hyperdrive ships it was all one neighborhood. I said, "Then why are we visiting Forward?"

"I still want to check my ideas with him. More than that: he probably knows the head ship eater, without knowing it's him. Probably we both know him. It took something of a cosmologist to find the device and recognize it. Whoever it is, he has to have made something of a name for himself."

"Find?"

Carlos grinned at me. "Never mind. Have you thought of anyone you'd like to use that magic wire on?"

"I've been making a list. You're at the top."

"Well, watch it. Sigmund knows you've got it, even if nobody else does."

"He's second."

"How long till we reach Forward Station?"

I'd been rechecking our course. We were decelerating at thirty gravities and veering to one side. "Twenty hours and a few minutes," I said.

"Good. I'll get a chance to do some studying." He began calling up data from the computer.

I asked permission to read over his shoulder. He gave it.

Bastard. He reads twice as fast as I do. I tried to skim, to get some idea of what he was after.

Collapsars: three known. The nearest was one component of a double in Cygnus, more than a hundred light years away. Expeditions had gone there to drop probes.

The theory of the black hole wasn't new to me, though the math was over my head. If a star is massive enought, then after it has burned its nuclear fuel and started to cool, no possible internal force can hold it from collapsing inward past its own Swartzchild radius. At that point the escape velocity from the star becomes greater than lightspeed; and beyond that deponent sayeth not, because nothing can leave the star, not information, not matter, not radiation. Nothing—except gravity.

Such a collapsed star can be expected to weigh five solar masses or more; otherwise its collapse would stop at the neutron star stage. Afterward it can only grow bigger and more massive.

There wasn't the slightest chance of finding anything that massive out here at the edge of the solar system. If such a thing were anywhere near, the sun would have been in orbit around it.

The Siberia meteorite must have been weird enough, to be remembered for nine hundred years. It had knocked down trees over thousands of square miles; yet trees near the touchdown point were left standing. No part of the meteorite itself had ever been found. Nobody had seen it hit. In 1908, Tunguska, Siberia must have been as sparsely settled as the Earth's moon today.

"Carlos, what does all this have to do with anything?"

"Does Holmes tell Watson?"

I had real trouble following the cosmology. Physics verged on philosophy here, or vice versa. Basically the

Big Bang Theory—which pictures the universe as exploding from a single point-mass, like a titanic bomb—was in competition with the Steady State Universe, which has been going on forever and will continue to do so. The Cyclic Universe is a succession of Big Bangs followed by contractions. There are variants on all of them.

When the quasars were first discovered, they seemed to date from an earlier stage in the evolution of the universe . . . which, by the Steady State hypothesis, would not be evolving at all. The Steady State went out of fashion. Then, a century ago, Hilbury had solved the mystery of the quasars. Meanwhile one of the implications of the Big Bang had not panned out. That was where the math got beyond me.

There was some discussion of whether the universe was open or closed in four-space, but Carlos turned it off. "Okay," he said, with satisfaction.

"What?"

"I could be right. Insufficient data. I'll have to see what Forward thinks."

"I hope you both choke. I'm going to sleep."

Out here in the broad borderland between Sol system and interstellar space, Julian Forward had found a stony mass the size of a middling asteroid. From a distance it seemed untouched by technology: a lopsided spheroid, rough-surfaced and dirty white. Closer in, flecks of metal and bright paint showed like randomly placed jewels. Airlocks, windows, projecting antennae, and things less identifiable. A lighted disk with something projecting from the center: a long metal arm with half a dozen ball joints in it and a cup on the end. I studied that one, trying to guess what it might be . . . and gave up.

I brought *Hobo Kelly* to rest a fair distance away. To Ausfaller I said, "You'll stay aboard?"

"Of course. I will do nothing to disabuse Dr. Forward of the notion that the ship is empty."

We crossed to Forward Station on an open taxi: two seats, a fuel tank and a rocket motor. Once I turned to ask Carlos something, and asked instead, "Carlos? Are you all right?"

His face was white and strained. "I'll make it."

"Did you try closing your eyes?"

"It was worse. Futz, I made it this far on hypnosis. Bey, it's so *empty*."

"Hang on. We're almost there."

The blond Belter was outside one of the airlocks in a skin-tight suit and a bubble helmet. He used a flashlight to flag us down. We moored our taxi to a spur of rock—the gravity was almost nil—and went inside.

"I'm Harry Moskowitz," the Belter said. "They call me Angel. Dr. Forward is waiting in the laboratory."

The interior of the asteroid was a network of straight cylindrical corridors, laser-drilled, pressurized and lined with cool blue light strips. We weighed a few pounds near the surface, less in the deep interior. Angel moved in a fashion new to me: a flat jump from the floor that took him far down the corridor to brush the ceiling; push back to the floor and jump again. Three jumps and he'd wait, not hiding his amusement at our attempts to catch up.

"Doctor Forward asked me to give you a tour," he told us.

I said, "You seem to have a lot more corridor than you need. Why didn't you cluster all the rooms together?"

"This rock was a mine, once upon a time. The miners drilled these passages. They left big hollows wherever they found air-bearing rock or ice pockets. All we had to do was wall them off."

That explained why there was so much corridor between the doors, and why the chambers we saw were so big. Some rooms were storage areas, Angel said; not worth opening. Others were tool rooms, life-support systems, a garden, a fair-sized computer, a sizable fusion plant. A mess room built to hold thirty actually held about ten, all men, who looked at us curiously before they went back to eating. A hangar, bigger than need be and open to the sky, housed taxis and powered suits with specialized tools, and three identical circular cradles, all empty.

I gambled. Carefully casual, I asked, "You use mining tugs?"

Angel didn't hesitate. "Sure. We can ship water and metals up from the inner system, but it's cheaper to hunt them down ourselves. In an emergency the tugs could probably get us back to the inner system."

We moved back into the tunnels. Angel said, "Speaking of ships, I don't think I've ever seen one like yours. Were those *bombs* lined up along the ventral surface?"

"Some of them," I said.

Carlos laughed. "Bey won't tell me how he got it."

"Pick, pick, pick. All right, I *stole* it. I don't think anyone is going to complain."

Angel, frankly curious before, was frankly fascinated as I told the story of how I had been hired to fly a cargo ship in the Wunderland system. "I didn't much like the looks of the guy who hired me, but what do I know about Wunderlanders? Besides, I needed the money." I told of my surprise at the proportions of the ship: the solid wall behind the cabin, the passenger section that was only holographs in blind portholes. By then I was already afraid that if I tried to back out I'd be made to disappear.

But when I learned my destination I got really worried. "It was in the Serpent Stream—you know, the crescent of asteroids in Wunderland system? It's common knowledge that the Free Wunderland Conspiracy is *all through* those rocks. When they gave me my course I just took off and aimed for Sirius."

"Strange they left you with a working hyperdrive."

"Man, they *didn't*. They'd ripped out the relays. I had to fix them myself. It's lucky I looked, because they had the relays wired to a little bomb under the control chair." I stopped, then, "Maybe I fixed it wrong. You heard what happened? My hyperdive motor just plain vanished. It must have set off some explosive bolts, because the belly of the ship blew off. It was a dummy. What's left looks to be a pocket bomber."

"That's what I thought."

"I guess I'll have to turn it in to the goldskin cops when we reach the inner system. Pity."

Carlos was smiling and shaking his head. He covered by saying, "It only goes to prove that you *can* run away from your problems."

The next tunnel ended in a great hemispherical chamber, lidded by a bulging transparent dome. A man-thick pillar rose through the rock floor to a seal in the center of the dome. Above the seal, gleaming against night and stars, a multi-jointed metal arm reached out blindly into space. The arm ended in what might have been a tremendous iron puppy dish.

Forward was in a horseshoe-shaped control console near the pillar. I hardly noticed him. I'd seen this arm-and-bucket thing before, coming in from space, but I hadn't grasped its *size*.

Forward caught me gaping. "The Grabber," he said.

He approached us in a bouncing walk, comical but effective. "Pleased to meet you, Carlos Wu. Beowulf Shaeffer." His handshake was not crippling, because he was being careful. He had a wide, engaging smile. "The Grabber is our main exhibit here. After the Grabber ther's nothing to see."

I asked, "What does it do?"

Carlos laughed. "It's beautiful! Why does it have to do anything?"

Forward acknowledged the compliment. "I've been thinking of entering it in a junk-sculpture show. What it does is manipulate large, dense masses. The cradle at the end of the arm is a complex of electromagnets. I can actually vibrate masses in there to produce polarized gravity waves."

Six massive arcs of girder divided the dome into pie sections. Now I noticed that they and the seal at their center gleamed like mirrors. They were reinforced by stasis fields. More bracing for the Grabber? I tried to imagine forces that would require such strength.

"What do you vibrate in there? A megaton of lead?"

"Lead sheathed in soft iron was our test mass. But that was three years ago. I haven't worked with the Grabber lately, but we had some satisfactory runs with a sphere of neutronium enclosed in a stasis field. Ten billion metric tons."

I said, "What's the point?"

From Carlos I got a dirty look. Forward seemed to think it was a wholly reasonable question. "Communication, for one thing. There must be intelligent species all through the galaxy, most of them too far away for our ships. Gravity waves are probably the best way to reach them."

"Gravity waves travel at lightspeed, don't they? Wouldn't hyperwave be better?"

"We can't count on their having it. Who but the Outsiders would think to do their experimenting this far from a sun? If we want to reach beings who haven't dealt with the Outsiders, we'll have to use gravity waves . . . once we know how."

Angel offered us chairs and refreshments. By the time we were settled I was already out of it; Forward and Carlos were talking plasma physics, metaphysics, and what are our old friends doing? I gathered that they had large numbers of mutual acquaintances. And Carlos was probing for the whereabouts of cosmologists specializing in gravity physics.

A few were in the Quicksilver Group. Others were among the colony worlds . . . especially on Jinx, trying to get the Institute of Knowledge to finance various projects, such as more expeditions to the collapsar in Cygnus.

"Are you still with the Institute, Doctor?"

Forward shook his head. "They stopped backing me. Not enough results. But I can continue to use this station, which is Institute property. One day they'll sell it and we'll have to move."

"I was wondering why they sent you here in the first place," said Carlos. "Sirius has an adequate cometary belt."

"But Sol is the only system with any kind of civilization this far from its sun. And I can count on better men to work with. Sol system has always had its fair share of cosmologists."

"I thought you might have come to solve an old mystery. The Tunguska meteorite. You've heard of it, of course."

Forward laughed. "Of course. Who hasn't? I don't think we'll ever know just what it was that hit Siberia that night. It may have been a chunk of antimatter. I'm told that there is antimatter in known space."

"If it was, we'll never prove it," Carlos admitted.

"Shall we discuss your problem?" Forward seemed to remember my existence. "Shaeffer, what does a professional pilot think when his hyperdrive motor disappears?"

"He gets very upset."

"Any theories?"

I decided not to mention pirates. I wanted to see if Forward would mention them first. "Nobody seems to like my theory," I said, and I sketched out the argument for monsters in hyperspace.

Forward heard me out politely. Then, "I'll give you this, it'd be hard to disprove. Do you buy it?"

"I'm afraid to. I almost got myself killed once, looking for space monsters when I should have been looking for natural causes."

"Why would the hyperspace monsters eat only your motor?"

"Um . . . futz. I pass."

"What do you think, Carlos? Natural phenomena or space monsters?"

"Pirates," said Carlos.

"How are they going about it?"

"Well, this business of a hyperdrive motor disappearing and leaving the ship behind—that's brand new. I'd think it would take a sharp gravity gradient, with a tidal effect as strong as that of a neutron star or a black hole."

"You won't find anything like that anywhere in Human space."

"I know." Carlos looked frustrated. That had to be faked. Earlier he'd behaved as if he already had an answer.

Forward said, "I don't think a black hole would have that effect anyway. If it did you'd never know it, because the ship would disappear down the black hole."

"What about a powerful gravity generator?"

"Hmmm." Forward thought about it, then shook his massive head. "You're talking about a surface gravity in the millions. Any gravity generator I've ever heard of would collapse itself at that level. Let's see, with a frame supported by stasis fields . . . no. The frame would hold and the rest of the machinery would flow like water."

"You don't leave much of my theory."

"Sorry."

Carlos ended a short pause by asking, "How do you think the universe started?"

Forward looked puzzled at the change of subject. And I began to get uneasy.

Given all that I don't know about cosmology, I do know attitudes and tones of voice. Carlos was giving out broad hints, trying to lead Forward to his own conclusion. Black holes, pirates, the Tunguska meteorite, the origin of the universe—he was offering them as clues. And Forward was not responding correctly.

He was saying, "Ask a priest. Me, I lean toward the Big Bang. The Steady State always seemed so futile."

"I like the Big Bang too," said Carlos.

There was something else to worry about. Those mining tugs: they almost had to belong to Forward Station. How would Ausfaller react when three familiar spacecraft came cruising into his space?

How did I want him to react? Forward Station would make a dandy pirate base. Permeated by laser-drilled corridors distributed almost at random . . . could there be two networks of corridors, connected only at the surface? How would we know?

Suddenly I didn't want to know. I wanted to go home. If only Carlos would stay off the touchy subjects—

But he was speculating about the ship eater again. "That ten billion metric tons of neutronium, now, that you were using for a test mass. That wouldn't be big enough or dense enough to give us enough of a gravity gradient."

"It might, right near the surface." Forward grinned and held his hands close together. "It was about that big."

"And that's as dense as matter gets in this universe. Too bad."

"True, but . . . have you ever heard of quantum black holes?"

"Yah."

Forward stood up briskly. "Wrong answer."

I rolled out of my web chair, trying to brace myself for a jump, while my fingers fumbled for the third button on my jumper. It was no good. I hadn't practiced in this gravity.

Forward was in mid-leap. He slapped Carlos alongside the head as he went past. He caught me at the peak of his jump, and took me with him via an iron grip on my wrist.

I had no leverage, but I kicked at him. He didn't even try to stop me. It was like fighting a mountain. He gathered my wrists in one hand and towed me away.

Forward was busy. He sat within the horseshoe of his control console, talking. The backs of three disembodied heads showed above the console's edge.

Evidently there was a laser phone in the console. I could hear parts of what Forward was saying. He was ordering the pilots of the three mining tugs to destroy *Hobo Kelly*. He didn't seem to know about Ausfaller yet.

Forward was busy, but Angel was studing us thoughtfully, or unhappily, or both. Well he might. We could disappear, but what messages might we have sent earlier?

I couldn't do anything constructive with Angel watching me. And I couldn't count on Carlos.

I couldn't see Carlos. Forward and Angel had tied us to opposite sides of the central pillar, beneath the Grabber. Carlos hadn't made a sound since then. He might be dying form that tremendous slap across the head.

I tested the line around my wrists. Metal mesh of some kind, cool to the touch . . . and it was tight.

Forward turned a switch. The heads vanished. It was a moment before he spoke.

"You've put me in a very bad position."

And Carlos answered. "I think you put yourself there."

"That may be. You should not have let me guess what you knew."

Carlos said, "Sorry, Bey."

He sounded healthy. Good. "That's all right," I said. "But what's all the excitement about? What has Forward *got*?"

"I think he's got the Tunguska meteorite."

"No. That I do not." Forward stood and faced us. "I will admit that I came here to search for the Tunguska meteorite. I spent several years trying to trace its trajectory after it left Earth. Perhaps it *was* a quantum black hole. Perhaps not. The Institute cut off my funds, without warning, just as I had found a real quantum black hole, the first in history."

I said, "That doesn't tell me a lot."

"Patience Mr. Shaeffer. You know that a black hole may form from the collapse of a massive star? Good. And you know that it takes a body of at least five solar masses. It may mass as much as a galaxy—or as much as the universe. There is some evidence that the universe is an infalling black hole. But at less than five solar masses the collapse would stop at the neutron star stage."

"I follow you."

"In all the history of the universe, there has been one moment at which smaller black holes might have formed. That moment was the explosion of the monoblock, the cosmic egg that once contained all the matter in the universe. In the ferocity of that explosion there must have been loci of unimaginable pressure. Black holes could have formed of mass down to two point two times ten to the minus fifth grams, one point six times ten to the minus twenty-fifth Angstrom in radius."

"Of course you'd never detect anything that small," said Carlos. He seemed almost cheerful. I wondered why . . . and then I knew. He'd been right about the way the ships were disappearing. It must compensate him for being tied to a pillar.

"But," said Forward, "black holes of all sizes could have formed in that explosion, and should have. In more than seven hundred years of searching, no quantum black hole has ever been found. Most cosmologist have given up on them, and on the Big Bang too."

Carlos said, "Of course there was the Tunguska meteorite. It could have been a black hole of, oh, asteroidal mass—"

"—and roughly molecular size. But the tide would have pulled down trees as it went past—"

"—and the black hole would have gone right through the Earth and headed back into space a few tons heavier. Eight hundred years ago there was actually a search for the exit point. With that they could have charted a course—"

"Exactly. But I had to give up that approach," said Forward. "I was using a new method when the Institute, ah, severed our relationship."

They must both be mad, I thought. Carlos was tied to a pillar and Forward was about to kill him, yet they were both behaving like members of a very exclusive club . . . to which I did not belong.

Carlos was interested. "How'd you work it?"

"You know that it is possible for an asteroid to capture a quantum black hole? In its interior? For instance, at a mass of ten to the twelfth kilograms—a billion metric tons," he added for my benefit, "a black hole would be only one point five times ten to the minus fifth angstroms across. Smaller than an atom. In a slow pass through an asteroid it might absorb a few billions of atoms, enough to slow it into an orbit. Thereafter it might orbit within the asteroid for aeons, absorbing very little mass on each pass."

"So?"

"If I chance on an asteroid more massive than it ought to be . . . and if I contrive to move it, and some of the mass stays behind . . ."

"You'd have to search a lot of asteroids. Why do it out here? Why not the asteroid belt? Oh, of course, you can use hyperdrive out her."

"Exactly. We could search a score of masses in a day, using very little fuel."

"Hey. If it was big enough to eat a spacecraft, why didn't it eat the asteroid you found it in?"

"It wasn't that big," said Forward. "The black hole I found was exactly as I have described it. I enlarged it. I towed it home and ran it into my neutronium sphere. *Then* it was large enough to absorb an asteroid. Now it is quite a massive object. Ten to the twentieth power kilograms, the mass of one of the larger asteroids, and a radius of just under ten to the minus fifth centimeters."

There was satisfaction in Forward's voice. In Carlos' there was suddenly nothing but contempt. "You accomplished all that, and then you used it to rob ships and bury the evidence. Is that what's going to happen to us? Down the rabbit hole?"

"To another universe, perhaps. Where does a black hole lead?"

I wondered about that myself.

Angel had taken Forward's place at the control console. He had fastened the seat belt, something I had not seen Forward do, and was dividing his attention between the instruments and the conversation.

"I'm still wondering how you move it," said Carlos. Then, "Uh! The tugs!"

Forward stared, then guffawed. "You didn't guess that? But of course the black hole can hold a charge. I played the exhaust from an old ion drive reaction motor into it for nearly a month. Now it holds an enormous charge. The tugs can pull it well enough. I wish I had more of them. Soon I will."

"Just a minute," I said. I'd grasped one crucial fact as it went past my head. "The tugs aren't armed? All they do is pull the black hole?"

"That's right." Forward looked at me curiously.

"And the black hole is invisible."

"Yes. We tug it into the path of a spacecraft. If the craft comes near enough it will precipitate into normal space. We guide the black hole through its drive to cripple it, board and rob it at our leisure. Then a slower pass with the quantum black hole, and the ship simply disappears."

"Just one last question," said Carlos. "Why?"

I had a better question.

Just what was Ausfaller going to do when three familiar spacecraft came near? They carried no armaments at all. Their only weapon was invisible.

And it would eat a General Products hull without noticing.

Would Ausfaller fire on unarmed ships?

We'd know, too soon. Up there near the edge of the

dome, I had spotted three tiny lights in a tight cluster.

Angel had seen it too. He activated the phone. Phantom heads appeared, one, two, three.

I turned back to Forward, and was startled at the brooding hate in his expression.

"Fortune's child," he said to Carlos. "Natural aristocrat. Certified superman. Why would *you* ever consider stealing anything? Women beg you to give them children, in person if possible, by mail if not! Earth's resources exist to keep you healthy, not that you need them!"

"This may startle you," said Carlos, "but there are people who see *you* as a superman."

"We bred for strength, we Jinxians. At what cost to other factors? Our lives are short, even with the aid of boosterspice. Longer if we can live outside Jinx's gravity. But the people of other worlds think we're funny. The women . . . never mind." He brooded, then said it anyway. "A women of Earth once told me she would rather go to bed with a tunneling machine. She didn't trust my strength. What woman would?"

The three bright dots had nearly reached the center of the dome. I saw nothing between them. I hadn't expected to. Angel was still talking to the pilots.

Up from the edge of the dome came something I didn't want anyone to notice. I said, "Is that your excuse for mass murder, Forward? Lack of women?"

"I need give you no excuses at all, Shaeffer. My world will thank me for what I've done. Earth has swallowed the lion's share of the interstellar trade for too long."

"They'll thank you, huh? You're going to tell them?"

"I—"

"Julian!" That was Angel calling. He'd seen it . . . no, he hadn't. One of the tug captains had.

Forward left us abruptly. He consulted with Angel in low tones, then turned back. "Carlos! Did you leave your ship on automatic? Or is there someone else aboard?"

"I'm not required to say," said Carlos.

"I could—no. In a minute it will not matter."

Angel said, "Julian, look what he's doing."

"Yes. Very clever. Only a human pilot would think of that."

Ausfaller had maneuvered the *Hobo Kelly* between us and the tugs. If the tugs fired a conventional weapon, they'd blast the dome and kill us all.

The tugs came on.

"He still does not know what he is fighting," Forward said with some satisfaction.

True, and it would cost him. Three unarmed tugs were coming down Ausfaller's throat, carrying a weapon so slow that the tugs could throw it at him, let it absorb *Hobo Kelly,* and pick it up again long before it was a danger to us.

From my viewpoint *Hobo Kelly* was a bright point with three dimmer, more distant points around it. Forward and Angel were getting a better view, through the phone. And they weren't watching us at all.

I began trying to kick off my shoes. They were soft ship-slippers, ankle-high, and they resisted.

I kicked the left foot free just as one of the tugs flared with ruby light.

"He did it!" Carlos didn't know whether to be jubilant or horrified. "He fired on unarmed ships!"

Forward gestured peremptorily. Angel slid out of his seat. Forward slid in and fastened the thick seat belt. Neither had spoken a word.

A second ship burned fiercely red, then expanded in a pink cloud.

The third ship was fleeing.

Forward worked the controls. "I have it in the mass indicator," he rasped. "We have but one chance."

So did I. I peeled the other slipper off with my toes. Over our heads the jointed arm of the Grabber began to swing . . . and I suddenly realized what they were talking about.

Now there was little to see beyond the dome. The swinging Grabber, and the light of *Hobo Kelly*'s drive, and the two tumbling wrecks, all against a background of fixed stars. Suddenly one of the tugs winked blue-white and was gone. Not even a dust cloud was left behind.

Ausfaller must have seen it. He was turning, fleeing. Then it was as if an invisible hand had picked up *Hobo Kelly* and thrown her away. The fusion light streaked off to one side and set beyond the dome's edge.

With two tugs destroyed and the third fleeing, the black hole was falling free, aimed straight down our throats.

Now there was nothing to see but the delicate motions of the Grabber. Angel stood behind Forward's chair, his knuckles white with his grip on the chair's back.

My few pounds of weight went away and left me in free fall. Tides again. The invisible thing was more massive than this asteroid beneath me. The Grabber swung a meter more to one side . . . and something struck it a mighty blow.

The floor surged away from beneath me, left me head down above the Grabber. The huge soft-iron puppy dish came at me; the jointed metal arm collapsed like a spring. It slowed, stopped.

"You got it!" Angel crowed like a rooster and slapped at the back of the chair, holding himself down with his other hand. He turned a gloating look on us, turned back just as suddenly. "The ship! It's getting away!"

"No." Forward was bent over the console. "I see him. Good, he is coming back, straight toward us. This time there will be no tugs to warn the pilot."

The Grabber swung ponderously toward the point where I'd seen *Hobo Kelly* disappear. It moved centimeters at a time, pulling a massive invisible weight.

And Ausfaller was coming back to rescue us. He'd be a sitting duck, unless—

I reached up with my toes, groping for the first and fourth buttons on my falling jumper.

The weaponry in my wonderful suit hadn't helped me against Jinxian strength and speed. But flatlanders are less than limber, and so are Jinxians. Forward had tied my hands and left it at that.

I wrapped two sets of toes around the buttons and tugged.

My legs were bent pretzel-fashion. I had no leverage. But the first button tore loose, and then the thread. Another invisible weapon to battle Forward's portable bottomless hole.

The thread pulled the fourth button loose. I brought my feet down to where they belonged, keeping the thread taut, and pushed backward. I felt the Sinclair molecule chain sinking into the pillar.

The Grabber was still swinging.

When the thread was through the pillar I could bring it up in back of me and try to cut my bonds. More likely I'd cut my wrists and bleed to death; but I had to try. I wondered if I could do anything before Forward launched the black hole.

A cold breeze caressed my feet.

I looked down. Thick fog boiled out around the pillar.

Some very cold gas must be spraying through the hair-fine crack.

I kept pushing. More fog formed. The cold was numbing. I felt the jerk as the magic thread cut through. Now the wrists—

Liquid helium?

Forward had moored us to the main superconducting power cable.

That was probably a mistake. I pulled my feet forward, carefully, steadily, feeling the thread bite through on the return cut.

The Grabber had stopped swinging. Now it moved on its arm like a blind, questing worm, as Forward made fine adjustments. Angel was beginning to show the strain of holding himself upside down.

My feet jerked slightly. I was through. My feet were terribly cold, almost without sensation. I let the buttons go, left them floating up toward the dome, and kicked back hard with my heels.

Something shifted. I kicked again.

Thunder and lightning flared around my feet.

I jerked my knees up to my chin. The lightning crackled and flashed white light into the billowing fog. Angel and Forward turned in astonishment. I laughed at them, letting them see it. Yes, gentlemen, I did it on purpose.

The lightning stopped. In the sudden silence Forward was screaming, "—know what you've *done?*"

There was a grinding *crunch*, a shuddering against my back. I looked up.

A piece had been bitten out of the Grabber.

I was upside down and getting heavier. Angel suddenly pivoted around his grip on Forward's chair. He hung above the dome, above the sky. He screamed.

My legs gripped the pillar hard. I felt Carlos' feet fumbling for a foothold, and heard Carlos' laughter.

Near the edge of the dome a spear of light was rising. *Hobo Kelly*'s drive, decelerating, growing larger. Otherwise the sky was clear and empty. And a piece of the dome disappeared with a snapping sound.

Angel screamed and dropped. Just above the dome he seemed to flare with blue light.

He was gone.

Air roared out through the dome—and more was disappearing into something that had been invisible. Now it showed as a blue pinpoint drifting toward the floor. Forward had turned to watch it fall.

Loose objects fell across the chamber, looped around the pinpoint at meteor speed or fell into it with bursts of light. Every atom of my body felt the pull of the thing, the urge to die in an infinite fall. Now we hung side by side from a horizontal pillar. I noted with approval that Carlos' mouth was wide open, like mine, to clear his lungs so that they wouldn't burst when the air was gone.

Daggers in my ears and sinuses, pressure in my gut.

Forward turned back to the controls. He moved one knob hard over. Then—he opened the seat belt and stepped out and up, and fell.

Light flared. He was gone.

The lightning-colored pinpoint drifted to the floor, and into it. Above the increasing roar of air I could hear the grumbling of rock being pulverized, dwindling as the black hole settled toward the center of the asteroid.

The air was deadly thin, but not gone. My lungs thought they were gasping vacuum. But my blood was not boiling. I'd have known it.

So I gasped, and kept gasping. It was all I had attention for. Black spots flickered before my eyes, but I was still gasping and alive when Ausfaller reached us carrying a clear plastic package and an enormous handgun.

He came in fast, on a rocket backpack. Even as he decelerated he was looking around for something to shoot. He returned in a loop of fire. He studied us through his faceplate, possibly wondering if we were dead.

He flipped the plastic package open. It was a thin sack with a zipper and a small tank attached. He had to dig for a torch to cut our bonds. He freed Carlos first, helped him into the sack. Carlos bled from the nose and ears. He was barely mobile. So was I, but Ausfaller got me into the sack with Carlos and zipped it up. Air hissed in around us.

I wondered what came next. As an inflated sphere the rescue bag was too big for the tunnels. Ausfaller had thought of that. He fired at the dome, blasted a gaping hole in it, and flew us out on the rocket backpack.

Hobo Kelly was grounded nearby. I saw that the rescue bag wouldn't fit the airlock either . . . and Ausfaller confirmed my worst fear. He signaled us by opening his mouth wide. Then he zipped open the rescue bag and half-carried us into the airlock while the air was still roaring out of our lungs.

When there was air again Carlos whispered, "Please don't do that any more."

"It should not be necessary any more." Ausfaller smiled. "Whatever it was you did, well done. I have two well-equipped autodocs to repair you. While you are healing, I will see about recovering the treasures within the asteroid."

Carlos held up a hand, but no sound came. He looked like something risen from the dead: blood running from nose and ears, mouth wide open, one feeble hand raised against gravity.

"One thing," Ausfaller said briskly. "I saw many dead men; I saw no living ones. How many were there? Am I likely to meet opposition while searching?"

"Forget it," Carlos croaked. "Get us out of here. Now."

Ausfaller frowned. "What—"

"No time. Get us out."

Ausfaller tasted something sour. "Very well. First, the autodocs." He turned, but Carlos' strengthless hand stopped him.

"Futz, no. I want to see this," Carlos whispered.

Again Ausfaller gave in. He trotted off to the control room. Carlos tottered after him. I tottered after them both, wiping blood from my nose, feeling half dead myself. But I'd half guessed what Carlos expected, and I didn't want to miss it.

We strapped down. Ausfaller fired the main thruster. The rock surged away.

"Far enough," Carlos whispered presently. "Turn us around."

Ausfaller took care of that. Then, "What are we looking for?"

"You'll know."

"Carlos, was I right to fire on the tugs?"

"Oh, yes."

"Good. I was worried. Then Forward was the ship eater?"

"Yah."

"I did not see him when I came for you. Where is he?"

Ausfaller was annoyed when Carlos laughed, and more annoyed when I joined him. It hurt my throat. "Even so, he saved our lives," I said. "He must have turned up the air pressure just before he jumped. I wonder why he did that?"

"Wanted to be remembered," said Carlos. "Nobody else knew what he'd done. *Ahh*—"

I looked, just as part of the asteroid collapsed into itself, leaving a deep crater.

"It moves slower at apogee. Picks up more matter," said Carlos.

"What *are* you talking about?"

"Later, Sigmund. When my throat grows back."

"Forward had a hole in his pocket," I said helpfully. "He—"

The other side of the asteroid collapsed. For a moment lightning seemed to flare in there.

Then the whole dirty snowball was growing smaller.

I thought of something Carlos had probably missed. "Sigmund, has this ship got automatic sunscreens?"

"Of *course* we've got—"

There was a universe-eating flash of light before the screen went black. When the screen cleared there was nothing to see but stars.

There Is a Tide

I

THEN, THE PLANET had no name. It circles a star which in 2830 lay beyond the fringe of known space, a distance of nearly forty light-years from Sol. The star is a G3, somewhat redder than Sol, somewhat smaller. The planet, swinging eighty million miles from its primary in a reasonably circular orbit, is a trifle cold for human tastes.

In the year 2830 one Louis Gridley Wu happened to be passing. The emphasis on accident is intended. In a universe the size of ours almost anything that can happen, will. Take the coincidence of his meeting—

But we'll get to that.

Louis Wu was one hundred and eighty years old. As a regular user of boosterspice, he didn't show his years. If he didn't get bored first, or broke, he might reach a thousand.

"But," he sometimes told himself, "not if I have to put up with any more cocktail parties, or Bandersnatch hunts, or painted flatlanders swarming through an anarchy park too small for them by a factor of ten. Not if I have to live through another one-night love affair or another twenty-year marriage or another twenty-minute wait for a transfer booth that blows its zap just as it's my turn. And people. Not if I have to live with people, day and night, all those endless centuries."

When he started to feel like that, he left. It had happened three times in his life, and now a fourth. Presumably, it would keep happening. In such a state of ano-

mie, of acute anti-everything, he was no good to anyone,
especially his friends, most especially himself. So he left.
In a small but adequate spacecraft, his own, he left everything and everyone, heading outward for the fringe of
known space. He would not return until he was desperate for the sight of a human face, the sound of a human
voice.

On the second trip he had gritted his teeth and waited
until he was desperate for the sight of a Kzinti face.

That was a long trip, he remembered. And, because
he had only been three and a half months in space on
this fourth trip, and because his teeth still snapped together at the mere memory of a certain human voice
. . . because of these things, he added, "I think this
time I'll wait till I'm desperate to see a Kdatlyno. Fe-
male, of course."

Few of his friends guessed the wear and tear these
trips saved him. And them. He spent the months reading, while his library played orchestrated music. By now
he was well clear of known space. Now he turned the
ship ninety degrees, beginning a wide circular arc with
Sol at its center.

He approached a certain G3 star. He dropped out of
hyperdrive well clear of the singularity in hyperspace
which surrounds any large mass. He accelerated into the
system on his main thruster, sweeping the space ahead
of him with the deep-radar. He was not looking for habitable planets. He was looking for Slaver stasis boxes.

If the pulse returned no echo, we would accelerate
until he could shift to hyperdrive. The velocity would
stay with him, and he could use it to coast through the
next system he tried, and the next, and the next. It saved
fuel.

He had never found a Slaver stasis box. It did not
stop him from looking.

As he passed through the system, the deep-radar
showed him planets like pale ghosts, light gray circles on
the white screen. The G3 sun was a wide gray disk, dark-
ening almost to black at the center. The near-black was
degenerate matter, compressed past the point where
electron orbits collapse entirely.

He was well past the sun, and still accelerating when the screen showed a tiny black fleck.

"No system is perfect, of course," he muttered as he turned off the drive. He talked to himself a good deal, out here where nobody could interrupt him.

"It *usually* saves fuel," he told himself a week later. By then he was out of the singularity, in clear space. He took the ship into hyperdrive, circled halfway round the system, and began decelerating. The velocity he'd built up during those first two weeks gradually left him. Somewhere near where he'd found a black speck in the deep-radar projection, he slowed to a stop.

Though he had never realized it until now, his system for saving fuel was based on the assumption that he would never find a Slaver box. But the fleck was there again, a black dot on the gray ghost of a planet. Louis Wu moved in.

The world looked something like Earth. It was nearly the same size, very much the same shape, somewhat the same color. There was no moon.

Louis used his telescope on the planet and whistled appreciatively. Shredded white cloud over misty blue . . . faint continental outlines . . . a hurricane whorl near the equator. The ice caps looked big, but there would be warm climate near the equator. The air looked sweet and noncarcinogenic on the spectrograph. And nobody on it. Not a soul!

No next door neighbors. No voices. No faces.

"What the hell," he chortled. "I've got my box. I'll just spend the rest of my vacation here. No men. No women. No children." He frowned and rubbed the fringe of hair along his jaw. "Am I being hasty? Maybe I should knock."

But he scanned the radio bands and got nothing. Any civilized planet radiates like a small star in the radio range. Moreover, here was no sign of civilization, even from a hundred miles up.

"Great! Okay, first I'll get that old stasis box." He was sure it was that. Nothing but stars and stasis boxes were dense enough to show black in the reflection of a hyperwave pulse.

He followed the image around the bulge of the planet. It seemed the planet had a moon after all. The moon was twelve hundred miles up, and it was ten feet across.

"Now why," he wondered aloud, "would the Slavers have put it in orbit? It's too easy to find. They were in a war, for Finagle's sake! And why would it stay here?"

The little moon was still a couple of thousand miles away, invisible to the naked eye. The scope showed it clearly enough. A silver sphere ten feet through, with no marks on it.

"A billion and a half years it's been there," said Louis to himself, said he. "And if you believe that, you'll believe anything. Something would have knocked it down. Dust, a meteor, the solar wind. Tnuctip soldiers. A magnetic storm. Nah." He ran his fingers through straight black hair grown too long. "It must have drifted in from somewhere else. Recently. Wha—"

Another ship, small and conical, had appeared behind the silvery sphere. Its hull was green, with darker green markings.

II

"Damn," said Louis. He didn't recognize the make. It was no human ship. "Well, it could be worse. They could have been people." He used the comm laser.

The other ship braked to a stop. In courtesy, so did Louis.

"Would you believe it?" he demanded of himself. "Three years total time I've spent looking for stasis boxes. I finally find one, and now something else wants it too!"

The bright blue spark of another laser glowed in the tip of the alien cone. Louis listened to the autopilot-computer chuckling to itself as it tried to untangle the signals in an unknown laser beam. At least they did use lasers, not telepathy or tentacle-waving or rapid changes in skin color.

A face appeared on Louis's screen.

It was not the first alien he had seen. This, like some others, had a recognizable head: a cluster of sense organs grouped around a mouth, with room for a brain. Trinocular vision, he noted; the eyes set deep in sockets, well protected, but restricted in range of vision. Triangular mouth, too, with yellow, serrated bone knives showing their edges behind three gristle lips.

Definitely, this was an unknown species.

"Boy, are you ugly," Louis refrained from saying. The alien's translator might be working by now.

His own autopilot finished translating the alien's first message. It said, "Go away. This object belongs to me."

"Remarkable," Louis sent back. "Are you a Slaver?" The being did not in the least resemble a Slaver, and the Slavers had been extinct for eons.

"That word was not translated," said the alien. "I reached the artifact before you did. I will fight to keep it."

Louis scratched at his chin, at two week's growth of bristly beard. His ship had very little to fight with. Even the fusion plant which powered the thruster was designed with safety in mind. A laser battle, fought with comm lasers turned to maximum, would be a mere endurance test; and he'd lose, for the alien ship had more mass to absorb more heat. He had no weapons per se. Presumably the alien did.

But the stasis box was a big one.

The Tnuctipun—Slaver war had wiped out most of the intelligent species of the galaxy, a billion and a half years ago. Countless minor battles must have occurred before a Slaver-developed final weapon was used. Often the Slavers, losing a battle, had stored valuables in a stasis box, and hidden it against the day they would again be of use.

No time passed inside a closed stasis box. Alien meat a billion and a half years old had emerged still fresh from its hiding place. Weapons and tools showed no trace of rust. Once a stasis box had disgorged a small, tarsierlike sentient being, still alive. That former slave had lived a strange life before the aging process claimed her, the last of her species.

Slaver stasis boxes were beyond value. It was known that the Tnuctipun, at least, had known the secret of direct conversion of matter. Perhaps their enemies had too. Someday, in a stasis box somewhere outside known space, such a device would be found. Then fusion power would be as obsolete as internal combustion.

And this, a sphere ten feet in diameter, must be the largest stasis box ever found.

"I too will fight to keep the artifact," said Louis. "But consider this. Our species has met once, and will meet again regardless of who takes the artifact now. We can be friends or enemies. Why should we risk this relationship by killing?"

The alien sense-cluster gave away nothing. "What do you propose?"

"A game of chance, with the risks even on both sides. Do you play games of chance?"

"Emphatically yes. The process of living is a game of chance. To avoid chance is insanity."

"That it is. Hmmm." Louis regarded the alien head that seemed to be all triangles. He saw it abruptly whip around, *flick,* to face straight backward, and snap back in the same instant. The sight did something to the pit of his stomach.

"Did you speak?" the alien asked.

"No. Won't you break your neck that way?"

"Your question is interesting. Later we must discuss anatomy. I have a proposal."

"Fine."

"We shall land on the world below us. We will meet between our ships. I will do you the courtesy of emerging first. Can you bring your translator?"

He could connect the computer with his suit radio. "Yes."

"We will meet between our ships and play some simple game, familiar to neither of us, depending solely on chance. Agreed?"

"Provisionally. What game?"

The image on the screen rippled with diagonal lines. Something interfering with the signal? It cleared quickly. "There is a mathematics game," said the alien. "Our mathematics will certainly be similar."

"True." Though Louis had heard of some decidedly peculiar twists in alien mathematics.

"The game involves a *screee*—" Some word that the

autopilot couldn't translate. The alien raised a three-clawed hand, holding a lens-shaped object. The alien's mutually opposed fingers turned it so that Louis could see the different markings on each side. "This is a *scree*. You and I will throw it upward six times each. I will choose one of the symbols, you will choose the other. If my symbol falls looking upward more often than yours, the artifact is mine. The risks are even."

The image rippled, then cleared.

"Agreed," said Louis. He was a bit disappointed in the simplicity of the game.

"We shall both accelerate away from the artifact. Will you follow me down?"

"I will," said Louis.

The image disappeared.

III

Louis Wu scratched at a week's growth of beard. What a way to greet an alien ambassador! In the worlds of men Louis Wu dressed impeccably; but out here he felt free to look like death warmed over, all the time.

But how was a—Trinoc supposed to know that he should have shaved? No, that wasn't the problem.

Was he fool or genius?

He had friends, many of them, with habits like his own. Two had disappeared decades ago; he no longer remembered their names. He remembered only that each had gone hunting stasis boxes in this direction and that each had neglected to come back.

Had they met alien ships?

There were any number of other explanations. Half a year or more spent alone in a single ship was a good way to find out whether you liked yourself. If you decided you didn't, there was no point in returning to the worlds of men.

But there were aliens out here. Armed. One rested in orbit five hundred miles ahead of his ship, with a valuable artifact halfway between.

Still, gambling was safer than fighting. Louis Wu waited for the alien's next move.

That move was to drop like a rock. The alien ship

must have used at least twenty gees of push. After a moment of shock, Louis followed under the same acceleration, protected by his cabin gravity. Was the alien testing his maneuverability?

Possibly not. He seemed contemptuous of tricks. Louis, trailing the alien at a goodly distance, was now much closer to the silver sphere. Suppose he just turned ship, ran for the artifact, strapped it to his hull and kept running?

Actually, that wouldn't work. He'd have to slow to reach the spere the alien wouldn't have to slow to attack. Twenty gees was close to his ship's limit.

Running might not be a bad idea, though. What guarantee had he of the alien's good faith? What if the alien "cheated"?

That risk could be minimized. His pressure suit had sensors to monitor his body functions. Louis set the autopilot to blow the fusion plant if his heart stopped. He rigged a signal button on his suit to blow the plant manually.

The alien ship burned bright orange as it hit air. It fell free and then slowed suddenly, a mile over the ocean. "Showoff," Louis muttered and prepared to imitate the maneuver.

The conical ship showed no exhaust. Its drive must be either a reactionless drive, like his own, or a kzin-style induced-gravity drive. Both were neat and clean, silent, safe to bystanders and highly advanced.

Islands were scattered across the ocean. The alien circled, chose one at seeming random, and landed like a feather along a bare shoreline.

Louis followed him down. There was a bad moment while he waited for some unimaginable weapon to fire from the grounded ship, to tear him flaming from the sky while his attention was distracted by landing procedures. But he landed without a jar, several hundred yards from the alien cone.

"An explosion will destroy both our ships if I am harmed," he told the alien via signal beam.

"Our species seem to think alike. I will now descend."

Louis watched him appear near the nose of the ship, in a wide circular airlock. He watched the alien drift gently to the sand. Then he clamped his helmet down and entered the airlock.

Had he made the right decision?

Gambling was safer than war. More fun, too. Best of all, it gave him better odds.

"But I'd hate to go home without that box," he thought. In nearly two hundred years of life, he had never done anything as important as finding a stasis box. He had made no discoveries, won no elective offices, overthrown no governments. This was his big chance.

"Even odds," he said, and turned on the intercom as he descended.

His muscles and semicircular canals registered about a gee. A hundred feet away waves slid hissing up onto pure white sand. The waves were green and huge, perfect for riding; the beach a definite beer party beach.

Later, perhaps he would ride those waves to shore on his belly, if the air checked out and the water was free of predators. He hadn't had time to give the planet a thorough checkup.

Sand tugged at his boots as he went to meet the alien.

The alien was five feet tall. He had looked much taller descending from his ship, but that was because he was mostly leg. More than three feet of skinny leg, a torso like a beer barrel, and no neck. Impossible that his neckless neck should be so supple. But the chrome yellow skin fell in thick rolls around the bottom of his head, hiding anatomical details.

His suit was transparent, a roughly alien-shaped balloon, constricted at the shoulder, above and below the complicated elbow joint, at the wrist, at hip and knee. Air jets showed at wrist and ankle. Tools hung in loops at the chest. A back pack hung from the neck, under the suit. Louis noted all these tools with trepidation; any one of them could be a weapon.

"I expected that you would be taller," said the alien.

"A laser screen doesn't tell much, does it? I think my translator may have mixed up right and left, too. Do you have the coin?"

"The *screee*?" The alien produced it. "Shall there be no preliminary talk? My name is *screee*."

"My machine can't translate that. Or pronouce it. My

name is Louis. Has your species met others besides mine?"

"Yes, two. But I am not an expert in that field of knowledge."

"Nor am I. Let's leave the politenesses to the experts. We're here to gamble."

"Choose your symbol," said the alien, and handed him the coin.

Louis looked it over. It was a lens of platinum or something similar, sharp-edged, with the three-clawed hand of his new gambling partner stamped on one side and a planet, with heavy ice caps outlined, decorating the other. Maybe they weren't ice caps, but continents.

He held the coin as if trying to choose. Stalling. Those gas jets seemed to be attitude jets, but maybe not. Suppose he won? Would he win only the chance to be murdered?

But they'd both die if his heart stopped. No alien could have guessed what kind of weapon would render him helpless without killing him.

"I choose the planet. You flip first."

The alien tossed the coin in the direction of Louis's ship. Louis's eyes followed it down, and he took two steps to retrieve it. The alien stood beside him when he rose.

"Hand," he said. "My turn." He was one down. He tossed the coin. As it spun gleaming, he saw for the first time that the alien ship was gone.

"What gives?" he demanded.

"There's no need for us to die," said the alien. It held something that had hung in a loop from its chest. "This is a weapon, but both will die if I use it. Please do not try to reach your ship."

Louis touched the button that would blow his power plant.

"My ship lifted when you turned your head to follow the *screee*. By now my ship is beyond range of any possible explosion you can bring to bear. There is no need for us to die, provided you do not try to reach your ship."

"Wrong. I can leave your ship without a pilot." He

left his hand where it was. Rather than be cheated by an alien in a gambling game—

"The pilot is still on board, with the astrogator and the *screee*. I am only the communications officer. Why did you assume I was alone?"

Louis sighed and let his arm fall. "Because I'm stupid," he said bitterly. "Because you used the singular pronoun, or my computer did. Because I thought you were a gambler."

"I gambled that you would not see my ship take off, that you would be distracted by the coin, that you could see only from the front of your head. The risks seemed better than one-half."

Louis nodded. It all seemed clear.

"There was also the chance that you had lured me down to destroy me." The computer was still translating into the first person singular. "I have lost at least one exploring ship that flew in this direction."

"Not guilty. So have we." A thought struck him, and he said, "Prove that you hold a weapon."

The alien obliged. No beam showed, but sand exploded to Louis's left, with a vicious *crack!* and a flash the color of lightning. The alien held something that made holes.

So much for that. Louis bent and picked up the coin. "As long as we're here, shall we finish the game?"

"To what purpose?"

"To see who would have won. Doesn't your species gamble for pleasure?"

"To what purpose? We gamble for survival."

"Then Finagle take your whole breed!" he snarled and flung himself to the sand. His chance for glory was gone, tricked away from him. There is a tide that governs men's affairs . . . and there went the ebb, carrying statues to Louis Wu, history books naming Louis Wu, jetsam on the tide.

"Your attitude is puzzling. One gambles only when gambling is necessary."

"Nuts."

"My translator will not translate that comment."

"Do you know what that artifact is?"

"I know of the species who built that artifact. They traveled far."

"We've never found a stasis box that big. It must be a vault of some kind."

"It is thought that that species used a single weapon to end their war and all its participants."

The two looked at each other. Possibly each was thinking the same thing. *What a disaster, if any but my own species should take this ultimate weapon!*

But that was anthropomorphic thinking. Louis knew that a Kzin would have been saying: *Now I can conquer the universe, as is my right.*

"Finagle take my luck! " said Louis Wu between his teeth. "Why did you have to show at the same time I did?"

"That was not entirely chance. My instruments found your craft as you backed into the system. To reach the vicinity of the artifact in time, it was necessary to use thrust that damaged my ship and killed one of my crew. I earned possession of the artifact."

"By cheating, damn you!" Louis stood up . . .

And something meshed between his brain and his semicircular canals.

IV

One gravity.

The density of a planet's atmosphere depended on its gravity, and on its moon. A big moon would skim away most of the atmosphere, over the billions of years of a world's evolution. A moonless world the size and mass of Earth should have unbreathable air, impossibly dense, worse than Venus.

But this planet had no moon. Except—

The alien said something, a startled ejaculation that the computer refused to translate. "*Secree!* Where did the water go?"

Louis looked. What he saw puzzled him only a moment. The ocean had receded, slipped imperceptibly away, until what showed now was half a mile of level, slickly shinning sea bottom.

"Where did the water go? I do not understand."

"I do."

"Where did it go? Without a moon, there can be no tides. Tides are not this quick in any case. Explain, please."

"It'll be easier if we use the telescope in my ship."

"In your ship there may be weapons."

"Now pay attention," said Louis. "Your ship is very close to total destruction. Nothing can save your crew but the comm laser in my ship."

The alien dithered, then capitulated. "If you have weapons, you would have used them earlier. You cannot stop my ship now. Let us enter your ship. Remember that I hold my weapon."

The alien sood beside him in the small cabin, his mouth working disturbingly around the serrated edges of his teeth as Louis activated the scope and screen. Shortly a starfield appeared. So did a conical spacecraft, painted green with darker green markings. Along the bottom of the screen was the blur of thick atmosphere.

"You see? The artifact must be nearly to the horizon. It moves fast."

"That fact is obvious even to low intelligence."

"Yah. Is it obvious to you that this world must have a massive satellite?"

"But it does not, unless the satellite is invisible."

"Not invisible. Just too small to notice. But then, it must be very dense."

The alien didn't answer.

"Why did we assume the sphere was a Slaver stasis box? Its shape was wrong; its size was wrong. But it was shiny, like the surface of a stasis field, and spherical, like an artifact. Planets are spheres too, but gravity wouldn't ordinarily pull something ten feet wide into a sphere. Either it would have to be very fluid, or it would have to be very dense. Do you understand me?"

"No."

"I don't know how your equipment works. My deep-radar uses a hyperwave pulse to find stasis boxes. When something stops a hyperwave pulse, it's either a stasis box, or it's something denser than degenerate matter, the matter inside a normal star. And *this* object is dense enough to cause *tides*."

A tiny silver bead had drifted into view ahead of the cone. Telescopic foreshortening seemed to bring it right alongside the ship. Louis reached to scratch at his beard and was stopped by his faceplate.

"I believe I understand you. But how could it happen?"

"That's guesswork. Well?"

"Call my ship. They would be killed. We must save them!"

"I had to be sure you wouldn't stop me." Louis Wu went to work. Presently a light glowed; the computer had found the alien ship with its comm laser.

He spoke without preliminaries. "You must leave the spherical object immediately. It is not an artifact. It is ten feet of nearly solid neutronium, probably torn loose from a neutron star."

There was no answer, of course. The alien stood behind him but did not speak. Probably his own ship's computer could not have handled the double translation. But the alien was making one two-armed gesture, over and over.

The green cone swung sharply around, broadside to the telescope.

"Good, they're firing lateral," said Louis to himself. "Maybe they can do a hyperbolic past it." He raised his voice. "Use all the power available. You *must* pull away."

The two objects seemed to be pulling apart. Louis suspected that that was illusion, for the two objects were almost in line-of-sight. "Don't let the small mass fool you," he said, unnessessarily now. "Computer, what's the mass of a ten-foot neutronium sphere?—Around two times ten to the minus six times the mass of this world, which is pretty tiny, but if you get too close . . . Computer, what's the surface gravity?—I don't *believe* it."

The two objects seemed to be pulling together again. Damn, thought Louis. If they hadn't come along, that'd be me.

He kept talking. It wouldn't matter now, except to relieve his own tension. "My computer says ten million gravities at the surface. That may be off. Newton's formula for gravity. Can you hear me?"

"They are too close," said the alien. "By now it is too late to save their lives." It was happening as he spoke. The ship began to crumble a fraction of a second before impact. Impact looked no more dangerous than a cannonball striking the wall of a fort. The tiny silver bead simply swept through the side of the ship. But the ship closed instantly, all in a moment, like tinsel paper in a strong man's fist. Closed into a bead glowing yellow with heat. A tiny sphere ten feet through or a bit more.

"I mourn," said the alien.

"Now I get it," said Louis. "I wondered what was fouling our laser messages. That chunk of neutronium was right between our ships, bending the light beams."

"Why was this trap set for us?" cried the alien. "Have we enemies so powerful that they can play with such masses?"

A touch of paranoia? Louis wondered. Maybe the whole species had it. "Just a touch of coincidence. A smashed neutron star."

For a time the alien did not speak. The telescope, for want of a better target, remained focused on the bead. Its glow had died.

The alien said, "My pressure suit will not keep me alive long."

"We'll make a run for it. I can reach Margrave in a couple of weeks. If you can hold out that long, we'll set up a tailored environment box to hold you until we think of something better. It only takes a couple of hours to set one up. I'll call ahead."

The alien's triple gaze converged on him. "Can you send messages faster than light?"

"Sure."

"You have knowledge worth trading for. I'll come with you."

"Thanks a whole lot." Louis Wu started punching buttons. "Margrave. Civilization. People. Faces. Voices. Bah." The ship leapt upward, ripping atmosphere apart. Cabin gravity wavered a little, then settled down.

"Well," he told himself. "I can always come back."

"You will return here?"

"I think so," he decided.

"I hope you will be armed."

"What? More paranoia?"

"Your species is insufficiently suspicious," said the alien. "I wonder that you have survived. Consider this neutronium object as a defense. Its mass pulls anything that touches it into smooth and reflective spherical surface. Should any vehicle approach this world, its crew would find this object quickly. They would assume it is an artifact. What other assumption could they make? They would draw alongside for a closer examination."

"True enough, but that planet's empty. Nobody to defend."

"Perhaps."

The planet was dwindling below. Louis Wu swung his ship toward deep space.

Safe at Any Speed

In the two hundred years between Beowulf Shaeffer and Louis Wu, little had changed on the surface. Known Space was somewhat larger. Most ships used a reactionless drive, the "thruster." The birthright lotteries had been in use on Earth almost since Shaeffer's time.

It was the birthright lotteries, which made being born a matter of sheer luck, that eventually created the Teela Brown gene. Teela Brown's story is chronicled in *Ringworld*. There were other teelas on Earth, and their effect was catastrophic, at least for a writer. Stories about infinitely lucky people tend to be dull.

One tale survives from the golden age that followed. *LN*

But how, you ask, *could a car have managed to fail me?*

Already I can see the terror in your eyes at the thought that your car, too, might fail. Here you are with an indefinite lifespan, a potentially immortal being, taking every possible precaution against the abrupt termination of your godhead; and all for nothing. The disruptor field in your kitchen dispose-all could suddenly expand to engulf you. Your transfer booth could make you disappear at the transmitter and forget to deliver you at the receiver. A slidewalk could accelerate to one hundred miles per hour, then slew sideways to throw you against a building. Every boosterspice plant in the Thousand Worlds could die overnight, leaving you to

217

grow old and gray and wrinkled and arthritic. No, it's never happened in human history; but if a man can't trust his *car*, fa' Pete's sake, what *can* he trust?

Rest assured, reader, it wasn't that bad.

For one thing, it all happened on Margrave, a world in the first stages of colonization. I was twenty minutes out of Triangle Lake on my way to the Wiggly River logging region, flying at an altitude of a thousand feet. For several days the logging machines had been cutting trees which were too young, and a mechanic was needed to alter a few settings in the boss brain. I was cruising along on autopilot, playing double-deck complex solitaire in the back seat, with the camera going so that just in case I won one I'd have a film to back up my bragging.

Then a roc swooped down on me, wrapped ten huge talons around my car, and swallowed it.

Right away you'll see that it couldn't happen anywhere but Margrave. In the first place, I wouldn't have been using a car for a two-hour trip on any civilized world. I'd have taken a transfer booth. In the second place, where else can you find rocs?

Anyway, this big damn bird caught me and ate me, and everything went dark. The car flew blithely on, ignoring the roc, but the ride became turbulent as the roc tried to fly away and couldn't. I heard grinding sounds from outside. I tried my radio and got nothing. Either it couldn't reach through all that meat around me, or the trip through the bird's gullet had brushed away my antennas.

There didn't seem to be anything else I could do. I turned on the cabin lights and went on with the game. The grinding noises continued, and now I could see what was causing them. At some time the roc had swallowed several boulders, for the same reason a chicken swallows grit: to help digestion. The rocks were rubbing against the car under peristalsis, trying to break it down into smaller pieces for the murky digestive juices to work on.

I wondered how smart the boss brain was. When it saw a roc glide in for a landing at the logging camp, and when it realized that the bird was incapable of leaving no matter how it shrieked and flapped its wings, would the master computer draw the correct conclusion? Would it realize the bird had swallowed a car? I was afraid not. If the boss brain were that smart it would have been in business for itself.

I never found out. All of a sudden my seat cocoon wrapped itself around me like an overprotective mother, and there was a meaty three-hundred-mile-per-hour Smack!

The cocoon unwrapped itself. My cabin lights still showed red-lit fluid around me, but it was getting redder. The boulders had stopped rolling around. My cards were all over the cabin, like a snowstorm.

Obviously I'd forgotten one teensy little mountain when I programed the autopilot. The roc had been blocking the radar and sonar, with predictable results. A little experimenting showed that my drive had failed under the impact, my radio still wouldn't work, and my emergency flares refused to try to fire through a roc's belly.

There was no way to get out, not without opening my door to a flood of digestive juices. I could have done that if I'd had a vac suit, but how was I to know I'd need one on a two-hour car trip?

There was only one thing to do.

I collected my cards, shuffled, and started a new game.

It was half a year before the roc's corpus decomposed enough to let me out. In that time I won five games of double complex solitaire. I've only got films for four; the camera ran out. I'm happy to say that the emergency food-maker worked beautifully if a little monotonously, the air-maker never failed, and the clock TV kept perfect time as a clock. As a TV it showed only technicolor ripples of static. The washroom went out along about August, but I got it fixed without much trouble. At 2:00 P.M. on October 24 I forced the door open, hacked my way through the mummified skin and flesh between a couple of roc ribs, and took a deep breath of real air. It smelled of roc. I'd left the cabin door open, and I could hear the airmaker whine crazily as it tried to absorb the smell.

I fired off a few flares, and fifteen minutes later a car dropped to take me home. They say I was the hairiest human being they'd ever seen. I've since asked Mr. Dickson, the president of General Transportation, why he didn't include a depil tube in the emergency stores.

"A castaway is supposed to look like a castaway," he tells me. "If you're wearing a year's growth of hair, your rescuer will know immediately that you've been lost for some time and will take the appropriate steps."

General Transportation has paid me a more than adequate sum in a compensation for the fact that my car was unable to handle a roc. (I've heard that they're changing the guarantees for next year's model.) They've promised me an equal sum for writing this article. It seems there are strange and possibly damaging rumors going around concerning my delayed arrival at Wiggly River.

Rest assured, reader. I not only lived through the accident without harm, but came out of it with a substantial profit. Your car is perfectly safe, provided it was built later than 3100 A.D.

Afterthoughts

I HAD BEEN writing about three years. You might say I was just getting into the swing of constructive daydreaming: letting my imagination flow until I had something, then guiding it.

I had a violent picture in my mind, and practically no story around it, at first. I saw men building a campfire out of what they did not know to be stage-tree logs . . .

The stage tree was part of the background of the novel *World of Ptavvs*. I had developed quite an elaborate background for the Thrintun, the race that ruled the galaxy one-and-a-half billion years ago. The stage tree was an organically grown solid-fuel rocket: tree on the outside, chemicals in the core around a star-shaped hollow. It bothered me, losing all those fascinating life forms . . .

. . . The campfire catches slowly, then burns briskly. And suddenly the logs are going off like so many sticks of dynamite!

Well, why shouldn't some of those life forms have survived in mutated form?

"A Relic of Empire" was the third story set in Beowulf Shaeffer's era. But it was the first of the Known Space Series, because it linked the cosmos of Lucas Garner with the cosmos of Beowulf Shaeffer. From that point on I was writing a future history. Later I included the Kzinti, who already existed via "The Warriors;" and the intermediate era of *A Gift From Earth;* and in *Ringworld* even the sunflowers of Kzanol's time were found to have survived. Early tales of planetary exploration became part of the fabric. It was fun, fitting the pieces together.

That was how the Known Space Series began. It ends with *Ringworld*. Though I've written stories in the series since *Ringworld*, writing that novel made me realize how tangled and complex my basic assumptions had become. There were too many unlikely miracles left over from individual stories. For example, from *World of Ptavvs* came a stasis field so useful that every story set later in time must be examined for reasons why a stasis field would not solve the problem. From *Neutron Star*, where it was introduced to create an airtight problem in logic, comes an invulnerable spacecraft hull—same remarks. For the Ringworld floor material I had to come up with still *another* unreasonably strong material.

And then there was the Teela Brown gene to consider. And I had to contend with the near certainty that the Ringworld had been settled, as was Earth, by Pak breeders and had been built by Pak protectors. But the story was already too complex; I couldn't open that can of worms too! I settled for letting Louis Wu deduce the wrong answer.

It's been fun. Unexpectedly, I've had a great deal of interaction with readers, and I pass along some of their more interesting suggestions:

Mathematically, the Ringworld can be treated very simply, as a suspension bridge with no endpoints.

The antimatter planet in "Flatlander" can be furnished with an experimental outpost, by setting the buildings on a metal base with a stasis field around it.

A fan named Dan Alderson has done a two thousand-word treatment of the Grog problem as raised in "Handicap." His conclusion: the Grogs can be controlled, if they need to be, by Bandersnatchi. The dinosaur-sized beasts are demonstrably immune to hypnotic telepathy. However, they must be spacelifted in from Jinx.

I keep meeting people who have done mathematical treatments of the problem raised in the short story "Neutron Star," from which the collection derived its title. Alas and dammit, Shaeffer can't survive. It turns out that his ship leaves the star spinning, and keeps the spin.

"There Is a Tide" was suggested by a conversation

with Tom Digby and Dan Alderson. Hank Stine suggested Matt Keller's interestingly limited psychic power, later known as "Plateau eyes."

Well, I've put these notes at the back of the book to avoid ruining your willing suspension of disbelief. If one must explain a magic trick, one should do so after the show is over. The Known Space series is now complete. If you want more stories in the series you can make them up yourself. I think I've given you enough background.

Bibliography

The Worlds of Larry Niven

Key

Collections

A1. *Neutron Star*
A2. *The Shape of Space*
A3. *All the Myriad Ways*
A4. *The Flight of the Horse*
A5. *A Hole in Space*
A6. *Tales of Known Space*
A7. *The Long ARM of Gil Hamilton*

Novels

N1. *World of Ptavvs*
N2. *A Gift from Earth*
N3. *Ringworld*
N4. *The Flying Sorcerers*
N5. *Protector*
N6. *The Mote in God's Eye*

AHM *Alfred Hitchcock's Mystery Magazine*
ASF *Analog Science Fiction*
DV *Dangerous Visions*
EPC *Epic*
EQM *Ellery Queen's Mystery Magazine*
FAN *Fantastic*
FSF *The Magazine of Fantasy and Science Fiction*
FU *Futures Unbounded*

GAL *Galaxy Magazine*
IF *Worlds of If*
Q4 *Quark 4*
TET *Ten Tomorrows*
TRM *Trumpet, No. 9*

TTT *Three Trips in Time and Space*
VER *Vertex Magazine*
WOT *Worlds of Tomorrow*

nov. novel
coll. collection
nSF not science fiction
UC has not appeared in a collection

Bibliography

Throughout, titles followed by asterisks appear in this collection. Italicized titles are those of collections or novels; all others are titles of stories or nonfiction articles.

Yr	Mon	Title	Orig. Publ.	Book	Series
1964					
	Dec	The Coldest Place*	IF	A6	Known Space
1965					
	Mar	World of Ptavvs	WOT	N1	Known Space
	Apr	Wrong Way Street	GAL	UC	Time Travel
	Jun	One Face	GAL	A2	Known Space
	Jul	Becalmed in Hell*	FSF	A3/A6	Known Space
1966					
	Feb	Eye of an Octopus*	GAL	A6	Known Space
	Feb	The Warriors*	IF	A2/A6	Known Space
	Apr	Bordered in Black	FSF	A2	Known Space
	Jun	By Mind Alone	IF	UC	Teleportation
	Oct	Neutron Star	IF	A1	Known Space
	Oct	How the Heroes Die*	GAL	A2/A6	Known Space
	Nov	At the Core	IF	A1	Known Space
	Dec	A Relic of the Empire	IF	A1	Known Space
	Dec	At the Bottom of a Hole*	GAL	A2/A6	Known Space
1967					
	Feb	The Soft Weapon	IF	A1	Known Space
	Mar	The Long Night†	FSF	A2	not series
	Mar	Flatlander	IF	A1	Known Space
	Apr	The Ethics of Madness	IF	A1	Known Space
	May	Safe at Any Speed*	FSF	A2/A6	Known Space

† Title changed for novelization or appearance in a collection; see "Title Changes," p. 231.

Jun	The Adults†	GAL	N5	Known Space
Dec	The Handicapped	GAL	A1	Known Space
—	The Jigsaw Man*	DV	A3	Known Space

1968

Feb-Apr	Slowboat Cargo†	IF	N2	Known Space
Apr	The Deceivers*†	GAL	A6	Known Space
Apr	Grendel	A1	A1	Known Space
Apr	Neutron Star	coll.	A1	Known Space
May	Dry Run	FSF	A2	not series
Jul	There Is a Tide*	GAL	A5/A6	Known Space
Aug	The World of Ptavvs	nov.	N1	Known Space
Sep	Like Banquo's Ghost	IF	A2	not series
Sep	A Gift from Earth	nov.	N2	Known Space
Oct	The Meddler	FSF	A2	not series
Oct	All the Myriad Ways	GAL	A3	Time Travel
—	Wait It Out*	FU	A3/A6	Known Space

1969

Jan	The Deadlier Weapon	EQM	A2	nSF
Jan	The Organleggers†	GAL	A2/A7	Known Space
Mar	Exercise in Speculation: The Theory and Practice of Teleportation	GAL	A3	nonfiction
Apr	Not Long before the End	FSF	A3	Warlock
Sep	Passerby	GAL	A3	Léshy Circuit
Sep	The Shape of Space	coll.	A2	
Oct	Get a Horse†	FSF	A4	Svetz
Nov	Down in Flames	TRM	UC	nonfiction

1970

May-Jul	The Misspelled Magishun (w. D. Gerrold)†	IF	N4	not series
Jun	There's a Wolf in My Time Machine	FSF	A4	Svetz
Aug	Leviathan	PLB	A4	Svetz
Oct	Bird in the Hand	FSF	A4	Svetz
Oct	Ringworld	nov.	N3	Known Space
Dec	Unfinished Story No. 1	FSF	A3	Warlock

---

† Title changed for novelization or appearance in a collection; see "Title Changes," p. 231.

1971

	Jun	Inconstant Moon	A3	A3	not series
	Jun	Man of Steel—Woman of Kleenex	A3	A3	nonfiction
	Jun	Theory and Practice of Time Travel	A3	A3	nonfiction
	Jun	What Can You Say About Chocolate-Covered Manhole Covers?	A3	A3	not series
	Jun	Unfinished Story No. 2	A3	A3	not series
	Jun	No Exit (w. Hank Stine)	FAN	UC	not series
	Jun	All the Myriad Ways	coll.	A3	
	Jul	For a Foggy Night	FSF	A3	Time Travel
	Aug	The Flying Sorcerers	nov.	N4	not series
	Nov	Rammer	GAL	A5	Léshy Circuit
	—	The Fourth Profession	Q4	A5	Léshy Circuit

1972

	Mar	Cloak of Anarchy*	ASF	A6	Known Space
	Sep	What Good Is a Glass Dagger?	FSF	A4	Warlock

1973

	Jun	The Alibi Machine	VER	A5	Teleportation
	Jun	All the Bridges Rusting	VER	A5	Teleportation
	—	Flash Crowd	TTT	UC	Teleportation
	Sep	The Flight of the Horse	coll.	A4	Svetz
	Sep	Protector	nov.	N5	Known Space
	—	The Defenseless Dead	TET	A7	Known Space

1974

	Jan	The Hole Man	ASF	A5	not series
	Mar	Bigger Than Worlds	ASF	A5	nonfiction
	Apr	A Kind of Murder	ASF	A5	Teleportation
	—	$16,940.00	AHM	A5	nSF
	Jun	The Last Days of the Permanent Floating Riot Club	A5	A5	Teleportation
	Jun	A Hole in Space	coll.	A5	various
	Aug	Night on Mispek Moor	VER	UC	Léshy Circuit
	Aug	Plaything	GAL	UC	not series

	Oct	*The Mote in God's Eye*			
		(w. Jerry Pournelle)	nov.	N6	not series
	Dec	The Nonesuch	FSF	UC	not series
1975					
	Jan	The Borderland of Sol*	ASF	A6	Known Space
	Aug	*Tales of Known Space*	coll.	A6	Known Space
		ARM	EPC	A7	Known Space
1976					
	Feb.	*The Long ARM of Gil Hamilton*	coll.	A7	Known Space

Title Changes

1967		original	becomes	in
	Mar	The Long Night	Convergent Series	A2
	Jun	The Adults	(incorporated into) Protector	N5
1968				
	Feb-Apr	Slowboat Cargo	A Gift from Earth	N2
	Apr	The Deceivers	Intent to Deceive	A6
1969				
	Jan	The Organleggers	Death by Ecstasy	A2/A7
	Oct	Get a Horse!	The Flight of the Horse	A4
1970				
	May-Jul	The Misspelled Magishun	The Flying Sorcerers	N4

Series

Known Space (stories in chronological order of appearance; righthand
column is *latest* publication)

1964
The Coldest Place   *Tales of Known Space*

1965
World of Ptavvs   *World of Ptavvs*
One Face   *The Shape of Space*
Becalmed in Hell   *Tales of Known Space*

1966
Eye of an Octopus   *Tales of Known Space*
The Warriors   *Tales of Known Space*
Bordered in Black   *The Shape of Space*
Neutron Star   *Neutron Star*
How the Heroes Die   *Tales of Known Space*
At the Core   *Neutron Star*
A Relic of the Empire   *Neutron Star*
At the Bottom of a Hole   *Tales of Known Space*

1967
The Soft Weapon   *Neutron Star*
Flatlander   *Neutron Star*
The Ethics of Madness   *Neutron Star*
Safe at Any Speed   *Tales of Known Space*
The Adults   *Protector*
The Handicapped   *Neutron Star*
The Jigsaw Man   *Tales of Known Space*

1968
Slowboat Cargo†   *A Gift from Earth*
The Deceivers†   *Tales of Known Space*
Grendel   *Neutron Star*
Neutron Star   *Neutron Star*

---

† Title changed for novelization or appearance in a collection; see
"Title Changes," p. 231.

LESHY CIRCUIT

SVETZ

----

† Title changed for novelization or appearance in a collection; see "Title Changes," p. 231.

TELEPORTATION

By Mind Alone (1966)	*If*, June
Flash Crowd (1973)	*Three Trips in Time and Space*
The Alibi Machine (1973)	*A Hole in Space*
All the Bridges Rusting (1973)	*A Hole in Space*
A *Kind* of Murder (1974)	*A Hole in Space*
The Last Days of the Permanent Floating Riot Club (1974)	*A Hole in Space*

TIME TRAVEL-PARALLEL UNIVERSE

Wrong Way Street (1965)	*Galaxy*, April
All the Myriad Ways (1968)	*All the Myriad Ways*
For a Foggy Night (1971)	*All the Myriad Ways*

WARLOCK

Not Long before the End (1969)	*All the Myriad Ways*
Unfinished Story #1 (1970)	*All the Myriad Ways*
What Good Is a Glass Dagger? (1972)	*The Flight of the Horse*

WORKS NOT PART OF ANY NIVEN SERIES:

The Long Night (1967)
Dry Run (1968)
Like Banquo's Ghost (1968)
The Meddler (1968)
The Deadlier Weapon (1969)
The Misspelled Magishun (1970)
No Exit (1971)
Unfinished Story #2 (1971)
Inconstant Moon (1971)
What Can You Say about Chocolate Covered Manhole Covers? (1971)
The Hole Man (1974)
$16,940.00 (1974)
Plaything (1974)
The Mote in God's Eye (1974)
The Nonesuch (1974)

NONFICTION

Exercise in Speculation: The Theory and Practice of Teleportation (1969)	*All the Myriad Ways*
Down in Flames (1969)	*Trumpet, No. 9*
The Theory and Practice of Time Travel (1971)	*All the Myriad Ways*
Man of Steel—Woman of Kleenex (1971)	*All the Myriad Ways*
Bigger Than Worlds (1974)	*A Hole in Space*

WORKS WHICH HAVE NOT APPEARED IN A NIVEN COLLECTIVE TO DATE:

Wrong Way Street (1965)
By Mind Alone (1966)
No Exit (1971)

STORY COLLECTIONS

A1. *Neutron Star,* Ballantine, April 1968
Neutron Star (1966)
A Relic of the Empire (1966)
At the Core (1966)
The Soft Weapon (1967)
Flatlander (1967)
The Ethics of Madness (1967)
The Handicapped (1967)
Grendel (1967)

A2. *The Shape of Space,* Ballantine, September 1969
The Warriors (1966)
Safe at Any Speed (1967)
How the Heroes Die (1966)
At the Bottom of a Hole (1966)
Bordered in Black (1966)
Like Banquo's Ghost (1968)
One Face (1965)
The Meddler (1968)
Dry Run (1968)
Convergent Series (1967)†

---

† Title changed for appearance in a collection; see "Title Changes," p 231.

The Deadlier Weapon (1968)
Death by Ecstasy (1969)†

A3. *All the Myriad Ways*, Ballantine, June 1971
All the Myriad Ways (1968)
Passerby (1969)
For a Foggy Night (1971)
Wait It Out (1968)
The Jigsaw Man (1967)
Not Long before the End (1969)
Unfinished Story #1 (1970)
Unfinished Story #2 (1971)
Man of Steel—Woman of Kleenex (1971)
Exercise in Speculation: The Theory and Practice of Teleportation (1969)
The Theory and Practice of Time Travel (1971)
Inconstant Moon (1971)
What Can You Say about Chocolate Covered Manhole Covers? (1971)
Becalmed in Hell (1965)

A4. *The Flight of the Horse*, Ballantine, September 1973
The Flight of the Horse (1969)†
Leviathan (1970)
Bird in the Hand (1970)
There's a Wolf in My Time Machine (1970)
Death in a Cage (1973)
Flash Crowd (1973)
What Good Is a Glass Dagger? (1972)
Afterword (1973)

A5. *A Hole in Space*, Ballantine, June 1974
Rammer (1971)
The Alibi Machine (1973
The Last Days of the Permanent Floating Riot Club (1974)
A *Kind* of Murder (1974)
All the Bridges Rusting (1973)
There Is a Tide (1968)
Bigger Than Worlds (1974)
$16,940.00 (1974)
The Hole Man (1974)
The Fourth Profession (1971)

---

† Title changed for appearance in a collection; see "Title Changes,"
p 231.

A6. *Tales of Known Space*, Ballantine, August 1975
The Coldest Place (1964)
Becalmed in Hell (1965)
Wait It Out (1968)
Eye of an Octopus (1966)
How the Heroes Die (1966)
The Jigsaw Man (1967)
At the Bottom of a Hole (1966)
Intent to Deceive (1968)†
Cloak of Anarchy (1972)
The Warriors (1966)
The Borderland of Sol (1975)
There Is a Tide (1968)
Safe at Any Speed (1967)

A7. *The Long ARM of Gil Hamilton*, Ballantine, February 1976
Death by Ecstasy (1969)
The Defenseless Dead (1973)
ARM (1975)

NOVELS

N1. *World of Ptavvs*, Ballantine, August 1968; a shorter version, "World of Ptavvs," appeared in *Worlds of Tomorrow*, March 1965; Known Space.

N2. *A Gift from Earth*, Ballantine, September 1968; originally appeared as *Slowboat Cargo* in *Galaxy*, February, March, and April 1968; Known Space.

N3. *Ringworld*, Ballantine, October 1970; original book publication, no serialization; Known Space.

N4. *The Flying Sorcerers* (w. David Gerrold), Ballantine, August 1971; originally appeared as "The Misspelled Magishun" in *Worlds of If*, May–July 1970; not part of a series.

N5. *Protector*, Ballantine, September 1973; the first half of the novel, "Phssthpok," appeared as "The Adults" in *Galaxy*, June 1967; Known Space.

N6. *The Mote in God's Eye* (w. Jerry Pournelle), Simon and Schuster, October 1974; original book publication, no serialization; not part of a series.

About the Cover

THE COLORED BAUBLES set against the background of a spiral galaxy represent some of the stars closest to our sun, the G-type star Sol. Many of them are the settings for stories Larry Niven has written dealing with a thirty-light-year diameter volume of the sky called Known Space.

Readers already familiar with the Known Space series will immediately recognize names such as Wunderland, Down, and Jinx as but a few of the fascinating and sometimes dangerous planets on and around which space-faring man has travelled.

The story of how the cover illustration came about is interesting in that it combined the talents of people in three different disciplines, all working in the field of science fiction: the author, editor, and art director; the artist; and a particular group of intelligent readers in Boston, Massachusetts, who have been busily cataloging everything in Known Space.

After a preliminary sketch of the galaxy was approved, I set out to try to render the local star group. When I approached James L. Burrows, a member of the New England Science Fiction Association who is conversant with computers, he had, not surprisingly, already written a program to produce the position map. What the computer gave him were the coordinates for the stars on a two-dimensional grid, as though viewed from roughly sixty-three degrees above the plane of the Milky Way. He put it simply: "Imagine traveling in space along the Earth's axis—pointed at the North Star—and looking back past the sun from a great many light years. This is what you'd see."

Just how big would Known Space be in this view of the galaxy?

Obviously the brightly painted stars in the foreground are part of an enlarged picture of the local neighborhood. If the Milky Way is 100,000 light-years across, then, at the size of a paperback cover, all of Known Space is a pinpoint .001″—a thousandth of an inch— from edge to edge.

One of the rewards of my kind of work is that I can add things to paintings that are visible on the original board, but not always in the reproduced version. Or are they?

If you look carefully, you'll find all fourteen black holes, two Puppeteer-built General Products spacecraft hulls, egg-shaped Jinx, and . . . there. The Ringworld, too, of course.

Rick Sternbach